I'LL
BE
WATCHING
YOU

COURTNEY EVAN TATE

mira

mira

ISBN-13: 978-0-7783-5129-0

I'll Be Watching You

Recycling programs
for this product may
not exist in your area.

For questions and comments about the quality of this book, please contact us at CustomerService@Harlequin.com.

BookClubbish.com

Printed in U.S.A.

To all the mamas in the world.

As Elizabeth Stone once said:

"Making the decision to have a child—it is momentous. It is to decide forever to have your heart go walking around outside your body."

I agree, Ms. Stone. I agree.

I'LL
BE
WATCHING
YOU

Ramblings from the Island

I fear that you won't like me much, dear readers.

I've been telling you lately of my escapades, and my choices, and they haven't all been good ones, have they?

I worry about that.

Culpability is a strange word, and one I've really never thought about before.

But I'm thinking about it now.

I've ended it with him, dear readers.

He wasn't happy.

But it wasn't right, was it?

He was scaring me, and fear should never be a part of love.

I'm glad I've come to realize that before things went even further.

I want you to know... I'm not a bad person. I swear to you, I'm not. You started my story at the point of my bad decision... My worst decision. A decision that seemingly only a bad person would make.

Please realize that when we're living our lives, sometimes we get swept up in choices, and making the wrong one is sometimes all too easy.

As I write this, I'm staring at the dream catcher that hangs over my bed. Its feathers are fluttering in the wind, and I have to think of the good dreams that seem so long ago. It seems lately that I'm living in a nightmare, in a web of bad decisions. I'd like to get back to the good dreams again.

Because in spite of what it seems, I'm a good person.

I promise.

Tags: bad decisions, bad love, abuse, inappropriate relationships, heartbreak.

CHAPTER ONE

August 9

"I'm nervous," Leah whispers to me. She's jittery, that is for certain.

She's curled into my side as we rock in the wooden double glider, her foot bouncing against the wood planks. My arm is around her slender shoulders, stroking her back, and it's private and quiet on our porch. The only noise comes from the crash of the ocean in front of us, as it repeatedly and violently kisses the shore.

"Why, sweetie?" I ask, glancing down at her innocent face. She's got just a smattering of freckles on her nose, the only imperfection on her entire body. Well, Leah thinks they are an imperfection. I think they're adorable. "Is it school tomorrow? It's your sophomore year. This isn't your first rodeo. You know everyone, everyone knows you. There's no reason to be nervous."

My daughter shrugs, and her arm drops over the edge of our chair so she can rest it on Bo. He rubs his giant body against her legs, wanting more attention. He's never satisfied with any amount. We figure that's because we adopted him from a refuge, where he'd been stuck in a cage in the back corner. He'll never get all of his loneliness filled up.

"I dunno," she answers simply. "You know how I get."

"I know." My daughter is thoughtful and pensive, deep and soulful. I tell her that she has the soul of an eighty-year-old crammed in her teenage body. She doesn't like that much, but it's true. She's a perfectionist, and she thrives on schedules. When they change, such as when the summer turns into the school year, it's unsettling for her. But she adjusts quickly.

The night breeze comes off the water now, smelling of salt and dark sea creatures, and lifts our hair off our faces. We both close our eyes, enjoying the break from the sultry tropical humidity.

The Florida Keys are beautiful, but excruciatingly hot in the summer.

"You know what your grandma Lola taught me before she died?" I ask her, knowing full well that I've told her time and time again.

"Which thing?"

"Well, she taught me three important things," I say and Leah nods. She knows. "First, if you're going to do something, *do it*. Do it all the way. If you can't, don't even bother."

Leah stares at me. "And that helps me for tomorrow, how? Are you telling me not to go to school?"

I chuckle. "Nice try. I'm reminding you because you're like her in that way. You do things all the way, babe. You're nervous now, but tomorrow afternoon, you'll come home and you will have owned that school. You do things all the way. Always."

She can't argue. She knows it's true. She doesn't know the meaning of the expression *half-assed*.

"She also taught you to fight for what you want," Leah tells me, because she has the three things memorized. She should, since she's heard them all her life.

My mom died when I was only twelve, so I've always clung to her lessons. They're all I have left of her fading memory.

"Yes, she did. She knew that better than anyone. As a poor girl growing up on this island back then...well, she had to fight for every ounce of respect she had."

"But then she threw it all away by sleeping with everyone's husbands," Leah points out, and even now, that fact stabs me in the gut. I know why my mother was the way she was. My gran told me a hundred times, and I repeat her words to my daughter now.

"She felt she had something to prove," I say softly. "She never felt like she was enough. So she tried to prove it by using her power over things—*men, specifically*—especially those who weren't hers. I'm not proud of it, but it's who she was."

She always wore red, my mother. Everyone who remembers her remembers her in red. It was Lola Casey's signature color, and it was, in fact, her third lesson to me: always wear red lipstick.

"Maybe that's why she killed herself," Leah muses, staring out to sea. "Because of guilt."

I pause, then shake my head. "No. I don't think so. I think she just got tired of trying to prove herself."

Leah grasps my hand, her fingers wrapping around mine. "I feel sorry for you, Mom. You lost her when you were so little."

I focus on the horizon, at where the moon's pregnant belly grazes the water. "It's okay," I say softly. "She wasn't really meant for this world. She was wild and erratic. She hated being a mother, even though she loved me. Gran and Grandpa raised me and made me feel loved. I couldn't have asked for a better childhood."

I don't tell her of the sadness...the all-encompassing sadness that consumed me for years after my mom died. She doesn't need to know about that.

"I shouldn't feel sorry for myself ever," my daughter decides suddenly, squaring her slim shoulders. "Not when I've been so lucky, with you as my mom."

A gush of warmth wells through me. "You think so?"

Leah nods. "I know so."

She's still holding herself rigid, her foot still thumping on the floor, but I smile at her.

"Thank you, honey. Were you feeling sorry for yourself?"

Her face is troubled, but then she wipes it away; whether she's hiding it, or I imagined it, I don't know.

Leah shakes away the sadness, changing the subject. "Mom. Look at the moon."

"I see it."

The light from it shimmers on the surface, turning everything an elegant shade of silver. It's magical.

"Let's go night swimming," she urges me now. "It will feel like fairy lights out there, with the moon on the water so bright. It'll be like we're swimming in moonlight, like an ocean full of stars."

I laugh again because my daughter has the best poetic imagination.

She pleads, her lower lip full as she tugs on it with her white teeth. Her smile cost me eight thousand dollars last year, but it's perfect now. I shake my head.

"Babe, I'm exhausted. And I still have wine left." I hold up my glass and swirl the red liquid around. "But you can go. Just for a while. You've got to get up early tomorrow."

She smiles, because she knew I would give in, because I rarely say no to her. I don't have to. She's a good kid and never asks for anything unreasonable.

She jumps up and runs into the house to change, up the three flights of stairs to our third-floor quarters.

Two minutes later, she returns, with Bo on her heels and her red paddleboard in tow. She's dressed in black bikini bottoms and a red bikini top. At fifteen, she's long and lean, with the perfect curves of the young.

She starts to bounce down the porch steps, but I remember what I'd seen earlier, when I took her clean laundry into her room.

"Leah?"

She turns, her innocent face tilted toward me, waiting for me to speak.

"I saw your latest pictures on your bed. What did I tell you?"

I'm stern, and she sighs.

"No taking pictures of the guests."

"Exactly. And why is that?"

"Because they come here to relax. Not to have their privacy infringed upon."

"Exactly," I agree. "So why are you still taking pictures of them?"

"I'm sorry, Mom." She meets my gaze. "It's just... You know how I am. I love to catch people in candid moments. It's when they're most truthful."

"But not the guests, Li-Li," I tell her firmly. "I mean it. Take pictures of Skye, take pictures of Liam. Hell, take pictures of everyone you know. But not the guests."

"Okay." Her shoulders slump because she's bored with taking pictures of her friends. She's told me that a hundred times since she picked up the photography bug a year or so ago.

"But they're really good," I tell her in a conspiratorial whisper. "You've got talent, little girl."

She grins now. "Yeah?"

"Oh, yeah. I think you should take pictures for the yearbook this year."

She beams at that, and heads toward the beach, pacified now. She jogs over the very same sand that I used to play in when I was little. Once upon a time, I spent all of my time out there, amid all the other little kids running through the surf while their parents drank mojitos on the shore. This is an inn, after all, and my family has always run it. There has never been a shortage of tourists to stay here within our rooms, or a shortage of tourists flocking to the Keys.

Hemingway himself lived here once, too, years ago. He fished and drank and scribbled his tomes. It wasn't until after he left that he blew his brains out.

I don't know if that was a coincidence, or not.

What I do know is that Key West isn't the perfect place the tourists believe it to be. They see the beautiful facade, the colorful houses, the foamy waves. They don't see the close-minded people, or the long hours people like me have to work in order to give them that perfect vacation.

But that's fine. I choose this life. My grandparents left me this inn on the water, the Black Dolphin; it was their greatest treasure. I treasure it, too. It's in my blood.

I watch Leah loop the ankle strap around her leg and swim out to the break, leaving Bo sitting on the sand. He tilts his big head and watches her, as a stream of drool drips from his jowl. I hope he shakes it away out on the sand rather than in the house later. I'm sick of finding dried dog spit splattered on the walls.

Leah slices through the water efficiently, her slender arms like silent knives. The water is quiet. But Leah doesn't care about that. She wants to sit and float on top of her board, staring at the moon, pretending the rays hitting her skin are fairy dust.

My daughter is a dreamer, just like me. I can't complain about that.

I watch her dark head bobbing in the water, swimming to and fro, until her shadowy form melts into the night sky. The splash of the sea against the shore is soothing and soft, and I am completely relaxed when my cell phone rings a mere moment later.

There's only one person who would call me this late.

"Hey, Nate," I greet my ex-husband. "How're things?"

People still marvel that we can be as close as we are, but the truth of the matter is, we're closer now that we're divorced and living thousands of miles apart than we ever were when we were married.

"Good," he answers in his husky voice. I always did love that voice. Raspy, like he'd been sitting in a smoky blues bar for hours. It immediately makes a person think of sexy things, of long nights and rumpled bedding. "How's Leah?"

"She's a bit nervous about the first day of school," I answer, watching her stand on her board for a minute, before she loses the small wave and crashes into the water.

"That's normal," he replies. "It happens every year."

"I know. She's been going to school with the same kids for years now. I don't know why she still gets the jitters."

"Because she's Leah," he says simply, and that really says it all.

"She'll be fine," I tell him confidently, and he agrees.

"She always is."

We're quiet for a second, in the familiar way that two people who have known each other forever can be.

"How's the mutt?" he asks next. "Still eating you out of house and home?"

I sigh. "Yeah. Thanks for that."

"Hey, Leah's the one who sent me the adoption notice, and kept texting all the sad pictures. What was I supposed to do?"

"*Not* send her the money to adopt a mastiff/Saint Bernard mix?" I suggest wryly.

"Now that's just crazy talk."

"How about...I'll send Bo to you and *you* can feed him?"

"Nope. It's too hot here in Phoenix for him. That wouldn't be fair to him." His answer was just a little too quick.

"That's convenient."

He laughs. "It's been well thought out, trust me."

"I'm sure."

"So, can I talk to her? I wanna wish her luck."

I glance back out at the water. Leah slaps at the surface, beckoning Bo closer. He hates the water. When he eventually does go in someday, it will only be because of her. He'll do anything for her. She'd won his loyalty quickly and absolutely.

"She's paddleboarding."

"In the dark?"

I can practically hear Nate slap his own forehead.

"I thought we talked about this."

"The water is quiet tonight. It calms her nerves."

He can't argue with that.

"I don't let her do it often," I add.

"You indulge her," he tells me.

"Says the man who bought her an elephant."

"Touché."

"What's she going to wear tomorrow? I'm sure she has it all picked out already."

"Oh, yes. The uniform of her generation. Maroon Hollister shirt, white cutoffs and white Converses."

"Classy."

I chuckle and he laughs, and for a minute, just a minute, I forget why we ever divorced.

My glass is empty and I decide to splash a little more in. I open the door with my foot.

"How's business?" Nate asks as I walk through the quiet lobby, back to the kitchen.

"We're half-full right now," I tell him. "It's to be expected this time of year."

"You still have that one guy living in a bungalow?"

I think of the recently divorced Derek Collins staying out in bungalow three by the shore. It's the farthest away and he rarely comes to the big house. He's been here for over a year, ever since he and his wife first separated.

"Yeah."

"He's an odd one."

"No, he's not." I don't know why I feel defensive of him. "He's just sad because his wife left him. I know how that feels."

There's a pause on the phone, and that wasn't fair of me.

"I'm sorry. You didn't leave me," I amend. "It was a mutual decision."

"We grew apart," Nate defends himself. "You know we did. I didn't want the Black Dolphin. You did. I couldn't make that commute anymore, Emmy. You know that. We just... We wanted different things."

He wanted another baby, and I didn't. But that's another thing entirely.

"I know, Nate," I say. "We're fine. I don't know why I snapped at you."

"You didn't." He's forgiving now. "I'm sure you've had a long day. That place works you to the bone."

"Yes, it does," I agree, and I gulp the last of the wine as I lean against the broad center island. The kitchen is dark; I didn't bother to turn on a light. The industrial stove looms large on the back wall, the copper pots glistening as they hang overhead. They cast ominous shadows onto the wall, the edges and handles jutting into the night.

I'm considering opening another bottle, when from somewhere outside, Bo barks, and I cringe.

"Ugh. I thought Bo wasn't a barker," I say to him. "That was your argument for getting him. That he wouldn't disturb the guests."

"The shelter assured me that he wouldn't bark much… It's not in his nature. Only when there's something to bark at. Regardless of his looks, and I do admit he's ugly, he's a gentle giant."

"Well, your gentle giant is barking his head off."

I'm annoyed and Nate laughs.

"He's *your* gentle giant now."

I growl at him. "I've gotta go before he wakes everyone up."

I hang up on Nate's laughing.

I stride though the first floor of the inn, throwing open the doors, and I find Bo pacing on the beach. He's furious about something, his hackles up, his muscles tight, his head enormous as he runs to and fro, barking incessantly in every direction.

"Bo, get in here," I shout, annoyed. "Now!"

He doesn't move toward me, and he doesn't stop barking. So I shout out to Leah.

She doesn't answer, and I don't see her, so I jog down the steps, ready to grab the giant dog by the collar and drag him into the house.

"Leah! Seriously! Get your dog and come in!" I holler, marching toward the sea, my feet sinking into the wet sand as I scan the water for her bobbing head. "No arguments."

The water is empty, though, a smooth sheen of dark glass. I pause, completely still, my foot ready to take another step. I search the water again, making sure I didn't just miss her.

But I didn't.

She's not there.

My own hackles are up now, and something heavy settles in my belly. Something…something…isn't right. An instinct, something innate in my mother's heart, seems to know it. It's heavy, crushing down on my chest, and I struggle to swallow, struggle to breathe.

That's when I see it.

My daughter's red paddleboard has washed up on the sand, the ankle strap ripped and empty.

Leah is nowhere in sight.

CHAPTER TWO

June 28

Leah listened for a second, her ears straining.

Nothing.

Only the sounds of the sea billowed in through her window, snapping her sheer curtains as the breeze came through. It rustled the dream catcher hanging next to her bed.

She looped her hair up into a bun on top of her head, getting it off her shoulders. Both she and her mother shared the same straight and silky dark hair.

Leah's skin was the most beautiful color imaginable, eternally tanned and glowing. It was her eyes, though…her eyes were the most magnificent of all. A unique grayish-blue that seemed impossible to be natural, but they were. She had a global look, and she loved it. There wasn't a single color she didn't look good in.

It was just one more thing to thank her great-gran for. Back in the day, her great-grandparents had bucked social norms and had gotten married, even though she was poor and he was rich. Great-Gran's family was Creole; they had come from New Orleans, hence the exotic good looks that both she and her mother had inherited.

If only they were still alive. Leah would give anything to sit on the porch again and listen to her great-gran's wisdom. She and Gramps would rock in those chairs and watch the sea, and talk to Leah as if she was an adult, even back when she was just a little kid. It was because of them that she had an extensive vocabulary and an old soul.

Those days with Gramps and Gran were long gone, though, and she lay on her belly now, her legs kicking one by one in the breeze, up, then down. Up, then down. Her calves stretched with the movement, relaxing the tight cord that ran up her leg.

Her mother was working late again, as she always did.

Emmy lived and breathed for the Black Dolphin, and Leah once again chuckled about the name. Gramps had named it for his dark-haired wife—the woman he had declared as the most beautiful woman he'd ever seen, and she'd been able to swim like a fish...like a black dolphin. It was a name people remembered.

Bo raised his head, at attention, and Leah glanced at him.

"What's wrong, boy?" She'd only had him for a month now, but he was her protector. It was as if he knew that she'd saved him from being put down in that rescue shelter. He'd only had days to live when she'd convinced her father to adopt him. No one else had wanted the giant dog with mastiff in his blood. He looked a bit terrifying, but Leah liked it. No one else knew that his heart was soft and sweet. It was her secret.

She got up and went to the window, unconcerned that she was only dressed in a sports bra and athletic shorts. Her room was on the third floor, and guests didn't come up this far. Settling into the window seat, she stared out…at the dark sky, at the dark water, at the dark treetops. Everything was dark, everything was quiet. But for bungalow three.

Derek Collins.

Mr. Collins had moved here during his divorce, and he had become a permanent fixture. He kept to himself and he was quiet and polite, mild mannered and tall. She liked him, even though she didn't know him well. He always smelled of peppermint, and he didn't bother anyone. He usually went to bed earlier, but not tonight.

Tonight, there was still a light on, and even though Leah couldn't see him through the drawn curtains, she suspected he was preparing for his son's arrival. Liam would come in a few days, at the end of the school year, to spend the summer with his dad. It would be their second summer here, and Leah was grateful.

Liam Collins had become one of her best friends, her link to the outside world. They were almost the exact same age, and throughout the year, she and Liam kept in contact via email and FaceTime. He told her of the artistic world in New York City, and she kept him abreast of the whole lot of nothing that happened on Key West. He envied the quiet here, and she envied the utter fullness and bustle of the city.

At the end of the day, though, Leah figured that everyone just wanted what they couldn't have. It was human nature.

"You want to go for a walk?" she asked her dog, and of course, his tail started wagging madly at the *W*-word. She smiled. "Okay."

Bo trotted heavily down the stairs, his nails clicking on the hardwood floors as they retrieved his leash from a cabinet in the kitchen. Mom insisted they keep Bo out of sight as much as possible, so as not to scare the guests. Because of that, Leah ended up taking him for walks on the beach at night.

She was just lucky to have him at all. She knew it was only because her parents felt guilty for getting divorced. Bo was a guilt gift, a momentary lapse in her mother's rigid demeanor under pressure from her dad. The inn was always her top priority. Anything that wasn't in the inn's best interest was usually shot down immediately. Bo had been a rare exception.

Leah patted Bo's head as she snapped the leash onto his collar.

"Let's go," she told him. She didn't have to say it twice. He pulled her out the back door and down the steps, yanking at her arm. Before she knew it, she was on the beach, her bare feet sinking into the sand.

Their private beach stretched over a hundred yards, which was a long piece of real estate, considering. Land here on the island was at a premium. People paid huge amounts of money to come here and disconnect from the outside world. Guests went so far as to hand their phones over to the Black Dolphin front desk…to be locked into tiny lockers, to protect themselves from the temptation to punch at the buttons, to scroll mindlessly through their newsfeeds, and to respond to the red notification symbols. Technology was like a drug, and people usually couldn't save themselves. They needed help for that.

Her mom was happy to oblige.

In fact, she limited Leah's online time as well, to only an hour per day. Leah felt that was too strict and, in fact, had campaigned her father to intercede. But he wouldn't. He and Emmy were both committed to being on the same team, and providing a "unified parental front," regardless of the thousands of miles between them.

Phoenix was a long way from Key West.

Bo stepped nervously around the lapping water, and Leah laughed.

"You're such a chicken," she told him. "Water isn't going to hurt you. It's nice. See?" She knelt and splashed at it, lapping it up onto her arms, cooling them down. It was only the end of June, and already it was hot and balmy. Summer was here.

Bo was skeptical and he wouldn't come near the edge. She rolled her eyes. "Fine. You don't know what you're missing, though."

He didn't care. He trotted on, and Leah followed, tethered by the long leash.

Around them, the sounds of the night were loud. Hawks and owls screamed and cried, and if Leah hadn't been so used to them, it would be unnerving. Lizards scuttled through the sea grass, and there was always something moving here in the landscape. Birds, lizards, bugs. *Big* bugs. Leah wasn't fond of the palmetto bugs—oversize cockroaches as long as her index finger. The sound they made when they flew in the air imprinted on a person's mind forever. It wasn't a thing you could forget. *Pfht, pfht, pfht.*

Leah and Bo walked to the edge of where their private beach ended, and then they even walked along the public section. Since it was almost midnight, there were barely any people out and about, short of the handful at the Cuban-style outdoor bar-restaurant at the end of the pier. Nico's. From here, Leah could hear the festive music, and the loud din of chatter. That came from the tourists having one too many mojitos. She was used to that sound.

This was a vacation destination, after all.

When they reached the large wet poles of the pier, they turned around and walked back, Bo leaving big paw prints in the sand. Leah smiled when she imagined what people must think when they saw the size of them. They probably thought there was a bear or a beast loose on the island. To be fair, Bo *was* a beast. Just not the kind they probably assumed he was. Even now, with his long strands of drool dangling from his jowls, he looked massive and mean.

She patted his head. "Let's go back, boy."

So they did. They headed for the inn, and when they were almost there, Leah caught sight of Derek Collins pacing behind his bungalow. All three of the bungalows were spaced evenly apart, lining the edge where the large lawns met the beach sand. They were framed by tall sea grass, and as isolated and remote as they could be.

"What time does your flight get in?" he asked in a low

tone, his phone to his ear. Leah paused now, interested. He was obviously talking to Liam. "Okay. I'll be at the airport. Have a safe flight, son."

He hung up, and a cherry burned bright in the darkness. He was smoking, Leah realized in surprise. She'd never seen him smoke before. Was he anxious about Liam coming? That would be absurd. Liam was the most laid-back boy she knew. Yes, he wore a bit of eyeliner and had shaggy hair, but that all worked with his rock-and-roll vibe. He had to dress like that, since he was the front man of the Roadrunners. Didn't all band members do that?

Looks could be deceiving, though, and Liam was a pussycat, just like Bo.

Leah kept walking now, satisfied that he'd be here soon. That excited her. Finally, something new to break the island monotony. Her best friend Skye would be excited, too. Leah knew that Skye had a crush on Liam, but she was pretty sure it wasn't reciprocated. In fact, she felt a strong suspicion that Liam was actually starting to like *her*.

That would complicate things eventually, but for now, she chose to ignore it. If she was lucky, it might go away on its own.

Derek noticed her now that she was close, and he raised his hand in greeting. She smiled at him, and he smiled back, and then he disappeared into his bungalow.

Her phone buzzed as she was climbing the back steps, with a text from her mother.

Where are you?

Just coming back from walking Bo, she answered. I'll be right up.

Her mother must've finally stopped working for the night. Leah knew that when her mom reached their owner's apartment, she would be exhausted and flopped on the couch with wine on the coffee table and some ice cream and a spoon in her hand.

Leah hoped it was Rocky Road.

CHAPTER THREE

August 9

The water flashes red and blue with the Coast Guard boats combing the area.

Their hulls skim the surface, their spotlights shining into the depths. It's been two hours since Leah's paddleboard washed up. They haven't found her yet. A scream has been poised in my throat for that same amount of time but it hasn't emerged.

My heart knows what my mind isn't ready to accept.

They're not going to find my baby.

I feel it in my bones. I see it on their faces. They all steal glances at me, as I sit here on the porch, a sweater gathered around my shoulders, and I see it in their eyes.

Leah is gone.

It's an impossible thing to grasp. She's such a strong

swimmer. Bo leans against my legs and I absently grip his shoulder, my fingers buried in his fur. It keeps my hand from shaking.

I see divers plunging into the water, oxygen tanks on their backs, and I know that if they don't find her by morning, they'll switch from a search-and-rescue mission, to recovery.

Oh, God.

My chest tightens unbearably, until I don't think I can breathe. I suck and suck, and nothing comes. Strong hands grip my shoulders, and I turn to see the youth pastor, Michael Hutchins.

"Focus on my face," he tells me. "Focus on my face."

His face blurs in and out, and my vision is rimmed in black ink. It bends and contorts, and then everything else is black, too.

When I open my eyes again, I'm in the house.

I'm lying on the couch and the pastor is sitting next to me. He's watching me, waiting. I can still see the red lights flashing on the walls of the den. I cringe.

"It wasn't a nightmare," I manage to say.

He shakes his head. "They called for a chaplain to sit with you," he tells me. "I'm the one on call tonight."

"They can't find her, Hutch," I say softly. "This can't be happening."

He reaches over and grasps my hand. His is warm and large. "We don't know anything yet," he says comfortingly, but we both know that in all probability if she were going to be found, they would've found her by now.

At least, if she is still alive.

"How long will they keep looking?" I ask, because I never want them to stop.

"I don't know," Hutch answers. He glances out the windows. "They're hard at it still."

"I shouldn't have let her go out there tonight," I tell him. "She wanted to paddleboard, and she wanted me to go with her. I should've gone. If I would've been there, this wouldn't have happened…" My words break off in a sob, and I press my fist to my mouth.

Hutch grips my shoulders, his eyes warm.

"Don't think like that," he says softly. "You can't do that."

But it's the truth, and we both know it. Who lets their kid go night swimming?

"We live on an island," Hutch says, as though he can read my thoughts. "We have a different way of life here. People swim at all hours of the day and night. You didn't do anything wrong."

I close my eyes. If I don't look, maybe nothing will be real. Maybe this really is a nightmare, and I'll wake up from it soon. Maybe if I just go to sleep, everything will be different when I wake.

"Maybe you should go change clothes," Hutch suggests. "You'd be more comfortable."

I'm still in the same clothing I plunged into the ocean in, when in a panic I looked for my daughter myself. I dove in and searched among the waves for several minutes before I called 911. Maybe if I called sooner…maybe…maybe…

"I'm fine," I say shortly. My jeans are uncomfortable plastered to my skin, but I deserve it.

I don't open my eyes.

"You don't have to wait with me," I add. "Truly."

Hutch shakes his head. "I'm here for the duration. Can I get you some coffee?"

"That might be good," I say, just because I'd like to be alone. I doubt I can even swallow coffee.

He nods and heads off for the kitchen. I get up and walk to the window, and see that a couple of the lifesaving boats are docked now. The divers are on the pier.

Have they given up?

One of them sees me and looks away.

My heart flutters.

No. It's too soon.

I feel like I'm not in control of my own body as I run down the steps and to the shore. "You can't stop!" I shout, the wind whipping my hair. "She's there. She's there somewhere. Please, please, keep looking."

I try to get into the water again so that I can keep looking myself, but someone grabs me and holds me tight.

"Don't," they say. "Don't."

"Let me go." I wrench away, and I plunge into the sea. I swim and swim, searching and searching. My fingers trail the sandy bottom, trying to feel for her. She's got to be here. She's got to be here. If I can find her, I can fix it.

Please God, please God.

I swim and swim in the darkness until I can't feel my arms and legs. I swim until my lips are blue and numb. I swim until I can swim no more. I'm limp as someone hauls me out of the water, and I'm a heap on the sand. Someone wraps me in a blanket and my teeth chatter.

"Don't stop," I beg them. "Please."

But their searchlights are dark now.

They're giving up for the night. I whimper and moan, and retch onto the beach.

"Call my ex-husband," I say aloud, to someone, to anyone. "Tell him to come."

I close my eyes and lie down, pressing my cheek into the sand.

Hands come and pull me away and lead me into the house, and I let them. Because nothing matters now.

Not anymore.

CHAPTER FOUR

June 29

Leah and Skye sunned themselves on the sand.
They knew that sunbathing could lead to wrinkles or
skin cancer, but they weren't old enough to worry about
it yet. They were still immortal.

"You have better skin than me," Skye grumbled.

"Yep," Leah agreed cheerfully. "Sorry about your luck."

Skye rolled her eyes. "You suck."

"Don't be salty."

Skye laughed. "If I didn't love you, I might hate you,"
her friend decided.

"Whatever." Leah wasn't worried.

Even the Black Dolphin's private beach was a bit crowded
today, since the weather was so perfect. Baby blue sky, cot-

ton clouds, a slight breeze. It was something straight out of a Jimmy Buffett song, and the tourists were eating it up.

The girls had been getting looks from most of the males on the beach, with Leah in her white bikini, and Skye in her red. They knew, but ignored it. They weren't here for boys today. Very seldom did they indulge in tourists. Too much drama for too little payoff.

"You're still coming to my parents' party tonight, right?" Skye asked with a yawn. "Don't leave me alone."

Leah nodded. "Yep."

"Is that your new favorite word?" Skye lifted an eyebrow and Leah opened her mouth.

"Y—"

"Don't even say it," Skye warned her. Leah grinned.

Skye looked down at the cast on her arm. "I'm going to have such a crooked tan."

"It's almost time to get the cast off," Leah reminded her. "It'll be fine."

Neither of them pointed out the fact that it was Leah who had accidentally dropped Skye during a cheer stunt at summer camp. Her hand had slipped, and Skye had fallen. It was an accident, and it didn't happen often. Leah felt terrible.

"Tonight is gonna suck so bad," Skye said instead, thinking again about her parents' cocktail party for her father's clients. "God. It's gonna be all business talk and kissing ass."

Leah laughed. "True. But we get to go out on a yacht, so that'll be fun."

"It's just a rented yacht," Skye reminded her.

"But still," Leah argued. "I've never been on a yacht. Not a fancy one anyway."

Skye seemed to cheer up a little. "What are you going to wear?"

"My little black dress," Leah answered. "It's my go-to. You?"

Skye nodded. "Same."

It was practically universal girl code. A fancy party = LBD.

They moaned about it awhile longer and debated which shoes to wear, and then they headed home to change clothes and get ready.

Leah stood in front of her bathroom mirror, twisting her hair up and then letting it down. She finally decided to wear it up. It would be breezy on the water, and she didn't want to deal with the tangles afterward.

"You look beautiful," her mother said from the door. "Here, I brought you a shawl."

"A shawl?" Leah arched an eyebrow at the old-fashioned term, and her mother laughed.

"It was actually your grandma Lola's." She handed the sheer slip of red lacy chiffon to Leah.

"It's really pretty," her daughter conceded.

"Yeah, it's timeless," Emmy agreed. "Just don't let your grandmother's behavior rub off on you." She arched an eyebrow sarcastically at her daughter. Leah laughed.

"Okay. I promise not to instantly become a bad decision-maker."

Her mom smiled. "Lord, you look just like her."

Leah imagined that to be a good thing. Lola Casey had

made poor decisions, but everyone to this day spoke of her beauty.

Her mother cleared her throat. "Now, tonight, don't get too close to the railings if the sea is rough."

"I know, Mom." Leah rolled her eyes good-naturedly.

"Are you staying over at Skye's afterward?"

"I think so."

"Well, text me when you get there safe."

Leah nodded, agreeing.

She soon found herself aboard the 150-foot *Happy Ending*. Skye was watching for her, and rushed to push a glass of punch into her hand. "Get me out of here," Skye said under her breath. "Mr. Bolton is smashed."

Leah glanced behind her friend to find the man staring lecherously at them both. "Gross," she muttered, steering her friend away.

A small band was playing on the bow, and the girls wove their way through groups of chatting people until they were next to the music. They swayed with the beat, staying a safe distance from the drunk elderly man who was looking for them with groping hands.

"Half the people from the island are here, I think," Leah observed, staring at all the finely dressed guests. She recognized a couple of teachers from school, a couple of pastors from her church, and even Liam's dad.

"You know my dad," Skye said wryly. "He's gotta schmooze."

"Yeah." Leah glanced at the Haydens, who were both

laughing with a client. "Your mom looks pretty good at it, too."

"Oh, yeah. She plays the part."

Mrs. Hayden caught Leah's eye and waved, with a smile. Leah waved back.

She and Skye danced as the sun set, dropping down over the horizon in an explosion of color, and it turned out to be not so bad, after all.

They met a couple of boys their own age, nephews of a new client here for the summer hunting for real estate investments. They hung out and talked and danced, and it was definitely better than sitting at home with nothing to do.

It was toward the end of the evening when Leah got the text.

She reached into the slim black clutch that she had borrowed from her mom and pulled her phone out. She expected it to be her mom, actually. Making sure she was okay.

But it wasn't.

Her eyes narrowed at the message. Not at the sender, because she knew him well, but because of his words.

You look stunning tonight, my dear.

She reread the message in confusion. Was she imagining that there was something new underlying there?

He'd never spoken to her in such a way.

A second text came through a few minutes later.

I hope it doesn't make you feel uncomfortable that I told you this. I just thought you should know.

She looked up, trying to find him among the crowd.

She wasn't exactly sure how it made her feel, to be honest. It felt different, almost wrong. But it was oddly exciting, too…to be noticed.

She wondered if that made her a bad person.

Or maybe she was just imagining that it meant anything at all.

CHAPTER FIVE

August 16

"Emmy."

Nate's voice is serious. I close my eyes. Somehow, I know I don't want to hear what he's going to say. He's been here for the past seven days, ever since *it* happened.

My ex-husband sits next to me now on the darkened porch, the crashing sea a perfect background for an ominous conversation. So many things pulled us apart over the years, so many "irreconcilable differences," but we have one huge commonality now.

Devastating, soul-wrenching grief.

"The sheriff's office is tentatively calling it a drowning related to a shark attack," he tells me, his voice decisively calm and steady. "There was an eight-foot bull shark sighted on the public beach earlier that day. The shredded ankle loop, the blood on the board, it all points toward the same thing."

"But she hasn't washed ashore," I say quietly, and my tongue is wooden. I can't feel it, and I swirl it around, trying to feel it, but it doesn't work. "There's no body, Nate."

Body. I'm talking about my precious girl in such strange terms. She's not a *body.* She's a person. She's *my* person.

Nate looks away, his mouth tight. "She might've been pulled out to sea, or…there might not be anything left."

Jesus God.

I exhale in a rush, and my breath feels sick. My hands shake, like they have every day since it happened.

"Go ahead and say it," I mutter. "This is my fault. If I hadn't let her go out that night…"

Nate puts a hand on my arm and his voice is stern. "Stop. I don't blame you, Emmy. It's something that happened. It's tragic. My heart is broken and life will never be the same, but it wasn't your fault. Of that, I am certain."

His absence of anger makes me feel even guiltier, because *I* know the truth. *I* know that it's all my fault. It was my job to not let her endanger herself in any way, and in one lapse of judgment, she paid the ultimate price for *my* mistake.

"I mean it, Em," he adds. "You need to believe that."

I don't, and I never will. But I don't argue with him.

"I think you should sell the inn," he says quietly a few minutes later. My hands clench around the arms of the rocking chair. "You would get top dollar for it, and you could get away from here, from this place. You could maybe even come to Phoenix. Maybe we could try again…"

His voice trails off and I fight the urge to laugh bitterly. A reunion? That was Leah's favorite daydream. I'd never do that now, not now that she isn't here to enjoy it. That would be an insult to her memory.

"We both know it wouldn't work," I tell him instead, my voice soft and even. "The death of a child…a couple rarely survives that. Besides, I don't want to sell the inn. Leah lived here. I'll never leave it. It's all I have left of her."

I haven't been in her room since the night she died.

Died.

Jesus. I can't say the word aloud, and I can barely even think it.

My daughter is dead. My beautiful, vibrant, strong daughter. It's unfathomable.

If I close my eyes and think hard enough, I imagine her like she was that night, poised on the steps and listening to me chastise her for taking photos again. Her face was soft and vulnerable, and all I'd done was come down on her. If I could just go back in time, I'd grab her and pull her away from the sea. I'd never let her swim in it again.

"You're too isolated here," Nate says, pulling me from my thoughts. His voice is firm, as though he has a say in it. "You need to be around people, Emmy."

"I am," I tell him. "I have guests here every day."

"Not the guests. I mean *real* people who you can talk to."

"What time does your flight leave?" I change the subject and Nate sighs.

"Six a.m. Are you sure you'll be okay?"

We've had this conversation at least ten times during the past week. I nod.

"Yes. We have to get back to normal. Our new normal."

It feels odd now, because when Nate leaves, our tie will be severed. Leah was our common bond, the last vestige from our marriage. Now that she's gone, there's no reason to stay in touch. It's as though he reads my mind, and he grabs my hand, squeezing it gently.

"We should…we should organize a memorial," Nate says now, and ice forms in my rib cage, stabbing my heart.

"No," I snap. "We can't. I can't do that yet, Nate."

He stares at me, his eyes filled with his own pain, yet so concerned with mine.

"Okay. We can wait. I'll come back whenever you're ready to do it. I'm always here for you, Em," he tells me. "I want you to check in with me, and we'll talk. Right?"

I nod. "Okay."

But I know what my intentions are. I'll phase him out, slowly but surely. Our calls will get further and further apart, until they disappear. He's too painful. He reminds me too much of Leah…the way he holds his mouth, the way he cocks his head. I can't do it.

"I can take Bo back with me," he offers, and this startles me. My gaze snaps up to where Bo is sleeping beneath a palm tree on the front lawn, his big head resting on his large paws. He sleeps there a lot nowadays, as though he's waiting for Leah to return. The thought of Nate taking him fills me with panic.

"No," I answer quickly. "It's too hot in Phoenix for him."

"It's hot here, too," Nate answers. I can see that we both

want this last piece of Leah. But Nate acquiesces. "But you can keep him, if you want. I just thought you hated him."

"Of course I don't hate him." Leah loved him, and now so do I. I owe that much to her. "He needs to be here in case we find her."

Nate arches an eyebrow but he doesn't say anything. He's being so careful, treading so cautiously, as though I might break.

And maybe I will. It's hard to say at this point.

"I love you, Em. I'll always love you."

"I know."

His eyes are mossy green, and for a minute, for just a minute, I want to lose myself in his arms, to forget my pain. I know those arms. I know the heat from his chest, the shape of his biceps, the beat of his heart. But taking comfort in him tonight won't help anything. Not really. It wouldn't bring Leah back, and in fact, it would only make things worse.

I shake my head, as though I'm shaking that option away. It's not an option. It will never be an option.

"Emmy," he says quietly. "Our daughter drowned."

My heart squeezes, and tears fill my eyes.

"She's gone," he continues. "But she died in the ocean that she loved. That's some consolation. It's small, but it's something."

"We don't know that," I insist. "Not for sure."

He's silent, and nods slightly. "We do, though."

"I'm gonna turn in," I say shortly. "I'll make you breakfast before you go."

"No, that's okay. I still don't like to eat that early." His smile is wry and I should've remembered that. But my brain is foggy still…cloudy with grief. I don't know when it will fade, when I'll be able to think straight once again. Because my daughter is dead. My heart knows it, even if my lips can't say it.

"Okay. Good night, Nate."

I pull my hand gently from his grasp and walk up to my owner's apartment, the one we used to live in as a family. It looms dark and lonely at the top of three flights of stairs, and I know that once Nate leaves, I'll probably start sleeping in an empty guest room. It's too lonely in my apartment without Leah. It feels too wrong to be here without her.

But then again, everything feels wrong without Leah.

I make myself a cup of chamomile tea, careful to move around the half-empty glass of water sitting on the counter. Leah had put it there a week ago, an hour before she'd gone out to paddleboard. Her hand had been on the glass, her lips on the rim, and I feel if I move it now, it will propel her memory even further away, or diminish her somehow. Right now, I still have things that she touched. If I don't move them, she will stay nearer to me. I can even pretend that she's coming back, that she'll just be gone for a while.

I know how illogical that is, and I ponder it as I sit in a chair by the window. There's a big difference between knowing and *caring*.

Across the room, her unused guitar still sits where she had it last, leaning against the wall. The rich brown wood gleams in the lamplight, and I remember when she sang and laughed as she played. She wasn't particularly good, but she didn't care and neither did I. We sang anyway.

It sits silent now.

Time was an enemy I hadn't expected. It raised its head and robbed me of my daughter. I only had fifteen years with her.

It wasn't enough.

If I'd known, I would've sang more songs, taken more walks, taken more time off work, made more breakfasts. I left her alone a lot because of my job, because that was what I thought was important. I wanted to leave her a legacy, and now there's no one to leave that legacy to.

I lived in a castle of glass and in one moment it all shattered.

I'm the queen of nothing, an empire without an heir.

Damn it.

I drop my head against the back of the chair.

If I close my eyes, I can remember the sound of her voice, the soft timbre, the melodious laugh. It seems to echo through the empty rooms. How long will that last? How long until I forget?

The idea of that, of forgetting, sets me into a panic. I jump to my feet and pace. I can't forget. Not *anything*.

As I walk to and fro, I pull out my phone and listen to the last voice mail I had from my daughter. *Hey, Mom. I'm stopping at Skye's for a while on my way home. I'll see you in a bit. Love you!*

I listen to it again, then again, then again a fourth time before I take a shaky breath and slide my phone back into my pocket.

I pause in front of a picture on the hallway wall, of Leah and her best friend Skye from last year. They are both in their freshman cheerleading uniforms, their faces painted, their hair in jaunty ponytails. They have their arms wrapped around each other's shoulders, two peas in a pod.

If only Skye had spent the night on the eve before school started, maybe it wouldn't have happened. Or if I had taken up her invitation and gone into the water with her. Sharks would've shied away from two people.

God. When will I stop with the "if only" scenarios? It is exhausting. If only, if only, if only.

If onlys are useless.

My pacing leads me down the hall toward our bedrooms. My door stands wide-open, and Leah's is tightly closed. I can't see in there. I can't see the furniture begging to be used, the bed waiting to be slept in, the Converses waiting to be worn by the door. It all haunts me, and so I keep it concealed. I'm not ready.

I practically leap past her door, and then close my own, so that I can't see outside, so that I can't see the door decorated with Leah's name in blue sparkles and dolphins, with school newspaper clippings and photos. I can't see it right now. Because I know she isn't behind the door.

Within the safety of my room, I undress and get ready for bed, collapsing into the soft sheets. But of course, I don't sleep. I don't sleep much anymore. My body is rebellious. I want to escape into the oblivion that sleep would bring, but my brain won't allow it. Instead, it tortures me with memories, with guilt.

I lie here, night after night, wide-awake.

Tonight, I hear Bo's toenails on the floor outside my room, and I sigh.

I forgot him.

I get up and let him in.

He lies down directly inside the door, and soon, I hear his even breaths. Even the dog is sleeping. I toss and turn, and when I get up to pace at 2:00 a.m., I wake him by accident. He watches me in the dark with big soulful eyes.

"Did you see it happen?" I ask him quietly. He cocks his head like he's trying to understand. "If you weren't so afraid of the water, maybe you could've saved her. You're worthless, you know that? You were supposed to guard her."

Another *if only*.

Bo drops his head onto his paws as though he already thought of that, as though he, too, carries that guilt.

It makes me feel bad, and I pat the space on the bed next to me.

Bo jumps up with me, and when I bury my face into his neck, I swear I can smell a hint of Leah…her coconut lotion and sunshine. It brings hot tears to my eyes and I can't control them. I sob, out of control, and Bo patiently allows it, even though his fur is soaking wet by morning.

CHAPTER SIX

June 30

"Leah!"

The voice, a blend of excited boy and mature man, carried down the beach, and Leah lifted her head. She was standing thigh-deep in the water, her board floating beside her. When she saw Liam striding toward her, dressed in black shorts and a black tank top, her face lit up.

"Liam!" she shrieked, and she sloshed onto the shore and propelled herself into Liam's waiting arms, soaking his shirt. Neither of them cared. "When did you get here?"

"Just now," he answered, and while he would've lingered in the embrace, Leah pulled away to look at him. She examined his angular features, his slant of a mouth, his dark eyes.

"You're not wearing eyeliner," she pointed out. He smiled.

"Why bother? It would just melt off here anyway."

"Good point," she agreed. "I'm pretty sure you've grown an entire foot."

"I'm six-one now," Liam acknowledged, and she gathered he was secretly proud of that fact. Somehow, being tall seemed to exude manliness. "I had a growth spurt."

"Yeah, you did," she agreed again, and her arm snaked through his, the paleness of his New York City skin in sharp contrast to hers. "What are your plans today?"

Before he could answer, Bo came barreling down the beach, growling the entire way, his gold eyes fixed on Liam. Liam froze and Leah laughed.

"Don't mind him," she said, but she moved in front of Liam just the same. "He's all bark. Bo, no. He's a friend. Pet him, Liam."

Bo sniffed at him suspiciously, but Liam obediently offered a hand. After a minute, Bo was satisfied, and flopped to the ground, allowing Liam to pat his belly.

"See?" Leah lifted an eyebrow. "Told you."

"Jesus. How much does he eat?" Liam asked, eyeing the massive dog. Leah laughed.

"More than you and I do put together. Mom complains about it all the time."

"I bet. How is she?"

"Mom?" Leah shrugged. "The same. Hard at work."

"I like her."

"She likes you, too." Leah glanced down the beach and

saw Derek behind his cabin, cigarette in hand. "When did your dad start smoking?"

Liam rolled his eyes. "I don't know. Since I was here at Christmas. His job is getting stressful, he says."

"Lung cancer is stressful, too," Leah pointed out.

"Hey, I'm not the smoker," Liam defended himself, his hands splayed wide. Leah smiled.

"What are your plans today? Wanna hang out?"

"Absolutely. Those *are* my plans."

He carried her paddleboard and they dropped it off behind the inn. Bo stayed with Liam as Leah changed into jean shorts and a T-shirt, and then the three of them set off toward Nico's on the pier for lunch. Bo waited at the door, flopping down in a heap as he eyed the food around him enviously.

At a nearby table, the pair ordered sandwiches and sodas.

"What's been happening? What have I missed?" Liam asked, his fingers drumming on the acrylic tabletop. Since they were seated on the pier, sea gulls perched nearby on the railings, waiting for crumbs that might be dropped.

"You mean since we chatted last week?" Leah reached for the soda from the waitress and sipped at it. "Nothing. Nothing ever happens here. You know that."

"How's Skye?"

"She broke her wrist at cheer camp," Leah filled him in, omitting the part where she had dropped her. "So that's new. I have to go help her wash her hair every other day. She won't let her mom."

"She hates her mom," Liam remembered.

"Yep. I don't think Christy's that bad, just annoying. But, man. She's hard on Skye."

"It's a mom-daughter thing," Liam said wisely. "None of them get along at our age."

He sounded so old, and Leah laughed when she told him so. He blushed, the red tinting his cheekbones. Leah couldn't help but notice how they seemed chiseled now, more pronounced. He'd definitely grown up this year, turning more into a man. She wasn't sure how that made her feel. He shifted in his seat, thinking she was offended.

"I mean, you and your mom do, but most don't."

She rolled her eyes. "I never see mine. So, we don't really count."

"My dad says she's the hardest worker he's ever seen," Liam told her. "And she's so pretty. I wonder why she doesn't just get remarried?"

Leah froze, her gaze on Liam. "You mean, so she can just be taken care of by a man? Are you sexist now?"

"No, of course not!" he said. "Never. I was just saying... It would be easier for her if she had someone, and..."

He trailed off and Leah laughed.

"I'm kidding. Calm down." She took another sip of her soda. "I don't know what's going on with that. She and my dad have a weird sort of attached relationship. I don't know why they don't just get back together and be done with it."

"Some people are happier apart." Liam nodded, a teenage sage. "Mine are. Of course, they hate each other, so..." He shrugged. His phone dinged. He glanced at it.

"Speaking of moms..." He punched at his phone, answering his mother's text.

Leah used the moment to check her own phone. She found several texts from *Him*. She didn't want to even think *His* name, because something felt off about the way he'd been texting her.

Today, he sent two photos of himself, just his torso, with two different shirts on.

Which one should I wear today? he asked.

She studied them, wondering why he wanted her opinion. But then chose.

The blue one, she answered.

Thanks, he replied immediately. I want to look good today. I never know what to wear.

What is so special about today? she asked, and her heart was going pitter-patter, and she didn't even know why.

I think I'll be seeing you, won't I? Her stomach lurched, but not in a bad way. It was a startling thing, to have things changing between them. He'd known her for so long, and now…it was different. But she had to admit, even though it felt weird, it felt good to have someone care about what she thought. He was even going to change his shirt because of her opinion.

"Here you go, *chica*." Nico delivered their food himself, and Leah and Liam both put their phones away.

"Plane food sucks," Liam said when Leah eyed him shoveling french fries into his mouth five at a time. "I haven't eaten all day."

She gave him her fries, too, and he ate every last one of them. "Do I want ice cream, too?" he asked Leah.

She rolled her eyes again. "No. You've forgotten the

heat here. Do you want to throw up on the sand from stuffing yourself?"

"You're right."

He paid the bill, insisting on paying for both of them. That gave Leah a funny feeling, too. Even though he'd done it in the past, it felt different now. While he was paying, she couldn't help but check her phone, anticipation flooding her.

Sure enough, *He'd* texted again.

I hope you don't think I'm a dirty old man.

Of course not, she texted back, while Liam handed Nico some bills. You're not old.

I just feel a connection to you. I've really noticed it lately. It feels different than before.

Her face flamed. Was this really happening?

Nico started chatting with her, bringing her attention away from the confusing texts. "I haven't seen you in a while," Nico said. "You need to come in more often and brighten this place up. I gave your monster here a beef bone."

She glanced down, and Bo moved to protect his new treasure, as though Leah might want the wet hunk of mangled marrow and bone.

"Thanks, Nico."

"*De nada, chica.*" He winked, his brown eyes sparkling, and she smiled back.

As they were clamoring down the wooden pier steps, Liam looked at her.

"That dude creeps me out. He's into you, and he's like... forty."

She smacked his arm. "Oh, my gosh. Forty isn't that old. And he's not into me. He's just friendly. He's *married*."

"That doesn't always mean anything." Liam was wry, and Leah felt awful.

"Oh, God. I'm sorry, Li." His mother had cheated on his father. She'd forgotten.

"No worries."

She knew he was used to it now, the fact that his mother had betrayed his father. But she should've remembered. She shouldn't have brought up anything related to cheating. To change the subject, she gestured toward the giant buoy in the bay. It tilted with the waves, the faded red and white paint peeling on top.

"Race you."

She took off running, with Bo on her heels. Bo, of course, skidded to a stop at the edge of the water, but Leah barely paused to pull off her shirt and toss it behind her on the sand. She dove into the waves in her sports bra, and didn't even check to see if Liam was following.

He wasn't.

Liam stood next to Bo, and when Leah reached the buoy and swung up onto it victoriously, he grinned at her beaming face. She did her victory dance while balanced on the slippery float, and he couldn't help but notice how beautiful she'd gotten. She looked like a younger version of her mother, Emmy, confident and exuberant. She had this glowing quality that he couldn't put his finger on. No one up north in the city had it.

Her wet sports bra was transparent in the sunlight. He noticed, and so did a couple of guys standing nearby who elbowed each other and eyed her pink nipples straining against the white fabric.

"Knock it off," Liam growled at them. "Fucking ass-holes."

They rolled their eyes and ignored him, and Liam motioned for Leah to come in. She took her time swimming in, and when she met him on the shore, he handed her her dry shirt.

"Put this on," he told her gruffly, unable to meet her eye. "You can see through your bra."

She was embarrassed as she put the shirt back on but laughed anyway. "Haven't you seen a nipple before?" She tried to laugh it off, but her cheeks were pink.

"Yeah. And now so have they." Liam gestured toward the guys nearby. "Yours."

There was a possessive quality to his voice, and for just a second, Leah liked it and didn't know why. It didn't make any sense. Why would she be satisfied with that? She didn't like Liam in that way, even if he *had* become hot over the winter. But the idea that she was desirable, that men might want her, it was a heady feeling. First *Him*, and now Liam. It was a little intoxicating.

She sort of wondered if her grandmother Lola had felt like this, if it had been the driving force in her apparently bad behavior. She shook her head. She had always been told she was nothing like her grandmother.

She chalked her feelings up to crazy female hormones and changed the subject, and they hung out in her room the rest of the day, listening to old Bob Marley vinyls and talking about life.

Life on the island was easy and slow, but having a friend to talk to made everything better.

When the text came in, she quickly and subtly shielded her phone from Liam's view. It was an instinct.

Do you mind that I've been texting you? I find that I rather like it.

Liam was scrolling through his own phone as Leah answered.

Of course not. Why would I?

Because my jokes are corny, he texted back. And I don't want you to feel weird.

I don't feel weird. Ok, maybe just a little. I don't know why things are changing.

I don't know why either, he texted. I only know that my feelings are changing, and I'm drawn to you and I don't know why. It's a little scary.

Yeah, it is.

But I never want YOU to be scared, he texted. Maybe

we're gravitating to each other because we're both lonely. I think you understand me.

He hit the nail on the head. She was lonely, and his attention was filling a hole. Maybe being lonely was normal, she decided. Everyone got lonely, right?

You're right, she told him. I'm lonely, too.

You'll never have to be lonely as long as I'm around. I promise.

Her heart glowed at his words. His promise buoyed her up, and she felt like floating. He was becoming a friend, somehow. It was different from before. She decided she liked it.

"Here, check out this clip." Liam thrust his phone at her, breaking up her thoughts. "It's hilarious."

She watched the video, and they laughed, and they fell down the rabbit hole of funny videos on YouTube for a long time. Her phone was tucked back into her bra, and even though it buzzed many more times with texts, she didn't pull it out to look with Liam sitting so close. It felt like a secret she should keep.

They were curled up on opposite ends of her bed sleeping when Emmy came looking for them at dinnertime. Emmy had no doubt that everything was on the up-and-up. They were just two buddies, exhausted from spending the day together.

Regardless, she left the door open when she went back down to work.

CHAPTER SEVEN

August 17

I stand outside Leah's door, my hand on the burnished copper knob. I'm determined this time.

I'm going to open it.

I stand forever, staring at the white wood in front of me.

It takes me a few minutes more of deep breathing, but finally...finally...I turn the handle, and push it open. It swings wide, and Bo barges in ahead of me, while I'm still frozen at the door.

Everything is how she left it.

I take a deep breath, inhaling the smell. It smells like her in here, of her perfume, her lotion, her hair. It's Leah.

The walls are aquamarine, the bedspread and window sheers white. She's got jars and jars of shells scattered here and there, having collected them over the years. Her white

Converses are by the door, her favorite hoodie is hanging on the back.

I swallow hard.

Jesus.

I try to enter, I really do. But my feet won't move. Inside, Bo sniffs at this and that, at her dirty clothes hamper and the volleyball next to her closet. Finally, he sits by the bed and whimpers, looking at me as if to ask, *Where is she?*

I gulp back a sob and I can't make myself go in there. Not yet.

So I do what I do best.

I go to work. But at least, this time, I leave the door open.

That's progress.

I take my frustration out on the empty rooms, pulling used bedding off beds, replacing it with clean, fresh linen. I scrub at the tubs, at the showers, at the sinks. I place fresh flowers in crystal vases on the nightstand in each room. When I'm done, each of the eight guest rooms is sparkling clean and waiting to invite the next guests.

Next, I take my beach cart, the one with the inflated wheels and loaded down with fresh towels, bedding and cleaning supplies, down the trail toward the bungalows. Only one is occupied at the moment, bungalow three, but I'm expecting guests for the other two later this afternoon when the plane comes in.

I stop at bungalow three first. I knock, three short raps, and Derek Collins answers immediately. He's dressed casually, in khaki shorts and a chambray shirt with the sleeves rolled up to the elbow. He's handsome. No one can deny that, not that I'm looking at anyone that way these days. My heart is closed and full of jagged edges, pieces that can't be reconstructed.

Derek smiles at me, and his dark eyes crinkle when he does.

"Good morning," he greets me. "You're up early. Would you like some coffee?" He gestures toward his little café-style table in front of the sliding glass doors. They face the sea, and the view is panoramic and breathtaking.

I shake my head. "No, thanks. I'm already caffeinated."

"Of course, you are," he agrees. "Do you ever sleep, Emmy?"

"Once every full moon," I confide, trying to joke. Humor doesn't reach my heart these days, but I can pretend.

He nods as if he understands, and takes the armful of fresh towels that I hand him. "The sheets don't need changing," he tells me, then glances at me. "How are you doing, Emmy?" he asks, and his voice is quiet now. He searches me with those dark eyes, and I find that I have to look away. I don't want people to know the depths of the pain I feel. It makes me vulnerable, and I don't like that.

"As well as anyone could," I answer. "I guess."

"If you need anything at all," he tells me, and I can see he means it. "An ear, someone to have a drink with…just come down. Sometimes a vodka tonic with a friend can help when nothing else will."

He should know. He experienced a different kind of pain when his wife cheated on him with his business partner.

"Thanks, Derek," I say, and I mean it. "I might take you up on it sometime."

Which is a lie. I won't. That was my grandmother's first rule. Never fraternize with the guests. Be social, not friends.

I leave him sitting at his table, and I finish up the other two bungalows. I'm thankful that I'll have an entirely full house this weekend. It's rare this time of year, right after the kids all go back to school. Things don't usually start to pick up now until after Thanksgiving.

When I see Skye rambling down the path waving at me, it startles me for a second. Shouldn't she be in school? But a quick check of my watch tells me that it's three thirty already. I'd spent more time cleaning than I thought. Time runs together these days. It's common for me to lose track of it, snippets and pieces and hours.

"Mom," Skye shouts, and that word cuts through my chest and impales my heart. I'm no one's mother now, not really. I don't correct her, though. She's called me that for years.

"Hey, sweetie," I answer. She's with Hutch. He was always good to Leah, and God knows he was good to me the night she…drowned. I smile at him now.

"Hi, Hutch."

Hutch smiles back at me, his eyes kind.

"I wanted to come call on you, Emmy. Skye was kind enough to bring me. I hope we're not an intrusion."

Yes, you are.

"Of course not," I answer aloud. "You're never an intrusion. Would you like a cup of tea?"

"That would be lovely," he answers. He and Skye accompany me to the kitchen, and we sit around the table. Skye wraps her arm around my shoulders, and I close my eyes for a minute, as my nose grazes her arm. That smell... of the slightly sweaty teenage girl skin. If I focus hard enough, I can pretend it's Leah.

"How are you doing?" Hutch asks me, bringing me out of my thoughts. "Is there anything I can help with?"

While it's nice that everyone cares, I wish they would all stop asking.

"I'm okay," I answer politely, pouring steaming water into their cups. Skye won't drink hers, but I pour her a cup anyway. "I'm surviving."

He nods, and grasps my shoulder in that sympathetic way that people do, as if he's trying to transfer comfort from his body into mine. Hutch came to Key West as the youth pastor a couple of years ago. His boyish looks, energy and charm had been an instant hit with the young people of the Vineyard Church, and Skye and Leah had rarely missed a meeting. Everyone loved him.

"We're going to hold a small candlelight memorial tonight at our meeting," he tells me now. "For Leah. I think...it will give some of the kids closure. It's been hard on them, too, Emmy." He pauses, and it takes me a minute to let the words soak in. A memorial. For my daughter. Because she's gone. My throat is instantly thick, and it's hard to swallow. Nate and I postponed doing this when he was here—not wanting to make our loss seem so final. I nod without a word.

"You're invited," he continues, and his voice is soft and

even. "I think it would be good for you to hear how much Leah was loved. How much she affected everyone around her."

My heart beats desperately now, trying to escape its cage of bones.

"I don't know," I manage to say. Of course I can't go to that.

"Please come," Skye says softly. "Please. I miss you, Mom."

My heart breaks a little. She's been a second daughter to me since she was in preschool. She and Leah bonded the very first day. I've baked her cupcakes, gone to her recitals, driven her to volleyball games. She's been part of my family, too, and I've been so busy isolating myself, I forgot about her, about how she must be struggling. She and Leah were closer than most sisters I know.

"Okay," I find myself agreeing. "I'll come."

She hugs me now, and I see the bags under her eyes. I missed them before. She hasn't been sleeping either.

"I love you," I murmur, and I cling to her for a second, her blond hair tickling my nose. She nods and a tear rolls down her freckled cheek.

"I love you, too."

After we pull ourselves together, she turns to me, her green eyes watery. "Leah has a picture of the two of us. On her nightstand. Do you think I can have it?"

She's expecting me to nod and tell her to go get it, but I can't. It makes me panicky just to think about someone else being in her room. But…Skye has a right to the picture. I know exactly the one she's talking about. They had their legs dangling off the pier, each wearing a matching anklet, and the afternoon light surrounded them in a halo.

"I'll bring it tonight," I tell her finally. Which means I'll have to go in and get it. My heart skips a beat.

"The memorial starts at seven," Hutch tells me on their way out. He hugs me quickly, in the way that pastors do, and I agree to be there. I watch them walk away, and Skye's shoulders sag, her steps are heavy. She's definitely suffering, too. I've got to make more of an effort to be there for her. She understands my pain in a way that most do not.

At four, the plane from the mainland arrives, so I spend the hour after that checking in guests and handing out mojitos.

"Would you like to check in your phone?" I ask a frazzled man. He looks up from his phone, his eyebrow lifted.

"We do have complimentary Wi-Fi here, but we also offer phone lockers...for those who need a break from technology and the frustrations of the real world." I smile, and his wife nudges his arm.

"Do it, Jim," she tells him. "I mean it. No work for the entire weekend."

He sighs and holds his phone out, and I take it. "I promise I'll keep it safe for you."

I place it in a tiny locker and close the door. He watches me, his eyes soulful, like I'm stealing his dog. I have to chuckle.

"You'll feel refreshed by Sunday."

He's not so sure, but he and his wife take their mojitos to stroll on the beach, arm in arm, and I'm left alone.

I glance toward the stairs and I can't procrastinate any longer.

I climb them, and pause in front of Leah's open door, not for the first time.

Her bed is rumpled, and I can see an indentation from where she lay on it. The pile of photos is still there.

I breathe in, then out.

I step over the threshold.

I don't move for several minutes. Instead, I soak in the room. I look at her notebooks, stacked neatly for the first day of sophomore year, and her backpack that she'd carefully prepared. Her first-day-of-school outfit is ready on the chair by the window.

My chest tightens, and I close my eyes, focused on relaxing those muscles.

I breathe in, then out. My ribs seem to creak with the effort.

When I reopen my eyes, I see the photo on the nightstand. It's in a seashell frame, and all I have to do is walk across the room to take it.

But it's hard. So hard.

I take a step.

Then another.

My toe nudges something metallic. Glancing down, I find Leah's laptop on the floor, tucked under the edge of the bed, still plugged in. I bend and pull it out. I remember how she'd been so diligent in keeping to my one hour of screen time a day. My little rule-follower.

My lips almost curve into a smile, but they can't.

Not yet.

It's too soon.

Instead, I sink to the floor, the computer on my lap.

With trembling fingers, I open it, and it comes to life. She didn't shut it down last time she used it. It had only been sleeping. My heart leaps at the thought that I'll get to be in whatever moment she was in the last time she used this machine.

It's such a small thing, but not to me.

It's all I have left.

As the screen brightens, I'm confused for a second.

Leah had been reading a blog.

Ramblings from the Island

The most recent entry was from the evening that Leah died, and I anxiously skim through it.

I was scared last night, she wrote. He choked me for the first time. We have a safe word, of course, but I didn't have enough air to say it. He was so rough, too rough. I thought for a minute he wasn't going to let go.

A sick feeling rises in my stomach, the bile into my throat. Who wrote this, and why would my daughter be reading about it?

The fingers of dread tighten up around my heart and the hairs on the back of my neck stand to attention as I click on the About Me tab. A picture grins at me from the page, a girl with a broad smile, gray-blue eyes, and glowing skin.

It was Leah.

CHAPTER EIGHT

July 1

The youth group room was full, filled with giggling teenagers and the smell of Doritos. On the wall, the movie projector flashed a movie, but the pictures weren't clear. They were fuzzy, the product of old, secondhand equipment. No one seemed to care. They were all immersed in their own chatter, in private conversations and recent gossip.

On one long sofa, Liam and Leah shared a blanket and a tub of popcorn, while Skye leaned her back against Leah's legs from the floor. From time to time, Skye glanced furtively toward Liam, unable to help herself. She'd noticed he'd changed so much this year. He'd left here as a boy last summer, and he'd returned as a man. He was only a year older than she, but he seemed so much more sophisticated.

And really into Leah.

Skye was annoyed by that. She loved Leah like a sister, but Leah didn't even like Liam in that way. *She* did, and he didn't even notice her. She nudged Leah.

"Hey. Are you staying over tonight?"

Leah nodded. "I planned on it. Is that still okay?"

"Yep. We can get up early and snag some sunrise pictures."

Leah growled, and Skye laughed. She was the sunrise girl; Leah loved the moon.

"Did your mom say okay?"

Leah nodded again. "Yep. I'm all set. I brought my bag." She motioned toward the door, and Skye saw her backpack there, loaded to the brim.

"Hey, kids," Hutch greeted them, pausing as he strolled through the throng of sprawled-out limbs. "Need some more popcorn?" He carried a big tub of it, a scoop in his hand. Liam glanced at their bowl.

"No, thanks."

"It's good to see you here," Hutch told him. "How was your flight?"

"Great. Not even a bump."

"That's what I like to hear." Hutch patted his shoulder, then turned to Leah. "Do you have your verse memorized?"

That had been the assignment this week. To memorize a scripture. They would each recite their chosen piece after the movie.

"I picked something from Song of Solomon," Leah told him, glowing. "Yeah, I'm ready."

"Oh, the *Song*," Hutch said, smiling. "Such romance. Which one did you pick?"

"You'll have to wait and find out." Leah grinned back, and their eyes lingered for just a second.

"You're such a tease," he laughed, and he continued on his way, dumping popcorn into bowls and making sure there was appropriate space between each prone body. He was cool, but he was still a pastor. He couldn't allow kids to make out in his youth group gatherings.

From across the room, Amber Fitzgerald rolled her eyes at their exchange. Was Leah really flirting with the pastor? God, Amber couldn't stand her. Leah pretended to be so perfect, and no one person could be as good as she tried to be. It was sickening. She strutted around the island with her ridiculously ugly dog. She probably got the dog just so that she could draw even *more* attention to herself.

What was worse, Leah could do anything she wanted, and Hutch never minded. Damn it. She uttered a quick prayer to God for swearing. It was a problem of hers. She was raised on the *F*-word. Her father was a mechanic and she'd heard it all of her life, every time he popped his knuckle on the hood, or rubbed oil in his eye. Fuck this, fuck that.

It was a wonder she was halfway decent.

But here she was, in the same youth group as all of the rich kids.

So you know what? Fuck them all.

Across the room, Liam's arm stretched out against the top of the sofa. Leah leaned into it, laughing up into his face, her cheeks rosy and pink. She was uninhibited, her laugh pealing throughout the space. She didn't try to be ladylike, or quiet. She was who she was.

Liam liked that about her.

Other girls tried to be what they *thought* they should be. Leah just…was.

"All right, all right, everyone." Hutch spoke above the din when the movie credits rolled. "It's that time. Everyone has their verse memorized, right?"

There were some groans, and some laughs. Hutch made a face.

"Uh-uh. We've got serious stuff to do, too," he reminded them. "Such as knowing God's word. We can't spread it if we don't know it, right?" He looked around. "Who wants to go first?"

There were no volunteers.

He sighed. "Okay. Leah. You can go."

She shrugged, unconcerned because she was ready. She stood and looked around the room as she spoke.

"'I am my beloved's, and my beloved is mine,'" she recited clearly, standing tall. "Song of Solomon 6:3."

Amber rolled her eyes. Leave it to Leah to memorize smut.

Hutch didn't say anything, though. He just nodded. "Memorized perfectly," he acknowledged. "What can we learn from those words?"

"To read romance books?" Amber piped up.

Leah rolled her eyes, and Amber grinned angelically at her.

"No," Hutch answered. "That when we choose a spouse,

a husband gives himself to his wife, and his wife gives herself back to him. You become one, forgoing all others." He looked around. "Okay. Who is next? Amber?"

She was annoyed, but she stood and recited her short verse from a chapter in John. She deliberately didn't look at Leah.

Liam scooted closer to Leah and whispered, "Did you pee in her latte or something?"

Leah laughed, rolling her eyes again. "No. She's always hated me. I've never done anything to her."

Liam considered that as Amber sat down, her nose in the air. She wore dingy clothes, although her hair was neatly combed and clipped to the side, perfectly parted. Her shoes were ratty, although that was okay. Converses shouldn't be pristine. But still. There was something about her that said she was poor. That she wasn't privileged at all, and Liam wondered if that was, in fact, her problem with Leah.

Leah wasn't rich, as far as he knew. But she lived in a beautiful inn on the edge of the sea. Anyone who didn't truly know her might think she was a spoiled brat. They would be wrong, though.

After everyone had recited their passages, Hutch stood in the middle of the circle again. "As you know, we have a project this summer. We're building a house for Habitat for Humanity. Be there Saturday morning at nine. Bring any tools that you might have. The address is on a sheet in the back, along with a permission slip for your parents to sign."

After he dismissed them, the kids milled outside. Amber stood alone on the periphery, waiting for her dad to pick her up.

"Doesn't she have a mom?" Liam asked Skye.

"No. She died when Amber was little. Cancer."

Liam felt a rush of sympathy. No wonder Amber was a bitch.

"I'll see you tomorrow." Leah hugged him. "I'm staying at Skye's tonight."

He nodded. "Want to surf in the morning?"

"Is Stephen the most underrated Marley son?"

Liam nodded again. "Of course."

Leah smiled. "There's your answer. See you at the beach."

She climbed into Skye's father's SUV, the one with the Jason Hayden, Realtor magnet on the door. Skye hated riding in this thing, even though everyone would recognize their car anyway. Jason was really the only Realtor on the island. There wasn't a real-estate deal that didn't go through him.

"Did you guys learn anything?" he asked, as he flipped on the turn signal.

Skye laughed.

"We learned that Amber Fitzgerald is a little witch," she told him, scrolling through her phone. Since they'd had to turn off their phones during the meeting, she had a lot to catch up on. Snaps and posts, pictures and quotes.

"I thought you already knew that?" He lifted an eyebrow. "I find it hard to keep up with you girls."

"It's okay, Mr. H," Leah told him from the back. "She's okay sometimes. Tonight she wasn't. She hates me."

"She's jealous of you," he corrected her as he turned into the slow traffic of the island. "There's a difference."

"There's nothing to be jealous of," Leah protested. "Seriously. I don't know what her problem is."

"You're kinder, prettier, more popular, and you have a mom. She doesn't. Trust me, she's jealous of you."

The mom thing gave Leah pause. "Sometimes I practically feel like I *don't* have a mom," she said. "She works so much."

"She has to," Jason agreed. "She runs that big place all by herself. Christy and I always wonder why she doesn't hire some help."

Leah shrugged. "My dad says the same thing. He wants her to at least get a housekeeper. But she's stubborn. She says my great-gran ran it alone, so she can, too."

"Your gran at least had your grandpa," Jason answered, and he met Leah's eyes in the rearview mirror. She shrugged again.

"I know. But like I said, she's stubborn."

"So that's where you get it from," Skye piped up. Leah laughed, and they faded into chattering about how much Liam had changed since the last time he was on the island. That conversation took up the rest of the ride to Skye's house on the edge of town. She, too, lived on the beach, but on the opposite side of the island. Her mom always called their houses bookends, although theirs was smaller since it wasn't an inn.

Regardless, it was still large. Her father, after all, made plenty of money.

"Girls, I have work to do," he said after they traipsed through the foyer. "Your mom is already in bed reading. If you need anything, just holler." He gave them each a hug, and turned for his den. Then paused. "There's cookie dough ice cream," he told them, and they both dropped what they were doing to run for the freezer.

He laughed because he didn't tell them Christy had already picked most of the dough pieces out. In this house, everyone fought over them. He smiled when he heard them groaning in discovery from the kitchen.

"Can I go with you to the beach in the morning?" Skye asked Leah, after shoveling a bite of ice cream into her mouth.

"Of course," Leah answered. "Why wouldn't you?"

Skye shrugged. "I dunno. It just seems like Liam wants you all to himself."

"Now you're crazy," Leah answered. But deep down, she knew it was true.

"Whatever." Skye let it go. "Are you going to volunteer on Saturday?"

"Yeah. I don't see why not."

"My dad is volunteering as one of the parents. You know him...if there's a house on this island, he has to have his name associated with it." She rolled her eyes and Leah smiled.

"He's like my mom. They both work a lot."

Skye didn't mention that he kind of had to. Her mom, Christy, was a stay-at-home mom, so he had to make all the money. Leah couldn't imagine sitting still that much. She'd get bored.

When they finished their ice cream, they retired to Skye's room, where they lay on the bed, listened to music, and scrolled through social media. They took a couple of selfies, and they each posted a pic of the other, with the caption Slay, girl!

Positive thinking was a good thing, as was propping up your best friend.

Skye fell asleep first, as she always did. She could sleep through a storm, with the lights on and the music blaring. Leah didn't know how she did it. She personally had to have it dark and quiet. So she carefully climbed up, turned off the light, turned off the music, and had just crawled back into bed when her phone buzzed.

Want to meet me tonight?

She answered immediately.

Yes.

The reply came in two minutes later.

See you there in ten minutes.

Careful not to wake Skye, Leah slipped out of the bedroom, and then out the back door, closing it quietly behind her. She made her way quickly and quietly to the Habitat for Humanity site, where the raw timbers loomed up into the night sky, the framework already completed.

She waited there for *Him*, in the shadows, her nerves on high alert.

She had sort of expected a message from *Him* tonight, but she never knew for sure.

She was happy it had come.

CHAPTER NINE

August 17

I'm not sure how long I sit staring at my daughter's sweet picture. Her eyes sparkle, her mouth curved into a smile, and she is so innocent.

But yet, apparently...she wasn't.

How did this happen? I thought she was a virgin. She'd never ever told me that she was involved with anyone. She told me everything, so if she didn't tell me this, then it was because she knew it was wrong. She knew I wouldn't approve.

Who was the man who had taken advantage of her?

Because having sex with a fifteen-year-old girl is criminal. She wasn't of age to consent.

My blood boils and my stomach churns as I scroll through the blog entries.

Ry, she calls him.

I don't know anyone by that name.

I grab my phone and send a quick text to Skye.

Hey, sweetie. Was Leah involved with anyone that you know of?

She answers immediately. Like…a guy?

Yes.

She replies instantly. Nope.

Are you sure? You can tell me.

Three bubbles. She's answering. I wait.

She would've told me if there had been someone. She told me everything.

That's true. She usually did. They giggled and chatted until late every night. But I'm staring at the evidence, and Leah hadn't told her. That's telling, in itself. To not tell her mother was one thing. To not tell her very best friend in the world…that's something else.

I scroll to an entry where he is mentioned. She doesn't mention him by name, but it's definitely about him.

I saw him today, World. I'm telling you because I can't tell anyone else. Because you don't know who I am, and so you can't tell anyone.

I'm not supposed to see him. People would say it's

wrong, but what no one understands is that I don't have anyone else. My mother is always working. My father lives across the country. My guy (and it feels so weird to call him that now!) understands me. All he wants to do is talk, and hold my hand, and tell me that I'm beautiful.

He's so patient with me. Not like the guys my age. They all want to have sex on day one, and then that's that. Not my guy. He's so sweet. So kind. If this is wrong, then the world itself isn't right.

My heart races and pounds, threatening to break free from my chest.

My baby. My baby. I didn't suspect a thing.

But how could I? As she says, I was always working. She was alone a lot.

This is all my fault.

Even the night she died... If only I had gone with her into the water like she'd asked. *If only.*

I would've saved her or—or I would've died trying.

I stare around Leah's room. It's the same as it always was, yet I see it through new eyes. This was a girl who was having a sexual relationship with someone. Yet, she still has teddy bears on her bed, and a pink penguin piggy bank on her shelf. This is the bedroom of a girl who was just turning into a woman, or at least, that's the way it *should've* been.

But someone...someone took it upon himself to speed up that process. And I want to know who. I know it won't change things now, but *I still have to know.*

I search through Leah's desk, through her notebooks, through loose papers in her closet, through jewelry boxes and storage cubbies. I look in every place I can think of, and I don't see any evidence of the man or his identity.

The only thing at all is the blog.

Ramblings from the Island

I perch on her bed again, on the sheets she slept in last, and read the very first entry.

Hi. You don't know me, and I don't know you. But that's best, isn't it? I can tell you all things and you won't judge me. And you can comment back, and I won't judge you.

You can call me Leah. I live on an island, and it's too quiet here. Nothing ever happens, although I do love the sea. My parents are divorced. I don't see my dad much because he lives in Phoenix now. He calls me every other day or so, but it's not the same. I have friends. I have a nice home. But I'm not very happy. I wonder why that is? Does anyone else out there ever feel the same?

My eyes well up when she says that she isn't happy.

God. The only reason I worked so hard was to grow the business at this inn and give Leah a legacy, something she could have and keep forever. Many would think growing up on an island was idyllic. It kills me that she didn't.

I'm wooden as I get up and walk down the hall. I'm silent as I comb my hair and pull it into a neat ponytail. I'm pensive as I drive to the church for Leah's memorial service.

I feel like a fraud. They are honoring a girl I thought I knew backward and forward, and it turns out there was a part of her I didn't know at all.

What kind of mother does that make me?

But somehow, I have to put that out of my mind and attend her memorial service, as though everything is the same as it was twenty minutes ago.

My legs are leaden as I climb the steps into the church, and I follow the soft music to the sanctuary. Candles are everywhere, flickering against the stained glass. Hutch stands at the front, and a crowd of teenagers fill the pews. A picture of Leah is on the overhead screen, smiling during a youth group meeting, and I slip into the back row, hoping no one notices me.

The picture is a slide show, and it turns from one image to the next. Skye must've provided the pictures. They're from everywhere. Skye's family boat, the cruise we took to Mexico, underwater while snorkeling, her hair a cloud around her face... God. My stomach clenches until it hurts.

Hutch begins the service, and shortly thereafter decides to have everyone stand up and share something about Leah.

"Emmy, would you start?" he asks me, his voice gentle.

Damn it. I'd hoped he wouldn't notice me. I stand up, my legs weak, and walk to the front of the room.

"My daughter was Leah." My voice sounds thick because I have to say *was* instead of *is*. "But you know that."

I clear the grief from my throat, and glance out at the sea of faces staring back at me. They're waiting. For me to say something, for me to be profound, for me to demonstrate the gravity of my loss. As if mere words can do that.

The back of my top is sweaty under the lights, and it smells in here, of teenage bodies compressed into too small a room, and too much cheap adolescent cologne. Leah should be here, crammed in among them. But she's not, and I am.

I swallow hard, nodding at the man running the media screen, and another picture of my daughter pops up, as large as the giant wall.

"That was her favorite T-shirt," I tell the faces. It's blue and tattered, and says LIVE LOVE REPEAT in peeling white letters. Her hair is long and dark, and her eyes are wide and gray, like a stormy day. *Were.* They *were.*

"She was running late the morning of these pictures. She didn't even have time for lip gloss. But she didn't need it. She was so pretty—but she was the kind of girl who didn't even realize it. But then, you guys know that, too."

The members of the massive youth group nod their heads solemnly. They know. Leah had come to every youth group meeting for two years. She'd started coming with Skye, but kept coming because she loved it. I failed her in that way. I never brought her to church, and I should have. What if her soul wasn't saved? What if she's in hell this very moment?

The thought catches the breath in my throat, freezing it still as stones.

"When you lose someone, even if you know that they are with God now, it takes your breath away. The pain, I mean," I tell the kids. "I'm not supposed to tell you this, probably. I should probably be telling you that everything happens for a reason, and that she's at peace now. But that's not how I feel. When I first realized she was gone, I couldn't sleep."

For a moment, I'm back there, frozen as the reality

crashed around me. My daughter, my life, was gone. Nate had come, and protected me from the reality too painful to accept.

Yet here I stand now.

I've managed to survive without her, a feat I once thought was impossible.

"It's only been a week," I say. "And the pain hasn't gotten better. I'm trying to learn to walk around with it."

The knot in my throat is back and I inhale around it slowly, then breathe it out before I continue.

"I want to thank you all for being her friends. Coming here to youth group was one of her favorite things."

I pause now, because what more is there to say? I can't ask them what I want to…whether any of them knew anything about her secret life.

"Anyway. I hope you are dealing with everything okay. If you're struggling, like me, just do what I do. Take it one day at a time, and know that Leah wouldn't want you to be sad. She would want you to remember something silly she'd said or done, and smile. Smile because she lived. I know that sounds cliché, but it really is what she would want."

The room is silent and I step away from the microphone now, and Hutch walks up to take over.

"Thank you, Ms. Fisher," he tells me, and his eyes are warm and brown. Sadness lurks there, and I know he truly cares about everyone around him. "Kids, if any of you are struggling, you can come to any of us for help. We'll talk with you, pray with you. Don't hesitate, okay?"

They nod and murmur and Hutch motions for the next person to speak.

A boy smiles and talks about Leah giving him her ice-cream cone last year when he dropped his own, and didn't have enough money to buy another.

The next girl tells a story about Leah being friends with her when she first moved to Key West, when no one else even glanced in her direction.

The next boy talks about always having a crush on her... and never having the guts to tell her.

His cheeks flare red, and the room closes around me, so I back away, into the hall of the church.

Leaning against the wall, I inhale the musty smell of the closed-up sanctuary as I try to gather myself. The memories...how people saw her...it's just too much.

Too much.

I allow the sanctuary to swallow me, to hold me in its arms, my eyes burning.

I don't come here often. This was Leah's thing. She was always volunteering for something. The soup kitchen, reading at nursing homes, the animal shelter. She thought it gave her life meaning, but what does that matter now?

I blink away the tears that threaten to fall again.

I suck in a breath, and it's hot and hard. I squeeze my eyes closed and slide down to the floor.

I don't know how long I stay here, still and silent.

All I know is that at some point, someone joins me.

A voice.

"Emmy."

It's Hutch. I recognize the kindness.

He puts an arm around my shoulder, and I lean into him, accepting the comfort.

"What you did tonight was brave," he tells me. "I know you were scared. I know you didn't want to. But it helped them. To see you coping, it gives them hope that they can cope, too."

He smells like Old Spice, and I open my eyes. It's such an old scent for someone so young. Well, youngish. He's my age. Thirty-six.

"I had to," I say simply. "Leah would've wanted me to."

Hutch thinks on that, staring at the giant crucifix hanging at the front. Jesus's face is so understanding, even though blood runs down his face from the thorns on his crown.

"Yes," he finally says. "She would've. But she wouldn't want you to torture yourself, Emmy. You've been through so much already. So very much."

I close my eyes, and lean my head on his shoulder.

"You're so strong, Emmy," he says quietly. "It's one of the things I admire about you."

I don't feel strong. On the inside, I'm a raging mess. It's disturbing to me that no one knows that.

"You've been so good to me," I finally answer. "I don't know why."

Hutch startles and stares at me, into my eyes. "Because you are a kind, beautiful soul, Emmy Fisher. That's why. Don't you forget it."

Maybe he knows something.

I don't know why this occurs to me now, but before I can think twice, I ask.

"Was Leah close to anyone here?" I ask curiously. "A man, I mean."

Hutch looks puzzled. "A man?"

I nod. "Yeah."

He thinks on that. "Well, there's only me and my assistant youth pastor, Daniel. Daniel isn't able to come to as many meetings now that he has evening classes."

"Is there anyone else?" I ask. "Anyone at all?"

"Is there some reason you're asking?" Hutch asks slowly, his eyes assessing me.

"Not really. I just… I want to find out what her last days were like. I *need* to know."

I want to say more, but a teenager pops up in the door of the sanctuary.

"Hutch," he calls.

Hutch stands up, offering me his hand. "I'm here, Jake," he answers as we stand up together. "If you need to talk," he says softly, his warm hand enclosing mine in that sympathetic way that clergy members do, "I'm available tonight."

"No, it's okay," I tell him. "But thank you."

He nods and his eyes are soulful, and he joins Jake. I watch them go, and then I bask in the quiet of the sanctuary for a minute longer.

It *feels* holy in here.

It's like I'm breathing in God, and he's filling up my lungs.

After a few breaths, I gather the strength to leave.

Church isn't where I belong. Not now. Not while I'm so angry at God for letting my daughter die.

I'm unlocking my car door in the dark before I realize I'm being followed.

It's a soft noise, maybe even a breath, that alerts me. I turn, and there's a girl in the shadows.

She's hesitant, pale. I recognize Amber, a girl from Leah's youth group.

"Hi there," I say softly, because what else should one say in a dark parking lot?

"Hi." She's soft, too. Hesitant.

My suspicions are immediately aroused. "Is there something you want to tell me?" I ask, trying to mask how eager I am.

The girl is quiet.

"Were you at the memorial?" I try to remember if I saw her face among the crowd, but they were all a blur under the lights.

She nods. "Yeah."

"Were you friends with Leah?" I'm waiting, fishing. Amber shakes her head.

"No. I hated her."

That startles me and my head snaps up.

"Don't worry, she hated me, too," the girl offers, as though that makes it better.

"Why?"

She shrugs. "I thought she was a poseur. I'm sorry. I know she was your daughter, and I'm very sorry for your loss."

I stare at her, and she does seem sorry, even if she *is* blunt. "You don't look like a mean girl," I offer.

"That's because I'm not."

I pause. My next question is unthinkable to me, but I ask it anyway.

"Was Leah?"

To my relief, she shakes her head. "No. We just had a mutual dislike. It happens."

"Yeah, it does," I agree. Thank God. I didn't think Leah was a mean girl, but at the same time, it turns out that I didn't know everything about my daughter.

"Why did you think she was a poseur?" I ask Amber. She stares at me.

"Because of the way she led people on. Liam, for one. She stomped all over him. There was no reason for that."

"She stomped all over Liam?" I'm confused. She thought the sun rose and set on him.

"Hey, is everything all right?" Hutch's voice comes from behind me, curious and clear, and I turn.

"Yeah, it's fine. This girl…" I turn back around, but she's gone. "Hey," I call out, into the shadows.

But she doesn't answer, and doesn't return.

"There was a girl, Amber," I tell him. "She said she hated Leah."

"Leah didn't like her either."

"That's what she said," I answer. "How much did they hate each other?"

Hutch reads my face. "It was normal teenage girl stuff, Emmy. Girls can get catty sometimes. Leah was a good girl, and Amber is, too."

His expression tells me that I'm reading too much into it, but I have that right, don't I? I just found out that my daughter wasn't who I thought she was. Don't I have the right to find out as much as I can?

Hutch helps me into my car, like a parent tucking his kid into bed.

"If you need me for anything, just call," he tells me firmly. "I mean it."

I nod, and drive away into the night.

CHAPTER TEN

July 1

As Leah waited at the Habitat site, she skimed through *His* text messages from the past few days, pausing on the highlights.

I love talking to you like this.

You really understand me, like no one else does.

Is this wrong?

Let's have code names. It will be fun. I'll call you Kitten, and you call me Ry.

I know we have an age difference, but age is just a number,

right? You already know me so well. This feels so natural. Don't you think?

She did. She agreed with everything he said. It all fell into place so quickly, so easily. At first it felt weird, but then it started feeling really right.

Something so right couldn't be wrong.

"Hey." His voice came from the shadow. Her head snapped up, searching the dark perimeter.

Leah smiled when she saw him, her lips curved, her eyes brilliant with excitement.

"Ry!"

She hugged him tight, the embrace just a little too long and close to be appropriate. It was searching, experimental. She wasn't sure how far to go. It was the first time she'd touched him since they'd been texting.

"I missed you."

"You see me all the time," Ry replied, his eyes crinkling at the corners. "Just today, actually."

She laughed, and leaned into him. She enjoyed the secret rush she felt just then when her breasts grazed his arm. She knew he noticed, too, because his breathing stuttered, just a bit. It gave her satisfaction that she affected him in such a way. It was exciting, and a little scary.

How had less than a week's worth of texting evolved into this amazing feeling?

"I saw a lot of people today," Leah told him, her fingers running down his arm. She wondered if it was okay to touch him like this, but he didn't stop her. It gave her a heady feeling.

"I hope you don't see anyone else quite like you see me,"

he said, his eyebrow arched and waiting. She couldn't tell if he was serious, or if he was teasing. To her, it was ridiculous. She would never. Everything had changed for them, and while it was still new and magical, it was solid.

"Of course not," she laughed. "There's only one you."

"Well, good. Because you're all I think about, Leah. Every minute, of every day. It's getting worse, not better."

"But isn't that a good thing?" She was confused now. She had ideas on how things were supposed to go, but he was older, more experienced. He knew so much more than boys her own age.

"It could be," he said and shrugged. "Except that I have to think on other things, too. I have responsibilities, you know. You're distracting."

"I'm sorry." She smiled, but she wasn't sorry. She knew it, and he knew it.

"You're impossible."

He drew her into his arms and held her there. She rested her head against his chest, listening to his strong heartbeat. This feeling was the best in the world. She loved the way she felt safe with him, the way she knew he'd never let anything happen to her.

"I know this is wrong," he said into her hair, his breath warm. "But God. I don't think I can give you up. I want to see where this goes, Kitten. Do you? Please, tell me you do."

A rush of warmth flooded her. She'd felt so expendable for so long. The idea that she could be so important to this man was...well, it was everything.

"Yes, of course I do." She wriggled closer, desperate for

his approval, and he kissed the top of her head. She wanted more, though.

She tilted her head, positioning herself for a kiss on the mouth. He stared at her lips intently, deciding. He swallowed hard.

"Not yet," he told her. "Not yet."

"Why?" She felt rejected. She had yet to have her first kiss, and she knew beyond any doubt that she wanted it to be with Ry. At fifteen, she was behind the curve anyway. All of her friends, even Skye, had had their first kisses long ago. Skye had been twelve when she kissed Danny Hodge behind the Dumpsters in junior high. Leah didn't want to kiss just anyone. She always knew, deep down, that she was saving herself.

Her mom always told her that.

Save yourself for someone who loves you.

She wasn't sure if Ry loved her yet, but she was sure that he would. They were on that trajectory already. She might be naive, but she could feel that much.

He ran his hands up and down her back, lingering in the recess at the top of her buttocks. His pinkie finger rubbed against her butt, but only slightly. Only enough to feel like an accident, and she wasn't sure if it was or wasn't.

"I want you to be my first kiss," she told him, and suddenly, she felt shy. She didn't know why; it was dumb. She'd known Ry for years now.

He smiled, his lips against her forehead. "Believe me, I want that, too. I just want to make sure you're ready. I don't want you to feel any pressure. When the time is right, we'll know."

Leah sighed and she laced her fingers with his, her forehead resting against his chest now. She didn't know what cologne he wore, but she'd never forget the smell. It was warm and welcoming.

"Have you talked to your dad lately?" Ry sat down on a stack of lumber nearby, and Leah sat next to him, her hand in his.

She nodded. "Yeah. Last night."

"You've got to be careful and not say anything to him," he cautioned. "I know you feel comfortable talking to him, but we've got to keep this quiet. Okay?"

She was annoyed by this. Of course she knew.

"We haven't done anything wrong yet," she pointed out.

"That's very true," he said, and he was soothing now. He even stroked at her hair, as though she needed calming. She wanted to pull away out of principle, but she liked it. What was it about him that always made her feel so safe?

"So, what have you and Skye got planned for the week?" he asked, trying to be casual now, as if he didn't realize that her hand was mere inches from his groin. She could move it over, just slightly, and everything would be different.

But she was too scared. Maybe he was right. Maybe she wasn't ready for that just yet.

"We're going paddleboarding in the morning with Liam," she answered, and she eyed him, waiting for his response. He always acted strangely when she talked about Liam.

"It'll be good for him to get out of the house and away from his makeup table."

He hated Liam's eyeliner because he thought it made him a pansy. Leah found that annoying.

"You're too hard on him," she said mildly. "But anyway, he's over that stuff. We're going paddleboarding."

"Can he even get up on a board?" Ry asked dubiously, and Leah found herself annoyed again.

"He's fine," she said sharply, and Ry knew to stop. One of the things he liked about Leah was that she was young enough that she hadn't mastered the art of playing games yet. But that also meant that she hadn't mastered her temper.

"Calm down," he said, his voice low. "I was just messing with you."

She rolled her eyes. "Whatever."

"Let's get back to where we were," he suggested, and his hand was on her back again. She was instantly putty in his hands, and he knew it.

"When can I see you again?" she asked him, because she could feel that this visit was drawing to a close. They'd been here almost an hour, just soaking in each other's warmth, and one of them was bound to be missed soon.

"As soon as possible," he promised. "I mean, if you want to see me."

"Of course I do." She was quick to answer. He smiled. She was so easy to figure out, so utterly without guile. It was intoxicating, and he couldn't help himself.

He kissed the tip of her nose.

She tried to pull him to her lips once again, but he pulled away.

"Not yet, Kitten," he said once again. "How about... next time."

"You'll kiss me next time?" Leah was doubtful.

But Ry nodded. "I will kiss you next time. So, think on that this week, little Kitten. Your first kiss is coming soon. I will kiss you as a woman is meant to be kissed."

Leah was breathless as she walked back to Skye's house alone, practically dizzy from excitement as she crawled back into bed with her best friend, her absence undetected.

He was going to be the one to make her a woman.

She could feel it.

CHAPTER ELEVEN

August 18

I've never been a whiskey drinker before, but tonight, it feels right. I pour a few fingers into a tumbler, and gulp at it. It burns like liquid fire blazing down my throat. That's fine. Maybe it'll dissolve the lump that lives there.

I stumble out onto the beach behind the house, and I don't know what time it is. Maybe one. Maybe 2:00 a.m. I'm never up this late, because I have to get up at four forty-five to prepare breakfast for the guests.

The sand is dark and wet, caking up onto my feet as I walk. There is barely a moon tonight, so the water looks black. Driftwood and seaweed litter the shore, and I carve a wide berth around them, eventually sitting on a dry patch down the way.

I sit the whiskey bottle next to me and swirl the liquid that is left in my glass. The smattering of stars above twinkle down and for just a minute, I try to remember which religion it is that believes that you turn into a star when you die.

Hinduism? Mormonism? Either way, that's not an ending I would choose.

That's my biggest problem now. The idea that Leah is gone. First she was here and burning bright, and now she's just...not. She's gone, and she's never coming back, and I didn't even get to say goodbye or tell her that I loved her. What if she didn't know?

The waves out there swell and swell, rising from the blackness, only to return to it, like the Sirens' call of the deep is simply too much to resist. I wonder if it hurt when Leah was taken off her board? Was it the shark that did it?

Lord.

I gulp at the whiskey. The not knowing is most certainly the worst part. I need to know, and yet, I'll never. I'll never know.

I'm so absorbed with my morbid thoughts that I don't hear the soft footsteps sinking into the sand until they are right beside me, two brown leather loafers.

I follow the legs up to the face.

Derek.

Damn it.

"You're up late," he observes, sitting next to me. He picks up the Dalmore bottle and looks at it. "Hmm. You have good taste."

"I serve it in the inn," I say needlessly. Is it me, or does my voice sound like a piece of dry wood splintering? Derek doesn't seem to notice.

"Can't sleep?"

I shake my head, and twirl my fingers through the sand, letting the tiny grains filter through my hand over and over like a waterfall of dirt.

"No. You?"

He laughs, sharp and short. "No. Unfortunately, sleep isn't one of my strong suits."

"I used to be great at it," I tell him, and I'm wry now. "Not anymore."

He looks away, uncomfortable now. Men are never comfortable when faced with a distraught woman. "I imagine."

"No, I don't think you can," I answer softly. "And I'm glad. How is Liam, by the way?"

Derek is still uncomfortable. I know he thinks that hearing about his healthy son will make me upset. That's far from the truth.

"I miss Liam," I tell him truthfully. "Even after he would go back to New York, I'd still see him from time to time when he and Leah FaceTimed. Now...well. Obviously, I don't."

I take another gulp, then another. I can't feel my throat now, so that's good.

Derek hesitates. I pat his hand.

"Seriously. Please tell me. Hearing about Leah's friends helps me, it doesn't hurt me."

That's not entirely true. There is a part of me, a hidden dark place, where I feel resentful when I see everyone else so alive and healthy. But it's only a small place, and I keep it secret. I'll never tell anyone about it, lest they think me a monster.

"Actually, he's struggling," Derek admits and his brow knits together. "I'm worried about him. He was struggling this past winter, and now he's floundering."

This takes me by surprise. I was so wrapped up in thinking he didn't want to tell me for other reasons.

"Oh, God. I'm so sorry," I say. "Is there anything I can do?"

"Brenda has him seeing a therapist, which I think is good," he answers. "And he's actually taking an antidepressant. But he quit his band."

"He quit the Roadrunners?" I suck in a breath. "He lived for that band. Leah talked about it all the time. I can't believe it."

"Yeah. Like I said, he's struggling. Now more than ever."

"Holy shit. I had no idea."

Because I've been unable to see anyone else's suffering other than my own.

Derek studies me, and his cheekbone cuts into the landscape. Behind him, the sea grass waves, and since my vision is becoming blurred, he's blending into it. I blink, and blink again harder. He's still surrounded by wavy lines and fuzzy colors. I should stop drinking.

I take another gulp instead.

"Did you think that no one else here cared?" he asks, and it's a real question. He's sincerely curious.

I shrug my shoulders. "I don't know. I mean, I know Skye does. But for so long, it's just been me and Leah here.

And her dad in Phoenix, of course. But I didn't know that it would truly impact other people like it does me."

Derek picks up my hand now, and I know he feels it shake. It always shakes nowadays, and he grasps it firmly to still it.

"Emmy, many, many people cared about your daughter. She was a gift, and you brought her into the world. You shared her, and for that, everyone will be forever grateful. Everyone misses her. I do, too. She used to joke with me about the New York Yankees every time she brought me towels."

"She didn't know a thing about baseball," I tell him.

He laughs. "I know. But she used to rag on the Yankees anyway, to get my goat. It was funny. I enjoyed it."

For a split second, I look at Derek as Leah might've. He's handsome, for sure. He looks almost like a modern Cary Grant, to be honest. But surely...the man she was involved with wasn't quite this old. That would've just been...gross.

"How old are you?" I ask bluntly, and my words are slurred now. Am I sitting up straight?

"Thirty-eight," he answers. "Why?"

"Jush wonderin'."

"How much have you had to drink tonight?" He raises an eyebrow now, and I think light comes out of his ear. Oh, wait. That's just the streetlight on the edge of the parking lot. I giggle at that.

All pain is gone at this point. Even the pain in my heart is dulled.

"Maybe I'll stay drunk forever," I confide in Derek. I'm

not sitting straight. I know this because I crash into his shoulder as I tip over. "Nothing hurts right now."

"You feel that way now, but you won't come tomorrow," he tells me, propping me back up. "Let's get you up. I'll help you to your apartment."

"How do you know I have an apartment?" I demand, trying to rear my head back in indignation. Unfortunately, it results in me landing on my back on the sand. I giggle again. "Fuck."

Derek rolls his eyes, I think. "I know because Liam hung out there a lot with Leah. Remember?"

My vision is tunneling now. "Oh, that's right." I'm pacified by that. He's not a stalker.

I think he sighs.

"Do you know if Leah stomped all over Liam?" I ask him.

He pauses, his shoulders square in the moonlight. He's in the shadow, and I can't really see his face.

"Why would you ask that?" he answers, a question with a question.

"Did she?"

"I think they were two kids just learning how to grow up. She was handling her hormones, he was handling his. Kids are inept at that age."

My drunk mind can hardly wrap itself around that answer, and I stare at him, trying to comprehend the riddle of his words.

"That wasn't really an answer," I try to tell him, but it comes out garbled.

"Come on," he says, and he's got my elbow. I can't see,

though. The ocean is spinning and the stars are too bright. I feel as if I'm in a snow globe, but the snow is actually stars. My eyes close.

"Do you believe that when we die we become stars?" I ask, and my voice is almost too thick to understand. Derek hefts me to my feet.

"No, I don't."

"Okay. Good."

That's when everything goes black. I feel his hand behind my head, and then nothing at all.

CHAPTER TWELVE

July 2

Liam lay on the beach, half beneath a blue umbrella. He couldn't stay in the direct sun as long as the girls could. His New York City skin couldn't take it. Not yet. In a few weeks, maybe, after his shoulders had tanned. Out at the break, where the sandbar met the deep, Skye and Leah floated on their boards, legs dangling in the water.

They laughed at something he couldn't hear, and then Leah jokingly pushed Skye off her board. Liam chuckled as she toppled off, her legs flying over her head. When she emerged, she was sputtering. She grabbed Leah, and the two began wrestling for the upper hand in the water. They were evenly sized, so the winner would be a toss-up.

He shook his head, gulping his water. He wasn't going to dehydrate and embarrass himself. He did that last year.

He'd pretended he was sick at the kickoff to the summer blowout that Leah had thrown for her friends, and had gone back to the bungalow and flopped onto his bed. The room had spun, he was dizzy and had the chills. It was humiliating.

No one would've known if his father hadn't ratted him out to Emmy. Emmy told Leah, and Leah told Skye, and before he knew it, everyone was teasing the city boy. The thing was, there was no reason for his father to tell. He could've just gone along with the story Liam told—that he was jet-lagged from the trip. But no. He had made sure to tell Emmy that his delicate son couldn't take the sun. Liam swore half the time that his father didn't even like him, although he didn't really understand why. He looked a bit like his mom, and he figured that might be it.

That was a bullshit reason, though. Liam hadn't asked for them to get divorced. It wasn't his fault that his mom had screwed his dad's business partner.

God, it was like a bad soap opera.

"Hey," a voice said from behind him. He looked over his shoulder to find Amber, a local girl he knew from youth group, holding a cooler and a beach towel. "Can I sit with you?"

He stared at her in surprise. "Yeah. Sure."

She sat next to him in a black one-piece. "How long have you been out today? You're getting kind of red."

"I'm fine," he said quickly, hoping he wasn't burning. She lifted an eyebrow.

"I've got some sunscreen. Here." She thrust it at him, and he put some more on his chest and arms.

"You don't like the water?" she asked, seemingly without judgment.

"No, that's not it. I just don't feel like swimming right now."

She shrugged.

They sat in silence for a while, and then Amber spoke. "Hey, if you're not doing anything later, would you like to come hang out and watch a movie or something?"

Liam froze. He didn't know what to say, he only knew what he felt. "Um, don't we have youth group tonight?" he answered her question with a question.

Her face fell. "No, not tonight." But before she could say anything else, he was saved by Leah and Skye.

"Li!" Leah waved her arms from the water. "Come out!" She and Skye had been joined by a couple of guys. Guys gravitated to them like the sun. Skye had that blonde island girl thing going on, and Leah was…Leah. She was glowing, and had the dark exotic looks of a mythical being.

"I'll see you later," he told Amber and he immediately got up and joined Leah and Skye, careful to position himself between the guys and Leah. Better to make sure they don't get *too* friendly. He'd been so very patient. He wasn't going to allow one of these idiots to just swoop in.

He floated on a board, although he knew he couldn't stand on it to save his life. Leah knew, too, but she never let on.

She was on her knees now, and Liam couldn't help but give her butt the side-eye. She'd been doing squats, and Lord, it showed. He swallowed hard.

She put him out of his misery by flipping onto her back

and staring at the sky. Reaching over, she grabbed his hand, holding it in the water between them.

"You might have culture in the city," she mused. "But you don't have this, Li."

"I definitely agree." He felt too much pleasure in the hand holding. It felt possessive, and he knew the other guys felt it, too. They glanced at it, and eventually, they floated away, leaving just Liam, Skye and Leah.

"You guys," Skye piped up, interrupting. "I have some tequila at my house."

Leah perked up her head. "Really?"

Skye nodded. "Yep. My dad got an entire case of it. Some client shipped it to him from Mexico. It's the real deal. Want to hang out and try it?"

Leah rumpled up her face. "We'll have to stop at the inn and get some orange juice or something. I'm not drinking it plain."

"You guys are lightweights," Liam interjected. "You've never tried it before? Not ever?"

Leah stared at him. "Don't judge."

He laughed. "I'm not."

"Then let's go," Skye urged them. She didn't have to twist their arms. They lugged their boards out of the water, dried off, and headed to the Black Dolphin.

Emmy was in the foyer, chatting with a pair of new guests, and she eyed them as they walked in. "Don't drip on the floor, kids," she called after them, then apologized to the guests. The guests smiled. *Kids will be kids*, their eyes said.

The trio of teenagers headed straight upstairs, where

Leah changed clothes and looked in the fridge. "No juice. We'll have to stop by the store."

"Fine. I've got money," Liam announced. The girls rolled their eyes.

"So do we," Skye told him drily. "But if you want to pay, be our guest."

Skye borrowed a dry outfit from Leah, and Liam stared at their legs, at the leather bracelets braided around their ankles.

"Twinsies?" he asked, his eyes twinkling. They rolled their eyes simultaneously.

"BFFs," Skye answered. "Suck it."

He laughed, and they clamored back down the stairs and out the door, heading down the road toward the supermarket. Once there, they picked up orange juice and a bag of chips. At the checkout, they found Amber, the strange girl from school and youth group, bagging up their groceries. She didn't look happy to see them and, in fact, wouldn't meet their gaze at all. Liam wondered if it was because he left her to join Skye and Leah in the water.

Leah forced her hand by saying hello, and Amber seemed annoyed when she answered.

"Hey," Amber said, shoving the chips into a bag.

Skye poked Leah in the ribs, as if to say *Don't bother*, but Leah ignored it, trying instead for some small talk.

"How's your summer so far?" Leah asked.

Amber was stone-faced. "Fine."

"Sounds exciting," Skye giggled and Leah stepped on her foot.

"We'll be hanging out this afternoon…in case you get bored," Leah offered.

This caught Amber's attention and her gaze shot up. "Yeah?"

Leah nodded. "Sure. We'll be at Skye's house."

"We will?" Skye asked, and she was giggling again.

Amber's face shut down again, as though she felt she was the butt of a joke.

"We will," Leah emphasized. "You're welcome to come, when you get off work."

Amber nodded and didn't say goodbye.

Outside, Leah turned to Skye. "I was trying to be nice," she said, nudging her friend. "It wouldn't hurt you either."

Skye snorted. "Why bother? That girl hates us."

"What did you do to her?" Liam chimed in. "She really does hate you."

Skye was unconcerned. "We've never done anything but exist. She blames us because her life is shitty and ours aren't, I think."

Leah agreed with that, and they finished walking in silence.

When they got to Skye's house, her dad was just getting into his car to go to a meeting. He waved at them as they climbed the steps. Her mom, Christy, was in the kitchen. They greeted her on their way through.

"You guys go wait in my room, and I'll go snag the bottle," she whispered. They did as she said.

Her room was an explosion of magentas and teals, an Asian tapestry hanging on the wall over her bed.

"Why do girls decorate like this?" Liam asked as he sat down. Leah raised an eyebrow.

"Like what?"

"Like...this." Liam gestured around the room, at all the baubles and knickknacks, and Leah just laughed.

"As opposed to a sterile environment?"

Liam grinned, because he knew as well as she did that his room was austere: black and white. Even the photos on the wall (Leah had taken them) were black-and-white. She knew him well, and had known he would like the beach still lifes she gave him...but only if they were colorless.

Skye was back within a minute, a tequila bottle tucked up under her shirt.

"Let's go out the back," she suggested.

They knew where they were going. There was a hangout room above the garage. Her father had had it built to keep their noise from disturbing him when he was watching football games.

It was private, yet close enough to raid the kitchen when they wanted.

It had three couches, two recliners, two ottomans, and a pool table against the back wall. They called it their Tree House.

Skye curled up on a couch, her knees tucked beneath her, and pulled out the liquor, while Leah produced the orange juice.

"We forgot cups." Liam sighed.

"It's okay. I'll go get some," Skye said. She rushed out, leaving Leah and Liam alone. Liam felt jittery, as though the air itself was tense, but Leah seemed perfectly comfortable.

"You should come over for dinner tonight," she told him. "Mom's been asking about you."

"Really?" Liam brightened up at that. Leah smiled.

"Yeah. She likes you."

"She feels sorry for me," Liam guessed. Leah was indignant.

"For what? You get to live in the city. There's nothing to feel sorry for."

Liam let that go because Leah's legs were very close to his own. He could feel the heat of her thighs against his, and he tried very hard to ignore it. She was his friend. She trusted him. He couldn't be a skeeze.

He looked determinedly at her face, and her eyes were wide and soft.

"So?" she asked, and the tone of her voice suggested this wasn't the first time she's asked.

"So what?" he answered dumbly.

"So will you come?" she repeated herself with a sigh. "You can bring your dad if you want. My mom won't mind."

"I don't want," he answered immediately. "I'll come alone."

Leah shrugged. "Okay. But make sure he knows I invited him so we don't seem rude."

Liam rolled his eyes. "Whatever. He won't even notice. But I'll tell him."

Skye was back, and she looked at them curiously, red Solo cups in her hand. "What did I miss?"

"Nothing," Liam answered, reaching for the cups. Within thirty seconds, he'd poured each of them a tequila and orange juice, filling them up to the rims. "To us." He held up his glass.

"To us." They toasted him. Leah was uncertain, but Skye dove right into hers. Leah sipped and made a face.

"God," she groaned. "This is terrible."

"Drink it anyway," Skye advised, so Leah did.

It burned her throat and singed her chest, but after a few minutes, it made her feel delightful. So light and airy. Leah got up and turned on the speaker on the wall. It was Bluetooth, so she was able to link it to the playlist on her phone. Soon, her favorite song was blaring, and she was dancing in the middle of the room, all alone.

"Come on," she urged her friends. Skye stood up on the couch, waving her hands in the air, and Liam shook his head. He sat back and watched the two girls sway like hippies. He hated to admit to himself that it was turning him on. He squeezed his eyes closed, but snapped them wide when he heard the door open.

Quickly, he tucked the tequila bottle behind his back.

Hutch, the youth group leader, stood there, chuckling as he saw the girls.

"Party?" he asked, with his brow lifted. "No one invited me."

That's how Liam knew he hadn't seen the tequila, thank God. The girls smiled, and honestly, it annoyed Liam how much the girls all smiled at Hutch. He was old enough to be their father.

"Good song, though!"

He smiled, and then protested when Leah tried to pull him into the circle created by the furniture. She persisted, though, and finally, he gave in. He danced in the middle, pulling Leah's hands and twirling her around, looping her over, under, through. To him, away from him, and back again.

Lyrics from the song floated around them, and laughter lingered in the air.

Skye giggled, and pulled Liam to his feet, and against his will, he danced. He wasn't going to be the only one sitting like he had a rod up his ass.

It was a moment to be remembered, honestly. A totally random spontaneous moment that seemed to personify sheer happiness.

When the song ended, Hutch walked to the wall and turned the music down. Turning around, he winked at the girls.

"Your mom told me you were up here," he said to Skye. "I was trying to track you down. Can I get your help with a project?"

"Something different from the Habitat project?" Skye asked, her brow wrinkled.

"Yeah," the youth pastor answered. "I'd like your help with Amber."

Leah's head snapped back. "We just saw her."

"I know. I was at the store, too. Behind you. I saw you try to be nice to her, and she wasn't interested."

Skye nodded. "She's always like that."

"Well, I was wondering…could you keep trying to include her? She's had a rough shake in life, and I think she's honestly just scared of letting people in. She doesn't want to get hurt or rejected." Hutch studied them. "I know it's hard to keep putting yourself out there, but I know she really needs friends."

Leah found herself nodding. "Sure, Hutch."

He grinned, and the room lit up. Skye practically preened in the glow from his smile.

"Thank you so much," he told them. "I knew I could count on you."

He looked at them with such gentleness that Liam wanted to vomit. He forced himself to answer.

"No problem, Hutch."

The youth pastor headed to the door, but paused. Turning, he looked them all in the eye. "You might want to chew some gum before you leave. You all smell like happy hour."

He left without a second glance, and the girls looked at each other, then laughed.

"Is he gonna tell?" Liam asked nervously.

"No," Skye answered confidently. "He's cool like that."

Leah was going to say something to the same effect, but her phone buzzed in her pocket, and she pulled it out to read the text.

You look lovely today.

She grinned and blushed, and put her phone away before anyone else saw it.

CHAPTER THIRTEEN

August 19

My head is exploding in bright shoots of pain when I wake. Light floods the window, and it's late. Very late.

I sit straight up and look at the clock. It's 8:11 a.m.

Son of a bitch.

Frantic, I pull on clothes and yank a brush through my hair, clattering down the stairs to the dining room, preparing to make my apologies to the hungry guests who are surely waiting for breakfast.

But instead, I find Derek pouring coffee and handing out sticky buns from the doughnut shop in town. He grins at me.

"I've explained that you're a bit under the weather

today," he tells me. "And that you asked me to help with breakfast."

I nod, dumbfounded, as the guests smile and offer me their best wishes. "I'm not contagious," I assure them. "Just a…migraine. I only get them once in a blue moon, but when I do…"

They're understanding, and I take over from Derek. He sits at a table by the window, and when everyone else has wandered out to get on with their days, I make myself go sit with him.

"Thank you," I say simply. "I don't know what came over me. I'm sorry. Really sorry."

"Do you remember much from last night?" he asks, lifting his coffee cup and meeting my eyes over the rim.

I shake my head. "Not after a certain point. If I spoke gibberish, I'm humiliated."

"Don't be," he says firmly. "You've earned the right to check out for a moment." I start to say something else, but he interrupts me. "Seriously. Don't even think on it."

"Can I at least pay you for the doughnuts?" I ask, and he shakes his head.

"Nope. No need."

"How did I get into my bed?" I ask him, and I'm pretty sure I know the answer.

"I put you there."

God. My cheeks flare into fire.

"Did you carry me up all three flights of stairs?"

"Yes. For such a little woman, you got pretty heavy by the third flight."

I want to die.

My head slumps, chin to chest, and Derek laughs.

"I'm just glad I came along when I did. Or you would've passed out on the beach alone."

"I would've been okay," I announce. "My beach is private."

"Yeah. But seagulls might've pooped on you, or something."

He's making fun of me, which does nothing for my humiliation.

"Lord, I'm so sorry," I apologize again. "Truly. That's not me. I promise."

"I know it isn't," he answers. "Please don't worry about it. I'm just glad to help. I've wanted to ask you ever since… for a while now, what I could do. I'm glad there turned out to be something."

"Well, it's not just anyone that I allow to carry me to bed," I quip, trying to make light of the awkwardness.

"I should hope not." He grins. Something in his tone, though, sends a shock through me, tingling my fingertips. He's a man. I'm a woman. That's to be expected. *He* was in my bedroom, my inner sanctum. It's so intimate.

"What do you do for a living, Derek?" I ask, trying to change the subject, because even though he's been here for months and months, I've never asked.

He's a Cheshire cat now, grinning widely, taking pleasure from my embarrassment. "I'm an investment manager. I handle people's money."

"That suits you," I tell him. "You have the look."

"The snobby look?" He lifts an eyebrow again.

"No. Just the whole…polished, put–together and confident thing."

"It's an act," he confides. "No one is truly confident. We all just pretend."

"Some do it better, then," I say. He smiles.

"I'm a great pretender. Anyway. Do you need anything else before I take my leave? I have a few conference calls this morning."

"Oh, no. You've done so much already."

He smiles again. "Anytime. I mean that."

He gets up and heads to the open terrace doors. "Hey, Derek?"

He pauses, then turns.

"Yes?"

"Is Liam coming back for fall break?"

"I hope so."

I nod, and he leaves, disappearing into the blue sky outdoors.

I head into the privacy of the kitchen and drop my head onto the table, utterly humiliated and completely hungover.

My ex–husband's worry comes through the phone.

"Em, I think you should cancel guests," Nate argues. "I mean it. You haven't taken any time off to grieve. It's all going to explode in your face."

"Did you hear what I told you?" I'm annoyed and tired. "I told you that Leah had an older boyfriend. That she wasn't a virgin. And you're worried about *me*?"

Nate is silent now, and then he sighs, loud and long.

"Does that eat at me? Do I want to find the fucking kid

and punch him in the fucking throat? Yes. Hell, yes. But that won't bring her back, Em. It won't. I think you're focusing on this in order to avoid your grief."

"But it might make me feel better," I say, and it's true. If I could just see the guy who inflicted pain onto her, the guy who desecrated her...the guy who took her innocence far too early. If I could spit in his face.

It might give me some peace.

Does that make me a monster?

"I think you should take some time off," Nate says finally. "I mean it."

"I can't. We can't have the reputation of closing our doors for any reason."

"You lost your daughter. Anyone...*anyone* would respect that. And let's be honest. Your heart isn't in it right now, and they're gonna know it."

"I'll think about it," I say finally. But only because he's right in one respect. I'm not able to do my job at a hundred percent. I can't let quality slip, or the guests won't return. Our future depends on repeat customers.

We hang up, and I step onto my bedroom balcony. It hovers over the back lawns, and I can see the sea. I spot a couple of guests out in the water, splashing in the waves in brightly colored swimsuits. They're smiling in the sun.

That's what the Black Dolphin is all about. Providing a respite. A soft landing place in the middle of the world's harsh troubles. A vacation from everything.

I slept through breakfast this morning. My heart is a piece of black stone, unable to feel anything but pain. Is

Nate right? Can I really offer them what they're coming here to experience?

I make my decision quickly, because that's what I do. I'm decisive, and once I decide, I act.

I go straight to my wood-paneled study downstairs, and I email all the guests scheduled to come in for the next month. I explain the situation, that my daughter has died and I need to grieve. I refund their money, then arrange for them to have accommodations at the resort on the other side of the island. I even give them vouchers to return here anytime in the next year at half price.

It's the first time in fifty years that the Black Dolphin has closed its doors for any reason.

When I'm finished with all of it, I sit back in my chair, almost stunned.

For ten days, I've immersed myself in doing a half-assed job at running the inn, hoping that I'd block out the pain...that I could somehow manage to skip the worst of the grieving.

It's not true.

All I've done is postpone it.

It's hitting me now, in flashes and bits and overwhelming rushes.

If I don't handle it, I'm going to lose my mind.

The sea breeze comes in through the open veranda doors, gently blowing the hair off my forehead. I breathe it in...the sweetly scented salty freshness.

As I stare out at the sea, Derek's tall form comes into focus, dressed only in a pair of swim trunks. He's surpris-

ingly fit. Even though he's trim, I never figured him to
be fit.

His face tilts up, and he meets my gaze.

I look away, and then realize... I have to do something
about him. He lives here. I can't quite kick him out for a
month.

With a sigh, I send another email. To him.

I explain I'm closing the inn for a month, but he's welcome to stay. The only way it will impact him is that I
won't be cooking breakfasts in the dining room.

He answers while still standing on the beach, his phone
in hand.

He looks up from his phone and stares at me, waiting
for me to read it. I click it open.

That's fine. I'll be happy to stay. Don't worry about not opening the dining room just for me. I'll be happy to join you in
your own from time to time.

(If you think I'm letting you close yourself away in the dark,
you're mistaken).

My head snaps up and I meet his gaze.

I don't know how to feel. He's just invited himself to
eat in my apartment, yet he only did it because he doesn't
want me to give in to the desperate swirl of grief that is
threatening to drown me.

How apropos is it that Leah drowned in the water, and
I'll drown in the grief?

I nod curtly toward Derek, in acknowledgment of his
email. He smiles, kind and secure.

I can't figure him out, and I don't have the energy to try. He's not my priority. Finding out who violated my baby is what will fuel me now.

With a deep breath, I head back down the hall toward her bedroom.

CHAPTER FOURTEEN

July 8

"It only takes one glance at you to make me forget everything else," Ry told Leah. It was dark, and they were finally meeting again in the darkened shadows at the Habitat site. She smiled up at him, flattered.

"Really?"

He stared into her eyes. "Really. I could look at you for hours. I thought you were never going to get rid of Skye and Liam tonight."

Leah rolled her eyes. "You knew that Liam was coming to dinner again."

"That doesn't mean I like it. You know, he's your age and everything. How do I know that you won't decide I'm too old? That you'd rather be with him instead?"

Leah's head snapped back because that thought had never crossed her mind.

"Oh, my God. That's crazy," she laughed, and he wrapped his arm more tightly around her shoulders. It was Florida, but for some reason this evening, the breeze was cooler than usual. His fingers stroked her bare arm, and goose bumps formed. She shivered in anticipation.

"You told me you'd kiss me tonight," she reminded him.

He smiled down at her, his eyes glinting in the moonlight.

"Ah, I see you didn't forget."

"Of course not!" She was indignant. "I've been looking forward to it."

He grinned again. "Good things come to those who wait, Kitten."

"But it will be tonight, right?" She blinked, and he kissed her eyelids.

"There you go. You've been kissed."

She glared and he laughed. "Okay, fine. You will get your *real* kiss tonight. I promise."

His groin was hardening at the mere thought, but Leah didn't know that. She was oblivious, wrapped up in her schoolgirl dreams of her first kiss. He smiled just a bit at that, at being her first.

She caught him. "What's funny?" she demanded.

He caught her hand and kissed her fingers. "See? I've kissed you twice now. Nothing is funny. You just make me happy."

She glowed at that, even in the dark.

"You'd better be careful texting me when I'm with Skye," she warned him. "She could see one of these times."

That sobered him up. "Hmm. We don't want that. How about... I'll get you a second phone. One that is your secret. Only take it out when you're alone."

Leah nodded. "That would work."

"Only use it to text me, though," Ry instructed. "I don't want you using it to flirt with anyone else."

Leah was annoyed now, and tried to pull her hand away. He held it fast. "I don't flirt with anyone else."

"You don't mean to flirt with anyone else," Ry corrected. "You can't help it. You're a teenager. You're just now learning what your sexuality can do."

"I'm an old soul," she told him.

She was angry for a minute, but then she paused, then scooted a little closer. Her hand was in his lap, and she pressed it against him, feeling his rigidity beneath her fingers.

"What can my sexuality do, Ry?" She asked it innocently, but the question was far from innocent. He breathed against her neck, warm and moist.

"It's everything, Leah."

"Everything?" she asked, and she splayed her hand wide over his crotch. His hardness startled her. She hadn't known it would be that stiff. It was a little scary, actually.

"Everything," he confirmed.

She exhaled against his cheek, because the sheer knowledge of knowing her effect on him was intoxicating. She leaned into his heat, and he accepted her weight, allowing her to melt into him.

"Let's make a deal," he suggested. She looked up at him through her fog.

"What is it?"

"I'll kiss you like you've never even dreamed of being kissed, if you send me a picture of yourself tomorrow."

"I've sent you tons of pictures," she laughed, shoving her hair out of her eye, tucking it behind her ear.

"Not those pictures," he corrected. "A naked picture. Be naked for me, Leah. Only for me."

Her breath caught, her words frozen on her tongue.

"Use your new phone to send me a beautiful picture of you, Leah. I want to be able to see you always, even when you aren't with me."

She blushed, flattered.

"What if you don't like it?" she murmured. "I don't know what to do in the picture."

"Are you serious?" he demanded. "I'll love it. Just stand there. Or lie there. Or anything you want to do. You're so beautiful, Leah. Inside and out—I just want to see you."

She nodded, and her insides felt like they would float away from happiness. To think, he would risk everything, his whole entire life, just to be with her. It was almost too much to wrap her head around.

"Why do you even like me?" she finally asked.

He was surprised again.

"I can't even believe you'd ask me that," he told her, and he used the side of his hand to stroke her face. "You're the kindest soul I've ever met. The happiest, the most beauti-ful. I shouldn't have become attracted to you. But I couldn't help it. You're like a light in the world, Leah. You are the personification of true joy."

Her reply to him was interrupted by her phone. She glanced at it.

"It's my mom…wondering where I am," she told him. "I've gotta go."

"Okay." He sighed. "If you must. One day, someday, we can be together as long as we want."

She was startled by this, and stared at him. "What do you mean? You mean…we can actually be together?"

He holds her hands tightly. "I'd like that. Would you?"

"Yes," she said immediately. "But I have to go to college. Maybe you can move with me."

He smiled and pressed his lips to her forehead. "Maybe so. We'll work it out."

They stood up, and she was nervous. He was going to kiss her, and she knew it. She wanted it, and she was scared of it.

The next thing she knew, his face was closer, then closer, and all of a sudden, she couldn't remember why she was so nervous in the first place.

It wasn't that big of a deal.

His lips were warm and soft, and his breath tasted like mint.

He opened his mouth a little, then pushed his tongue into hers, swirling around her own. She adjusted to the feeling and was distracted by it, when his hips jutted into her, and she could feel his hardness again.

He pulled away. "See how much I want you, Leah? Surely you can't doubt me now."

And she couldn't.

She was light-headed as she said goodbye, and dizzy as she walked home.

He was so mature. He'd been with so many people, and he still wanted her more than anything in the world.

It was almost unimaginable.

CHAPTER FIFTEEN

August 22

My daughter's love of simplicity bites me in the ass now.

Once, I was thankful for it. I never had to chide her for a messy room the way everyone else with a teenage daughter did. Instead, hers was always neat and tidy, everything in its place. She said it was because her brain was creative, and she couldn't think when her surroundings were chaotic.

But now, as I search carefully through her things yet again for clues about her secret life, I come up empty. I don't want to read through her blog posts. I will, but not yet. They will chew my heart up and spit them out. Each word is a painful assault to my memory of her. I'm not ready.

So instead, I sift through her belongings. Her notebooks, her journals, even the crumbled up paper in her trash can.

I don't find much.

I find a phone number scribbled hastily in pencil, which is a bit odd, since kids these days just put them immediately into their phones.

Oh, my God. Her phone.

Why haven't I looked at her phone?

It's lying on top of her desk, and it's completely dead.

I swallow hard at the irony, and plug it in.

Carefully, I lie on her bed, on the part that is rumpled… the place she lay upon last. With my hand, I feel the bedspread, the ridges and the texture. Her hand was here, in this exact spot. I close my eyes and imagine it.

When I reopen them, I look up at the dream catcher hanging over the headboard.

She brought it back from Phoenix when she vacationed with her dad for a week. Made from brown felt, silver wire, white feathers, and beautifully unique turquoise beads, she'd bought it from a Hopi woman on the side of a road. She informed me that it would keep her nightmares at bay. I wonder now if it did.

I also wonder if it would help with mine?

I dream over and over, when I actually do sleep, that Leah is drowning and I can't save her. It's a truth I'll never escape. The look on her face as she reaches her arms out to me… I can't shake it. Even if it wasn't real.

But *was it*? Did she reach for me when she was drowning? Was she hoping I'd come and save her?

Her phone cord stretches to the bed, so I pick it up. I know the passcode, so with four clicks, I'm staring at her photo wallpaper—she and Skye on the beach, blue sky above, sand below them.

I click into her text messages, afraid, so afraid, of what I will find.

She has 402 new messages from Liam.

Puzzled, I click into them. They begin the day after she died.

I miss you.

I can't believe this happened.

I want to say... I love you. You didn't know it, but it's true. I'll never love anyone the same way. I'm afraid of that.

They go on in much the same way, for dozens and dozens of messages.

I know you won't see these, but it makes me feel better to talk to you. Even if you can't answer.

I miss you.

God, I miss you.

I'm sorry.

I'm sorry.

I stare at the screen, and my vision blurs for a minute. What is he sorry for?

Can it be... Liam? Is he the one?

He's only older by a year. And from the posts that I read, Leah referenced a *man*, not a teenager.

The Liam I know is gentle, even if he wears black and acts like he's edgy. We all know that people wear masks. As Derek said, everyone pretends. Liam is kind. I've seen it in his eyes. Could he hide something darker there?

There are no texts that are abnormal. Skye, Liam, Anna. All kids from school, all talking about innocuous things.

This phone is no help. I scan the pictures, too.

There's nothing.

I know what I have to do. With trembling fingers, I open her laptop and find her blog.

It didn't happen suddenly.

It happened slowly, like the tide turning. He listened to me. I mean, really listened. I've never really met someone who does that. When I said something, he turned his whole body toward me, and soaked up every word, like he'd rather die than not hear what I said. He watched my mouth, like he could hear better if he saw my lips.

He still does, you know.

He treats me like a Goddess, like I'm the most amazingly beautiful thing he's ever seen. I know it's wrong. And I didn't choose this. I didn't mean for this to happen. But it did. I don't have any regrets, I just don't want anyone to hate me.

Honestly, though, how could I help falling for him? He's here for me when no one else is.

That last line impales my heart, and shatters it into pieces.

My daughter had felt so alone, and that's my fault. I practically chased her into the situation. I'm to blame.

I curl up on her bed, her phone in my hand, and I sleep for the first time in days, breathing in my daughter's scent, and surrounded by her memories.

It's impossible for anyone else to understand the pain I'm in.

I decide this as I wait for the kid at the grocery store to bag up my lettuce and onions and tomatoes.

They look at me and smile, and ask how I am, and I see in their eyes that they're scared.

They're scared I'll actually tell them.

"Have a good day, Mrs. Fisher," he says, and I think he was a grade younger than Leah, and when he wishes me a good day, he cringes, as though it was the stupidest thing he could've said. He probably doesn't think I'll ever have a good day again, and he's probably right.

Also, I think my existence scares people because it reminds them that they are mortal. If Leah can die—a beautiful, healthy girl—they can, too.

People don't want to think about that.

As for me, sometimes, it's all I think about.

The day that I finally get to die and see my daughter again.

There are times when I entertain the idea of just ending it now and getting it over with. But I can't. I have to retrace Leah's last steps, the last few weeks of her life. I have to know who she had been with. I have to know. Something inside me tells me that it was criminal, that the man had been of criminal age, and if that's true, he needs to pay.

It becomes my driving force, the one thing I can focus on without wanting to cry. It turns my mind red with lust for revenge, it shields me from the pain, at least a little bit, because it gives me purpose. Without it, I'm just a mother without her child, which isn't really even a mother at all anymore.

The inn is lonely and quiet when I unlock the back door and step inside with my groceries. I don't know why I bothered. I'm not hungry much anymore. I abandon them in the kitchen, shoving them hastily in the fridge, and head back out toward Nico's.

I notice the time on my way out, but I don't care that it's only 2:00 p.m.

I will do what I must to dilute the pain, and alcohol works as well as anything.

I might be developing a problem. I might not. I don't really care.

I walk up the wooden pier steps into Nico's, and for once, it's pretty dead. Usually, even in the middle of the afternoon, tourists linger here.

Today, the bar is empty, with plenty of seats to choose from. I pick one near the end, beside the window so I can stare out to sea.

Nico comes in from the back room, wiping his hands on his pants, and when he sees me, he smiles warmly.

"Ah, *bonita*," he says, grinning. "What a pleasure to see you today! What can I get for you?"

He leans against the bar, his face propped into his hands. Nico has a way of focusing in on you and making you feel like you're the only person on the planet. Sometimes, it's charming. Sometimes, like today, it just makes you feel like a bug under a microscope.

I squirm.

"I'll have a whiskey sour, please."

"You're so easy." He winks. "Coming right up."

He makes a show out of pouring it, with the bottles held high in the air. All I notice is the whiskey he splashes onto the bar top. So wasteful. But that's the innkeeper in me, I suppose.

When he hands it to me, his fingers linger on mine for a second. I roll my eyes at him, pulling the glass (and my hand) away.

"Nico, has your wife kicked you out yet?" I ask him, smiling sweetly.

He cocks his head. "Are you saying she should?"

"I'm saying I probably would. You're a hopeless flirt."

He laughs in delight. "But see, *mamacita*, my wife understands. She knows I'm a Cuban stallion."

I'm frozen, though, by *mamacita*. "Mommy." He's called me that for ages, and I'm sure he calls every woman the same. But today, now, it hurts me.

I toss back the whiskey like it's nothing.

I find that I like the burn as it blazes down my throat.

I like that pain. It distracts me from my *real* pain.

It's odd how little everyday things are so noticeable now. So painful.

I shove my empty glass at him. "Another please."

He lifts an eyebrow, then shrugs. "Of course."

He pours it without fanfare this time, and hands it back, serious now.

"Should I make you a sandwich to soak it all up with?" he asks. "I make a delicious Cuban. I use the best meats."

I think he's almost worried now.

"I'm not going to pass out in your bar," I assure him. "I'm perfectly fine."

He waves his hand. "No, no. I wasn't worried about that. I just noticed that you've lost weight. You're starting to get the legs of a chicken now. I thought maybe I should feed you."

I shrug, and look down. My chest does seem bony, and I suppose I have lost weight. I haven't felt like eating. Sitting at my dinner table alone only amplifies my loss.

"A sandwich would be good," I tell him. "Thank you. But can you wrap it up to go?"

He nods and disappears into the kitchen.

I wonder if it should alarm me that two whiskeys hasn't affected me at all. My senses are a bit dulled. That's all. A couple months ago, the room would be spinning.

I shake my head, determined not to worry about it. I have plenty of other things to worry about.

When Nico returns and hands me the bag with my sandwich in it, he also gives me a hug. Not a sexual hug, or even a lingering one where he discreetly feels me up. But a sincere hug.

"If you need anything, let me know," he tells me, and his eyes are warm.

I nod. "Thank you."

He watches me as I leave, and I inhale deeply when I'm outside. Bars always smell the same, even when they have open windows on the end of a pier. Like…old peanuts and neon lights, and felt-top pool tables and desperation.

I shake it off, soaking in the salt in the air instead.

My feet sink into the sand as I walk toward home and the sandwich actually smells amazing. I find that I'm a bit hungry, for the first time in days.

As I get closer, I notice something on the beach. Something white. I focus on it. Is it a heap of clothing?

That would be odd.

A few more steps, and I can see that it's flowers. A heap of white lilies.

Left right on the beach, right behind my house.

Right where Leah drowned.

I gulp hard, drop my sandwich on the sand, and run inside.

CHAPTER SIXTEEN

July 9

L eah sat on her bed, sprawled out.

Her mother was working, of course, and she was alone in the apartment. The new cellphone lay on her lap; Ry had hidden it by the garage last night, and she'd retrieved it this morning. The thing was...she didn't know how to take the picture.

She posed in one way, then another, and looked into the camera to see how it would look. But she couldn't tell for sure unless...unless...she took her clothes off.

So, she did.

It felt strange to take them off in the daylight in the middle of her room, for a purpose other than to get dressed. The sunlight shone upon her skin, illuminating any peach fuzz that grew on her skin, and highlighting any bump. It was actually liberating.

She stood there for a moment, enjoying the sense of freedom, and then took two pictures before she could think twice. One standing, one lying down. She pressed the send button quickly, then put the phone away.

She got dressed, and paced, and sat, and paced, and sat, and paced.

When her phone buzzed, she almost leaped to get it.

Sweet mother, he answered. You are the most beautiful creature I've ever seen. More please.

She grinned, her nervousness gone. How could she be nervous when he liked them so much? Photography was her favorite thing in the world, and so she could use her skill to her benefit. She took at least twenty more, in various angles, in various lighting, including one in her shower, leaning against the tile.

She sent them happily, secure in the knowledge that he was going to love them. And he did.

Leah, you're killing me, he answered.

Her heart fluttered at his words. She felt heady with power, and she wished she could tell someone. It was so exciting, yet there was no one she could tell. Everyone would tell her that it was wrong, or they would be angry.

All she wanted was for someone to listen.

The idea of a blog came to her like a bolt of lightning. Of course.

Surely no one from this island would come across it. She could pour her heart out, and she wouldn't have to risk getting Ry caught or in trouble. It was perfect. The only thing she'd have to do was be careful her mom didn't find it, but that wasn't likely. Her mom never snooped. But just in case, she'd clear her history after every time she used it.

She felt a twinge of guilt over lying to her mom.

They'd always shared everything, but they couldn't share this. Her mother would never understand.

She opened her laptop, and built a blog within minutes. It was incredibly easy to use a design template, and she was working on her first post before she knew it.

How it started, she typed.

It started easily, over a period of years. I didn't know it had begun, and maybe he didn't either. I knew him, he knew me. We liked each other. We teased, we joked. But nothing changed until recently.

I found him watching me once. I was with Skye, and his eyes were just frozen on me, like he couldn't look away. I was at a football game, and I was cheering. After that, he was the only one I could look at in the stands. Every move I made, I made it for him. All of a sudden.

I felt guilty. I felt weird. But more than any of that, it felt right.

Don't judge me, dear reader. I know it would hurt a lot of people, and I don't pretend to think that I'm above worrying about that. I'm not. I worry about the consequences a lot, actually. The problem is, I want to be with him more than I worry about the damage it might cause. I hope I don't burn in hell.

The cursor blinked, over and over, and she stared at the page, trying to decide if she wanted to write anything more. For a first entry, she thought this was pretty good. It was an introduction, after all. She could get more involved in the details later. She carefully chose tags for the post, so that it could get found by search engines. *Older boyfriend. Minor girlfriend. Inappropriate relationships.*

She hated that last one.

Inappropriate relationships.

Something that felt so amazing shouldn't have a label so ugly. She closed the lid on her computer, and picked up her phone.

He had texted again, and she hadn't heard it. When she saw the words, she sucked in her breath.

Touch yourself for me, Leah. Pretend your hand is mine. Let me see.

Her heart beat fast, then faster. He knew what he wanted, and he wasn't afraid to ask for it. She loved that. She smiled as she slid her pants off once more.

CHAPTER SEVENTEEN

August 23

"I don't know why it bothered me so much," I confide in Nate. "Seriously. I might be losing it. I should be happy that someone wants to remember her. But instead, seeing those flowers… It was like…it was like…"

Tears well up and my throat seems to swell. I swallow, then swallow harder.

"It's like a reminder?" Nate guesses.

I nod, then remember that he can't see me.

"Yeah. I guess."

"I feel the same way," he tells me. "People here at the office have sent me cards or flowers, and I don't even like looking at them. They mean well, and it's so nice of them. But…"

"Yeah. I know."

We're quiet for a while. I hear him breathe, and I absently stroke Bo's head.

"Do you need me to come back out, Emmy?" he finally asks. "Because I will. It wouldn't be a problem. I can come help you box up Leah's room, or whatever you need."

"I'm not boxing up her room yet." My answer is immediate and sharp. "It's too soon."

I'm not sure if I'll ever be ready. But I don't mention that.

Nate is placating. "Of course. Whatever you want. But when you're ready, just let me know. I'll come out and help."

"Okay." I barely manage to get the word out. The mere thought of getting rid of Leah's things—it makes me panicky.

"I still call her phone sometimes, to hear her voice mail," Nate tells me. He sounds ashamed, as though he should be stronger than that.

"I still listen to the last voice mail she left me," I admit. "Just hearing her voice…"

"Yeah. I know," he says quietly. "The reality of it is setting in now. It's so hard, Em."

He's crying, I realize. I hear the wetness in his voice, and the knowledge almost guts me. He never cries. Never.

"We'll be okay," I tell him, comforting him through the phone. "We will be. I'm strong, you're strong."

He calms himself, and is quiet.

"You're stronger," he finally says, and his voice is steady again. "You always have been."

"I think I'm just better at pretending," I answer, remembering Derek's words from the other night. "Let's just leave it at that."

"We'll get through this, Emmy," he tells me, and I agree. "Can you promise me you'll get out of the house? Don't just stay holed up there alone."

"Hey, make up your mind," I chuckle, trying to lighten the mood. "First you wanted me to cancel the guests, and now you don't want me alone."

"I'm serious. Get out into the sunshine. Promise?"

"Yeah."

"Good. I'll talk to you later." He hangs up, and I'm alone in the house again. It's funny how you never realize how quiet the silence actually is until you're the only one left in a home. Leah always filled up the space with singing, and laughing, and chatting on the phone. If she was home, the radio was on, or the TV. There was always noise.

Now, there is none.

I pad through the apartment, and even more feet don't make a sound.

It's honestly enough to drive a person mad.

Bo waits by the door, as if he can read my mind.

"You want to go out?" I ask him. He hasn't been walked since Leah died. His big tail thumps against the floor like a giant piece of rope. "Okay."

I grab his leash, clip it to his collar, and we set out.

He's as strong as he looks, and for a while, I'm a balloon on a string as he yanks me along. We don't walk on the beach. I don't want to look at the water today. Instead, we head for downtown, the small main street lined with touristy shops.

We stop at the local coffee shop, the one lined with velvet couches and where the local teenagers hang out on hot days. Leah always had a Joe's cup in her hand, it seemed like. I never did. I always just made my own at home.

But today, it's time for something new.

I order my coffee and when they hand it to me, I take it to an outside table to drink it. Bo sits on my feet, and I have to smile at the way people skirt around him, giving him a wide berth. What they don't know is that he'd just as soon lick them to death as anything else.

"Mom?"

The word is murmured from near my elbow, and I turn to find Skye behind me. She's so pale that I do a double take. She looks awful.

"Skye? Honey, have you been sleeping?"

She sits at the table with me, stooping to pet Bo. She doesn't answer; instead, she silently shakes her head. She's got dark circles beneath her eyes, and her shoulders are skinnier than ever.

My heart constricts.

"Babe," I whisper. "You have to take care of yourself. Leah would want that."

"When I sleep, I dream," she tells me, and her voice sounds choked. "I dream about Leah. I dream that I should've helped her and didn't."

"But you weren't there," I reason with her. "You couldn't have helped her. I was there, and I couldn't."

"It's not the same." She sighs, and I can see that she means it. She truly feels guilty. "She was my sister, in every way that mattered."

"Honey, she was my *daughter*. And I couldn't save her. Bad things happen sometimes. We can't change that."

Very bad things. I hesitate, fighting the urge to ask Skye once again about Leah's private life. She doesn't know. She already told me. I've never known Skye to lie, so I have to trust that.

"I was talking to Liam last night," she says, and she's hesitant now. She's not meeting my gaze, her eyes frozen on Bo. "He said he thinks something was going on with her before. That maybe she even…"

She swallows hard, and blinks fast.

"That she even…what?"

Skye exhales, allowing her cheeks to fill with air, then deflate.

"He's worried that she might've…killed herself."

I startle, and then shake my head in relief. "There's no way. No. She wouldn't. We were talking right before she went into the water. She wanted me to go with her. Plus, there was blood on her board, and the tether was ripped. There was a shark. The sheriff's office has confirmed that."

"I know." Skye nods. "I don't think so either. It's just… He's so convinced that she was into something bad before."

"Bad?"

"He thinks she was involved with someone she shouldn't have been," Skye finally says.

Now I'm the one exhaling.

"I'm concerned about that, too," I tell her. "That's why I asked you the other day."

"Liam says she was really upset that night. I didn't even

know." Her shoulders slump, and she turns her tear-filled eyes to me. "Did you?"

"No." I shake my head. "She seemed fine."

But I guess we all pretend.

My heart batters against my chest, straining to get out. I can't help but wonder what else I don't know.

CHAPTER EIGHTEEN

July 10

Leah decided her bedroom was utterly childlike.

She sat on the bed and stared around, at the sea-colored walls and princess white furniture. It didn't feel like her anymore. She didn't feel like a child. She felt like an adult.

She held in her hand a text that contained a picture of a grown man's penis. It was huge and rigid, and it was meant for her.

That idea turned her stomach over and over in anticipation.

When it had first come through, she was a little terrified. But after studying it, she decided that it wouldn't be any worse than inserting a tampon. A penis was bigger, of course, but her body adjusted for a tampon, and it would adjust for a penis.

Millions of women had sex every day and they were just fine. If it wasn't fine, or even better than fine, no one would want to do it.

Her first kiss had certainly been better than fine.

She decided to blog about it.

Our first kiss, she typed.

It was my first kiss ever. Our first kiss together. It was everything I hoped it would be and more. Who knew that a pair of lips would feel like that? After all, they're just lips. I have them, you have them. Everyone has them. But when they meet like mine and Ry's did... Lord. I think we shocked each other from the electricity. My lips tingled for hours, and I kept touching them to make sure they were still there. I felt like I could still feel his lips upon mine. If that is what sex is about, then sign me up. I know it will be amazing with him. I foresee it being ethereal, almost. Surreal. Otherworldly. My mom always says that I'm too poetic, that I keep my head in the clouds. But this time, I think it served me well. I didn't want to kiss some sweaty junior-high kid after ball practice behind the gym. I wanted to wait until it was special, and it was.

She tagged it *older man, younger woman, first kiss.*

Publish.

It was out in the world.

That felt good. She might have to keep Ry a secret

around here, but the world was a big place, and she could release her secret to faceless readers.

She started to close her laptop, but noticed that she had a comment on her very first post.

Intrigued, she clicked on it to see it.

SammySea32 wrote: Girl, how much older is he? I'm all for older men, but there is a point where it is criminal, you know? You have to be a certain age for him to not get jailed for statutory rape. You better check it out.

That made her pulse pound and she exited her blog immediately for a search engine. She punched in rape guidelines for Florida. Eighteen was the age of consent in Florida, although there was a stipulation that sixteen- and seventeen-year-olds could sleep with someone up to the age of twenty-three without prosecution.

She stared at her screen for a while, at the guidelines.

She was so lost in thought that she didn't hear her mom approach until Emmy stuck her head in the door.

"Hey, babe," she greeted her, and as she walked in, Leah closed her laptop.

"Hey, Mom," she answered with a smile.

"I have a few minutes of blessed free time. Want to walk downtown for some ice cream?"

Leah grinned. "Do I have two X chromosomes?" She stood and yanked a brush through her hair. "I hope they have Death by Chocolate this week."

"And the cute guy behind the counter?"

Her mom looked knowing, and Leah knew what she was talking about. A kid was here for the summer, and he'd gotten a summer job at Clark's, the ice-cream shop. He was good-looking. And maybe, once upon a time, she would have been interested, but not now. She rolled her eyes.

"Quit trying to match-make," she told her mom. "I'm a strong independent woman. I don't need a man."

Emmy laughed and they headed out. The quaint downtown wasn't busy with tourists for once, and when they opened the door to Clark's, they inhaled the familiar smell of sugar and refrigeration. They found a table directly inside, and to Leah's utter satisfaction, they did in fact have Death by Chocolate.

She was eating a double-scoop when the bell jingled as the door opened again, and looking up, they found Derek and Liam walking in.

Liam was entirely in black, and Derek was in khaki shorts and a linen shirt. They were polar opposites in the truest sense of the term.

Liam's face lit up when he saw Leah, and so after he ordered his milkshake, they sat down next to the ladies.

"I didn't know you were coming here," he said, but his delight was unmistakable. Emmy and Derek stared at each other knowingly. Liam's crush on Leah was visible to everyone but Leah herself.

"We didn't either," she told him, chocolate on her lip. "Spur-of-the-moment."

Emmy reached over with a napkin and dabbed at the ice cream before it dripped on her daughter's shirt, and Derek had to excuse himself to take a call outside. He left his ice cream on the table.

As the minutes passed, it melted more and more.

Emmy glanced outside and saw Derek pacing in the sun,

his phone to his ear, his mouth pursed. He was upset about something. Liam and Leah were oblivious, as they happily chatted next to her, and it wasn't until they were ready to leave that Liam even noticed his father was still outside.

Looking out, he frowned.

"He must be talking to my mom," he decided. "They've been fighting lately."

"What about?" Leah asked, unafraid of being too nosy.

"Dad wants me to stay here with him full-time," Liam explained, and his cheeks flushed a bit at that.

"Really?" Leah exclaimed. "That would be amazing, Li."

He nodded. "Yeah. But my mom obviously doesn't want me to, and she'd have to agree. So…" His voice trailed off, and they stepped outside.

Derek was angrily saying, "Listen. Think about someone other than yourself for one goddamned minute. I'll keep paying you child support, if that's what the issue is."

He glanced up, though, and saw them standing there, and he curtly dismissed her. "I've got to go. I'll talk to you later."

His face was flushed, too, and he tried to pretend as though nothing was wrong, but everyone knew otherwise.

They walked back toward the Black Dolphin together, but Derek's thoughts were a million miles away.

"Wanna get your board?" Leah asked Liam when they were on the property. He nodded.

"Yup." They each left to get their suits and boards.

Derek was standing still, staring into the gardens. Emmy stopped with him.

"You okay?" she asked gently. He shook his head as though he was shaking troublesome thoughts away.

"Yeah. Ex-wives suck."

"I've heard that," she agreed.

"What about your ex?" he asked. Emmy shrugged.

"We're friends. We actually get along better now than before." Derek all but glared at her and she laughed. "I know. We're an anomaly."

"He'd be better off here with me," Derek said, and his expression was mulish. Emmy thought about that.

"You're a great dad," she said. "But is his mom neglectful?"

Derek shook his head, no.

"Abusive?"

He shook his head no again. Emmy bit her lip.

"Well, the thing is, his school is there. Everything he knows. Unless you have a pretty amazing reason for wanting to uproot that, it might not be the best idea. I know you miss him when he's gone. But he needs consistency, too."

Derek scowled. "You sound like his mother."

Emmy flinched. "I don't mean to upset you. But having gone through a divorce…"

"Yeah, but you got to keep your kid," Derek answered. "You don't have to watch him growing up through Skype."

"He's here now," Emmy reminded him.

"I'm sorry, Emmy," he finally said. "I didn't mean to take it out on you. I know you're only trying to help."

She nodded, and he offered a small smile.

"Our kids are trying to become fish, I think." He

pointed toward the ocean, where the two of them were leaping in and out of the waves. Emmy grinned.

"Leah is already part fish," she acknowledged. "I've come to terms with it."

Derek stared at them for a bit longer. "I'm still thinking I might look into buying a house here on the island. I should have a more permanent residence in case...well, in case I do move forward with trying to sue for more custody."

Even though the loss of his monthly rent would be a financial hit for her, Emmy nodded. "Sure. I understand. Do whatever you need to do. In fact, I know the best Realtor on the island. Leah's best friend Skye...it's her father. You've probably seen Jason driving around—he's got big magnets on the side of his SUV with his face on them. I can text you his number."

"Thanks," Derek answered curtly. "It won't be anytime really soon. But I thought I should give you a ton of notice."

"I appreciate that," she replied honestly. "And I mean it, I just want what is best for you and Liam. You know, if he ever decides on his own to want to live with you, you won't have to sue for custody. Not at his age. The judge would take his wishes into consideration. Have you ever just asked him?"

Derek's gaze is frozen on the pair in the water. "Not yet. I don't want him to feel torn, like he has to choose."

"I totally understand that," Emmy answered. "I respect it."

"I was thinking, though..." He turned to her, and his eyes were lit up. "What if Leah mentioned it? Maybe she could just casually mention that it would be great if he moved here full-time. You know how much he likes her. Her opinion would carry a lot of weight."

Emmy narrowed her eyes. "So you basically want my daughter to do all of the heavy lifting for you?"

Derek sighed. "Well, if you put it that way, it sounds bad."

She couldn't help but chuckle.

"You know, you could always ask her first, if he has said anything to her. Maybe he has already? We're standing here speculating, but it's possible they've already talked about it," Emmy suggested. Derek's eyes widened.

"You know, that's true! Maybe they have. Would you want to ask her?"

Emmy rolled her eyes. "Man, you're not wanting to do any of the work, are you?"

He smiled, but then sighed again. "You're right. I need to do it myself, don't I?"

"It would be best," Emmy answered. "It's not hard. Just pull Leah aside and tell her what you told me. She's a mature kid, Derek. She'll understand the delicate nature of the conversation, and I'm sure she wouldn't share it with Liam. Not if you told her to keep it between the two of you."

"So you're suggesting that I keep secrets with your daughter?" Derek lifted an eyebrow.

Emmy rolled her eyes once again. "There are some things that are better off not getting shared," she replied. "I'm sure Liam would hate it if he knew you were asking about him to other people. So if you don't want to do the direct approach and go straight to him, Leah is probably your second best option."

He agreed. "Thanks, Emmy. I don't know why I didn't think of that before."

"Well, you probably aren't in the habit of propositioning teenage girls before," she joked, and they both laughed.

"No, not usually."

The moment seemed oddly intimate, Emmy decided as they stood together and watched their children laugh together out at sea. They were confiding important things, talking about their kids, offering advice. She was dangerously close to breaking her grandmother's number one rule: never make friends with the guests.

CHAPTER NINETEEN

August 25

The Haydens' house is opulent. A little over-the-top, but I wouldn't expect anything less. Jason Hayden is a Realtor, the best Realtor on the island, and he told me once... *Perception is everything.* He had to look successful in order to *be* successful.

As I stand at the front door, I wonder once again if I should even be here. Is it traitorous to Skye? But simply remembering her tortured face from the other day is enough to spur me on to ring the doorbell. Her parents should know how hard she's taking it, if they don't already.

Inside, I hear someone moving about, and within a few seconds, the door opens. Christy Hayden stands there, and when she sees me, her eyes get that alarmed look... like she is a deer and I am a car. But she quickly smiles,

and I know she's like everyone else. They just don't know
what to say.

"Emmy," she gushes as she grabs my elbow and hauls
me inside. "Come in. Oh, my gosh. You've been on my
mind so much. Come have some coffee."

She tugs me along until we get to their massive kitchen
and are surrounded by granite and luxury. After shoving
me into a chair, she turns around to grab coffee cups.

"Are you okay?" she asks when she returns to the table
with two steaming cups, setting one in front of me. "Cream
or sugar?"

"Both," I tell her, reaching for them. "And...as well as
can be expected. Thank you."

She nods and her hands flutter around her hair, as though
she doesn't know what to do with them.

"I'm so sorry, Emmy," she continues. "I should've come
to see you already."

"It's okay," I assure her. "I promise." She nods, uncon-
vinced, and I take a breath.

"Look, what I'm coming for today...it's not about me.
It's about Skye."

"Skye?" Christy is surprised by this. "Do you need her
for something? Anything you want her for, I know she'd
love to do it. She misses you."

"It's not that," I say. "It's... I'm worried about her. I saw
her a couple of days ago, and she told me she'd been struggling. I'm embarrassed to say that I haven't checked on her
like I should have."

Christy's brow wrinkles, then tightens.

"She's okay," she says slowly. "She's been sad, of course. But how could she not be?"

I glance over Christy's shoulder. In the hallway beyond, there are pictures of Skye and Leah together, happy, carefree.

"I don't know what to do for her," I confide. "I want her to come spend time with me, but at the same time, I don't want to cause her pain by being around Leah's things or pictures."

Christy fidgets. "I know," she finally agrees. "I don't know what the right answer is either. She was over at your house almost as much as she was home."

I look at the clock on the wall. It's 11:00 a.m.

"How about…can she come over tonight and spend the night? She and I can hang out, and I'll try to help her in any way that I can." I have suggested this before I thought the better of it. Being with Leah's best friend all night will hurt my heart, for sure.

"Of course," she agrees quickly. "I'm sure she'd love that."

We sit and chat for a little bit more, and as the minutes pass and I act as normally as anyone else would, Christy relaxes.

"How's Jason?" I ask as I sip the last of my coffee. Christy rolls her eyes.

"He's a man. Enough said."

She shrugs dramatically, and I have to laugh.

"Clothes on the floor next to the hamper, not *in* the hamper? Spills on the counter, not wiped up? The toilet seat always up?"

"Oh, yeah," she says, nodding. "And that's just the start."

We laugh like coconspirators, and for a minute, I feel normal. When I realize it, I'm startled, then feel guilty. I shouldn't get to laugh.

I sober myself up, and finish my coffee.

"We'll bring Skye over this afternoon," Christy tells me at the front door a little bit later. "Thank you so much for doing this."

"Thank *you*," I answer.

I head to my car, and as I open the door, something moves in the corner of my eye. I glance up at the house, and I see a curtain moving at a second-floor window. I pause, frozen. But I can't see anything there.

Was Skye home this entire time?

I'm cooking for the first time in weeks. Heretofore, I've been eating tuna straight out of the can, or a random Lean Cuisine meal. Tonight, I'm determined to have a girls' night with my daughter's best friend. Leah would want this.

So I make Skye's favorite. My famous lasagna, garlic bread, and I stock up on soda. The house smells like an Italian restaurant when the doorbell rings at 6:00 p.m.

I find Skye on the porch with her dad, and she looks sheepish when I ask why she rang the bell.

"I don't know," she answers, her cheeks flushing. "It felt weird to just come on in now that Leah's…"

Gone.

I shake my head. "Please don't change that," I urge. "You've been running in and out of here since you were five years old. I love it."

She grins and hefts her bag on her shoulder. Jason eyes me.

"You're sure you're up for this?" he asks, one eyebrow lifted. "You don't have to have her."

"It was my idea," I insist. "I miss my Skye."

She grins again, and for just a second, I see the sadness lift in her eyes.

"I'm making you lasagna," I add. She grins even bigger.

"My favorite," she sings.

"I know."

"I'm jealous," Jason announces, and I turn to him.

"You're welcome to stay, too." I invite him. But he's dressed in a tie, and he shakes his head regretfully.

"I've got an open house, but thank you anyway."

"I'll be home in the morning," Skye calls over her shoulder and she disappears into the house. I'm left with Jason alone, and without Skye's presence, I feel a little awkward, like he is examining me for cracks. I don't blame him, I guess. He is leaving his daughter with me overnight, after all.

"I'm fine," I assure him softly. "Truly. Skye is safe here."

He looks appalled. "Oh, I never doubted that. I was just concerned for you, Emmy. I can't imagine..."

No, he can't. No one can.

"Thank you," I say instead. "I can bring her home in the morning after breakfast, if that's okay?"

"I have to go out anyway. I can stop and get her around nine, if that works."

"Sure," I answer.

"Have a good night," he tells me, and walks away.

I turn, and stare at my home, willing myself to enter. There is a girl inside, alive and warm, who needs my help. I feel it in my bones, and I am not qualified to give it, but no one can understand like I can.

"Hey," I call to her. "How do you feel about ice cream for dessert? Triple Chocolate Threat?"

"Yessssss," she answers, and I think she's in Leah's room.

My heart pounds at that because what if she moves something?

I bound up the stairs, all three flights, and I'm out of breath at the top. The light from Leah's room slants across the floor, and I gulp as I cross the threshold.

Skye is sitting on Leah's bed, disturbing the way Leah left it. I want to protest, I want to say something, but I can't.

I have to help Skye. Not alienate her. I bite my tongue and perch carefully on the foot of the bed.

"I miss her," Skye says softly. She's not meeting my gaze, and her hands are gripping one of Leah's pillows.

"I know, babe," I answer. I reach over and grasp one of her hands. "Me, too."

"There are days when I can't believe she's gone," she continues. "I pick up my phone to text her, and then remember, and it's awful."

"I know. I do that, too."

"You do?" Her eyes are watery.

I nod. "Yeah."

"Are you…" Her voice trails off, and I nudge her.

"What is it?"

"Are you going to get a grave for her? It would be nice to have someplace to visit. To talk to her."

I think of the flowers on the beach.

"Did you leave flowers on the beach for her?" I ask. "Because you didn't have anywhere else to go?"

Skye nods. "Yeah."

A grave makes everything too real. And I don't want to do it. But maybe it's only fair.

"I'll think about it," I promise. "Soon."

I hold her hand and we sit in silence for a while.

"You've got to start taking care of yourself better," I tell her. "Your hand is bony."

She nods. "I haven't felt like eating."

"I know. Me either. But you know what? Leah would hate that. She wouldn't want you to be sad."

"Then she'd be crazy," Skye decides. I smile.

"She wouldn't argue with that."

She releases my hand, and grips the pillow in her lap, twisting the edge in her fingers nervously. She stares out the window toward the sea.

"I should've been with her," she says. "She wanted to come over that night and stay the night, to get ready for our first day of school. Dad said it was fine, but Mom said no. She said she wanted me to get plenty of sleep." There's resentment in her voice, and I can tell she's angry at her mother.

"Babe," I say. "That was reasonable. I would've done the same thing. Don't be mad at your mom."

"I can't help it," she whispers. "If only Leah had come over, she wouldn't have drowned."

For a scant minute, my unreasonable side is angry with Christy, too. But I tamp it down. That's crazy.

"It's not your mom's fault," I tell her, and myself, as well. "It just happened."

"But why do bad things happen to good people?" Skye asks me, her eyes wide. "It's not fair."

I reach over and hug her, stroking her hair. "It's not. I agree," I say.

Something scrapes my belly, and I look down.

The edge of something is poking out of the pillow sham.

Curious, I draw back to examine it.

It's a small stack of photos, stuffed inside the pillow covering.

"What the…" I pull them out.

Skye and I bend over them and my hands shake.

Blurred images are in the first one. A face, a long body, a man's shirt.

"Who is that?" Skye asks, alarmed.

"I don't know." I flip to the second picture.

A man's hand is twirling a piece of dark hair.

The third one. A man's hand is sitting on my daughter's leg, gripping her thigh.

My heart constricts.

The fourth one. My daughter's cheer uniform is in the corner, along with a pile of male clothing: slacks, a dress shirt, and a tie with shamrocks.

The pictures are black-and-white, artistic, and, very deliberately, they don't reveal the man's identity.

"What's going on?" Skye breathes, and I don't know.

I do know.

I hate it.

"Leah was involved with someone," I say shakily. "I just don't know who."

"But that's impossible," Skye says, and she sounds hurt. "She told me everything."

"She didn't tell you this," I answer unnecessarily.

"But why? Didn't she trust me?"

I look at her. "She wanted to hide this because it was wrong, and she knew it."

"Who is it?" Skye asks, scanning through the pictures again.

"I don't know. But I want to know."

"We have to talk to Liam. He might be able to help. Let's show him these and see what he says..."

Skye's voice trails off and she stares at me, and I think we both feel the same exact thing.

Something is so very, very wrong here. The knowledge of that threatens to swallow us both whole.

Liam was sleeping when we FaceTimed him.

I can tell because his clothes are rumpled and his hair is mussed. He's confused as his face comes into focus on the screen.

"Hey, Mrs. Fisher!" His gaze flits to Skye. "Skye."

He's curious.

"Liam, we're sorry to disturb you, but we are concerned about something, and are wondering if you can help."

"Sure," he says instantly. "Anything."

Skye holds up the pictures, and flips through them, one by one. Liam peers at his screen, his eyes widening, then narrowing.

"We found these in Leah's room. She was definitely involved with someone, just like you thought. But it looks like...well, it looks like an older man. We were wondering if you had any idea who it might be?"

Liam swallows hard. I see his Adam's apple bob up, then down.

"He looks older, for sure," Liam answers as he studies the dress shirt tossed on top of my daughter's cheer uniform. It's a plain white button-down, common to any man's wardrobe.

"Did she say anything to you?" I ask painfully. I want the answer, yet I don't want the answer.

"Not exactly," he replies and he sounds like he's in physical pain. "She said...a few things that made me worry."

"Like what, Liam?" Skye demands. "Please tell us. This is important."

"Why, though?" he asks, and his eyes are tortured. "She's gone now. It won't help anything."

"There are a number of reasons. First, I'd like to know about my daughter's last days. It seems there was a lot going on that I wasn't aware of. And second, it could've been criminal. This guy looks much older."

"Leah thought she was old enough to consent," Liam says reluctantly. "That's what she told me once."

God.

"But she was wrong," Liam quickly added. "I checked it myself. The age of consent in Florida is eighteen, but there is a Romeo and Juliet clause. A sixteen- or seventeen-year-old can consent to have sex, but only if their partner is no older than twenty-three."

"What makes you think he wasn't?" Skye asks, and her voice is amazingly steady. "What makes you think he was older?"

Liam is studying the photo in Skye's hand again.

"Well, first, there's those shoes," he points out. "They're dress shoes, and very polished. Unless a kid is going to prom, there's no way he's wearing those shoes."

I have to agree with that.

"And second, she told me once that she thought she had 'daddy issues,' because she was finding herself attracted to older guys. Much older."

My stomach clenches.

"When was this?" I ask, my lips tight.

"Just a few months ago."

Liam's shoulders are slumped, but Skye stares at him harshly.

"How do we know the man in the picture wasn't you? You had a thing for Leah. I know you did. I saw it."

Liam's face burns red, and he glares at Skye.

"It wasn't me. In fact, I'm afraid it might've been my father."

CHAPTER TWENTY

July 16

Derek sat in his living room.

He had taken Leah and Liam to youth group earlier, and a car pulled up to his bungalow. He heard kids laughing, and a male voice teasing them.

Intrigued, he went to the window and peered outside. The youth pastor was standing next to his car, laughing with the kids.

Something about the guy had always made him uncomfortable, although he couldn't put his finger on it. He stood too close, maybe? He laughed too much? He was too comfortable with teenagers. Maybe that was it. Although, then again, that was his job. He was supposed to make them feel comfortable.

The pastor, Hutch, leaned over and hugged Leah, and then slapped Liam on the back.

"Memorize your verses," he instructed them as he got back into his car. "See you next week."

They headed for the door and Derek rushed for his chair. He absolutely didn't want them to see him staring at them through the window.

"Leah's going to stay for a movie, is that all right?" Liam asked when he came in, forgoing a greeting.

"Of course," Derek agreed. "That's fine. Want me to make popcorn?"

"No," Liam answered, at the same time as Leah answered, "Please."

They looked at each other and laughed, and Derek stood up.

"No problem. I'll make some for the little lady, and I might even put M&M's in the bottom of the bowl."

She stared at him. "You're a genius, Mr. Collins."

He laughed. "Please call me Derek."

"Okay."

"Want to watch *The Blind Side* again?" Liam asked her. She lit up. "Yes."

Derek groaned jokingly. It was Leah's favorite movie and so he'd been forced to watch it over ten times since he moved into the bungalow the previous summer. They laughed, and went to find it, and curled up on the sofa. He watched them from the kitchen.

They sat a respectable distance apart, but they were so familiar with each other. They were like a couple already, and he found himself wondering if she really could be interested in his son? He didn't personally understand Liam's black clothes and his dabbling with eyeliner, but maybe Leah did. Maybe it was truly a generational thing.

He bustled about in the kitchen, making popcorn and, true to his word, dropping candy in the bottom of the bowls. He took them the snack, and when he did, Leah patted the couch next to her.

"Want to watch it, too?" she asked, glancing up at him when she took the bowl.

He shook his head. "Um, I'm pretty sure I could recite the words by heart nowadays."

She giggled, and he had to admit it to himself, she was stunning. Dark hair, those eyes. Legs that went all the way up. He checked himself. Lord, man. She was a teenager. But still. He wasn't blind, and if Liam had a brain in his head, he'd pursue Leah to the ends of the earth.

"Dad, you're in the way," Liam grumbled, and Derek moved. He went back to the kitchen, and then out to the patio. He found the hollow rock where he kept his smokes when Liam was here, and lit up a cigarette.

He didn't know why he didn't want anyone to know. He just felt gross about smoking. Everyone knew it caused cancer, and he was a bright guy. But he couldn't manage to shake the addiction, and that made him feel weak.

He didn't like things that made him weak.

Nonetheless, he puffed away into the night, the ocean a calming backdrop to his churning thoughts.

What should he do about Liam? Should he approach Leah about it? Should he sue his ex for full custody? Or maybe Emmy was right. He just didn't know, and he sure as hell wished there was a handbook for this kind of thing.

He was on his second smoke when the door slid open, and he threw his cigarette down in a hurry, stamping on it with his foot.

"Mr. Coll—er, Derek," Leah greeted him, stepping out into the night. "There's something wrong with the DVD player. Liam's trying to fix it, but I think he might need your help."

"Sure," he answered, and though he started to go inside, Leah leaned against the railing, staring out at the water.

"We should go night swimming," she mentioned, and Derek looked at her.

"That sounds dangerous."

She glanced at him, and laughed. "Maybe a little. But not tonight. There's barely a current. The moon is so big. Have you looked at it?"

He had to admit, he hadn't. He looked up now, though, and she was right. It was big and yellow, like something out of a movie.

"A perfect moon for a horror film," he agreed.

"Come on. Come out with us, Mr. C. My mom wouldn't be mad if you came with us."

He was already shaking his head. "I don't swim, Leah."

She cocked her head, not believing him. "You don't, or you can't? There's a big difference."

"I don't because I can't," he clarified, and she was taken aback.

"I didn't know there were really people who couldn't

swim," she said. "I could teach you, you know. It's not that smart to live on an island when you can't swim."

"That has been pointed out to me," he acknowledged. "By my ex-wife."

"Well, the offer is open," she told him. "Anytime. I helped teach a swim class last year at the YMCA."

"I'll think about it," he promised. She smiled.

"So, I guess that means not tonight?"

"Absolutely not."

He was pleasant, but firm. She smiled anyway.

"Okay." She started for the door, but he touched her arm.

"Hey, Leah… Has Liam ever mentioned wanting to live here permanently?"

Her head snapped back, and Derek took that to mean that he hadn't.

"Not really," she answered. "But we've never talked about it. Why? Is it a possibility?"

Derek shrugged. "I'm playing with the idea. But your mom thinks he needs the consistency of his life in New York."

"My mom never does things based on emotion," Leah agreed. "She's always based on logic. But I'd personally love it if he moved here." Derek studied her, and she eyed him curiously. "What?"

"Nothing," he answered. "I'm just curious about you and Liam."

He was direct and she flushed.

"What do you mean, me and Liam? We're friends. That's all."

"Does he know that?" Derek's question was blunt and Leah flushed again.

"I think so. He should."

Derek nodded. "Okay. I've overstepped, I'm sure. I'm not good with teenage girls. You're probably more sensitive than my teenage boy. I'm sorry."

"Don't apologize," she rushed to answer. "It's fine."

"I'd be forever grateful if you could listen to Liam about this subject," Derek continued. "I mean, if he said anything about maybe living here. I'm trying to decide if I should approach him or not. I don't want to put him in an awkward situation."

"You mean, kind of like this one?" Leah asked drily.

"Are you uncomfortable?" he asked quickly. "I didn't mean to do that."

"I was just kidding," she assured him. "I'm fine. And yeah, I can listen for you. I like to be a sounding board for him. He says he doesn't have many people to talk to."

Derek jolted at that, because he always thought he was someone Liam could talk to. Leah noticed, and cringed. "I'm sorry. I didn't mean it that way."

He smiled. "It's fine. I'm going to give you my cell number, so you can text me if he mentions it, okay?"

She nodded and pulled out her phone, and he put his number in.

She glanced at it when he handed it back. "DRC?" she asked, her eyebrow lifted.

"Yeah. I sorta feel like we're on a secret mission or something. I don't want him to see my name and start wondering."

"Ohhh, good thinking."

She slides her phone back in her pocket and opens the door. "Text me anytime," Derek tells her. "I appreciate your help."

"No problem."

Liam came looking for her at just that moment, and he looked quizzically at the two. "I fixed it," he announced, and the two of them went back into the living room, while Derek stayed outside to smoke just one more.

CHAPTER TWENTY-ONE

August 25

"**W**hy would you think it was your dad?" I manage to say around the pulse bounding in my neck.

Liam shudders.

"It's a feeling. I don't have proof. And I'd appreciate if you didn't tell anyone. Because I don't know. And my dad will hate me if I say anything."

"But you already have said something," Skye points out.

"Why do you feel this way?" I ask him. "Please. Specifics."

I'm only able to speak in one-word sentences now. Derek Collins is still down in my bungalow by the sea, and did he defile my baby?

"I don't have specifics," Liam says slowly. "It's just a feeling. My dad used to mess around with her all the time, about sports and stuff. It was flirty. She flirted back. It gave me a weird feeling. He watched her sometimes. I caught him. And...he has a shirt like that."

He points at the photo, and my heart lurches, but then I calm myself. "A lot of men have shirts like that," I answer. "It's a wardrobe staple."

Liam shrugs. "Like I said. It's just a feeling."

"Did you ask him about it?" I ask. "Confront him?"

Liam shakes his head. "No."

"Why not?" Skye demands. "We should know if there's something to this."

"Because—" and Liam lifts his gaze to meet hers "—I don't know if I want the answer. I could never forgive him if it's true."

"Thank you, Liam," I tell him.

He ends the call, but not before his tortured eyes sear into my soul.

Skye and I are left alone, staring at each other.

"I feel like I didn't know her at all now," Skye says and she chokes back a sob.

"Don't," I say. "This was a small chapter in Leah's life. You knew her far longer than this. You were so important to her, Skye. Maybe she didn't tell you because she didn't want you to feel conflicted, or to get into trouble."

"Maybe," she sniffs.

"She loved you like a sister," I assure her. I stand and pull her to her feet. "Let's go get something to eat. A full belly makes everything better."

That's a lie, but it convinces her to follow me to the kitchen.

I dish up plates and we eat on the veranda, watching the moon reflect off the surface of the water. The palm trees rustle in the breeze, and above us, I hear bugs chanting in the trees.

A light is on in bungalow three.

I can see it from here, and my blood is buzzing with the need to unravel all of this.

Is Derek involved?

The mere thought turns my stomach, and I have to be honest with myself. Is it only because I hate the thought of someone with my daughter, or did I, for just a moment, have an interest in Derek myself?

I'm appalled at my train of thought and try to change it, trying instead to chat with Skye about school.

She tells me about cheerleading, and having lunches without Leah, and how all of the teachers watch her for signs of depression, and I realize how much I've been neglecting her.

I engulf her in a bear hug.

"I'm sorry that I've been so distant," I tell her. "I've been struggling. But being here with you, it's helping me. I remember that life still goes on. You've got so much to live for, young lady."

"You only called us young ladies when we were in trouble," Skye remembers with a watery smile.

"Well, that wasn't very often," I point out. "You've always been good girls."

Except… Leah wasn't. Not at the end.

I can hardly fathom it.

Skye and I finish our dinner, then curl up in the living

room to watch a movie. It's a lighthearted chick flick, and Skye is asleep before the end, curled up on the end of the sofa. I cover her with a blanket and quietly make my way to the window.

A light is still on in bungalow three.

Without another thought, I head outside and down the path to the ocean. The light from the bungalow seems to burn brighter with every step I take, and before I know it, I am knocking on the door, three small raps in the night.

Derek opens it immediately, dressed in a pair of chambray shorts and a white button-down shirt. It's unbuttoned, as though he may have been getting ready for bed. It's also the same exact style of shirt that was in the photo.

"Emmy," he says in surprise, swinging his door open wide. "Come in."

I do, and the rooms are spotless, completely clean and neat, but for a small stack of folders next to the laptop on the table.

"To what do I owe this pleasure?" he asks, and he's automatically reaching for a bottle of wine. I start to stop him, but change my mind. I might need wine.

I take the glass of red, and he gestures for me to sit down. When I do, I suddenly find that I'm at a loss for words.

"I'm just restless," I manage to say, and I gulp at my wine. "I hope I'm not intruding."

"Of course you aren't," Derek says easily. He sits with his legs crossed at the ankles, studying me. I study him, too. Blatantly. He's tanned and slim. He looks outdoorsy, but he's not. I know that. Did he attract Leah? He's refined and polite, charming and upscale. Did that appeal to her? Did it remind her of Nate?

I feel sick, and leap to my feet, rushing to his back veranda. I throw open the French doors and let the breeze hit my face, and for a minute, I think I'm having a panic attack. My chest is heavy, I can't seem to breathe. Everything has a halo of light around it, fading in and out. I squeeze my eyes closed.

Derek is there next to me all of a sudden, and he's talking to me in smooth calming tones.

"You're okay. It's okay. Breathe. Take a breath, Emmy."

The fog eventually lifts a little, and I'm back in my body, and I can breathe again.

"You feeling better?" Derek asks me, and he's right next to me, his hand on my back.

I nod. "Yeah."

He doesn't ask me what triggered it. Instead, he just goes to get me a glass of water, brings it back and presses it into my hand.

I sip at it, reveling in the cool liquid as it slides down my throat. Focusing on that keeps me in the present.

"Better?" he asks, and his eyes are kind. I nod.

"Yeah. Thank you."

I walk back to the sofa and sit, my legs weak. I feel such conflicting emotions here. He's so kind, so how can he be the one?

He sits next to me and watches me curiously. "What's wrong, Emmy?"

"Am I that transparent?"

He nods. "A bit."

I sigh, because honestly, I don't know what to say. "I guess, I've just found out lately that Leah wasn't who I thought she was. At least, part of her wasn't. And it's killing me."

He's quiet now and studies me, his hand on his leg. "You found out she wasn't perfect?"

"The way you say it makes me sound bad."

"Not at all," he rushes to clarify. "It's just that Leah was a good kid. She had a good heart. Not a one of us is a completely open book for everyone to read, not even to those closest to us."

"Are you speaking from experience?" I can't help but ask.

He smiles ever so slightly. "Perhaps."

That could mean any number of things. His wife cheated on him, and I know it blindsided him. Or it could mean that he has secrets. How big are his secrets, though?

"Do you want to talk?" he asks politely, but I think he's also sincere. I do. But not about what he thinks.

"How well did you know Leah?" I ask him abruptly. No reason to pussyfoot around. His head snaps back.

"Um. A little. I joked around with her when she came to give me fresh towels. Stuff like that. You know I asked her about Liam sometimes."

"Did you like her?"

"Of course I did. I already said, she was a good kid. Emmy, where are you going with this?"

"Nowhere," I lie. "I just… I'm struggling. With trying to figure out who she really was."

That part is true.

"You know who she was," he tells me firmly. "She was your daughter. She loved to swim, she loved to smile. She was a gentle soul. She was a good friend to my son. You knew her, Emmy."

"I thought I did," I answer.

"You did," he replies firmly. "So she might've had a secret or two. What teenager doesn't?"

"Does Liam?"

Derek laughs. "Holy lord. I cringe to think of what that boy might be hiding from me. You do know he wore eyeliner until this summer."

I smile weakly. "It's very rock-and-roll."

"Maybe."

"I'm sorry," I tell him, and I mean it. "I didn't mean to barge in here and speak nonsense."

"You're not," he points out. "You make perfect sense. You're grieving. You have a right to question things. Just make sure to hold on to what really mattered...you loved her, and she loved you."

It sounds so simple when he puts it that way.

It almost makes me want to drop this whole quest for information, and to just let her memory rest...the way I always knew her. A bright, sweet, innocent girl. My girl.

But then, then...as I stand to leave, my eye catches on a piece of leather lying next to a lamp on an end table. A bracelet.

A woven bracelet, identical to the one that Skye wears.

It's Leah's.

I'm frozen, and Derek follows my gaze.

"I found that on the beach," he rushes to tell me. "I

wasn't sure whether to give it to you or not. I didn't know if it would upset you."

I turn to him. "But how did you know it was hers?"

He pauses at that, and am I imagining the hesitancy?

"I saw her wearing it a few times," he answers slowly. "I have a good memory."

"Okay."

But I'm not sure that it is.

I pick it up and run my fingers over it. "It doesn't look like it's been washed up on the beach," I point out.

"I don't know that it was," he replies. "Maybe it came off in the sand. I have no idea. I saw it, and picked it up. I knew you'd want it. I just didn't know when to give it to you."

But something about his face, the startled expression, bugs me long after I go home and drop into bed. I lie in bed for hours thinking about it, staring at the bracelet on my nightstand.

Was that guilt in his eyes?

How did he really come by the bracelet?

Something deep in my gut whispers that he's lying.

CHAPTER TWENTY-TWO

July 18

Leah's eyes flashed open at the sound of the phone vibration. She looked at the clock. It was 2:00 a.m. Sitting up, she picked up the phone.

Come see me.

I want to. But I don't think I can. My mom will hear.

Three bubbles.

Then be quiet. ;)

Her pulse raced while she thought about it. It would be risking a lot. If her mom caught her sneaking down the stairs, she would be sunk. Her mom trusted her now. She couldn't ruin that.

Don't you want to see me?

Her heart twinged. Of course she did.

I'll try, she texted back.

She crept to the door and quietly opened it, listening.

There was no noise but for Bo rumbling to his feet to follow her. She held a finger to her lips.

"No. Shhh. Stay."

He lay down with a groan.

"Shhh," she told him again. He cocked his head.

She tiptoed down the stairs, careful not to make a sound. At the bottom step, she straddled it because the middle would creak.

She was home free.

She slipped out the back door without a second glance and hopped on her bicycle. It only took her ten minutes to ride to the Habitat site. He was waiting for her there.

When he saw her, he grabbed her and kissed her long and hard, without even waiting for her to get off her bike. She slumped into him, his excitement igniting her.

"What's this all about?" she asked him breathlessly when he finally pulled away. His cheeks were pink, his eyes bright.

"I've been wanting you all day," he admitted. "You're all I can think about."

She almost purred at that. It was such an amazing feeling, almost overwhelming.

"I have something I want to try," he told her. "Can you keep an open mind?"

She nodded, hesitant.

He smiled.

"I have to confess something. Over the years, I've kind of gotten a penchant for rough things. Do you know what I'm saying?"

She stared at him.

He continued, "Rough sex, Leah. I know. Don't look at me like that." She was gaping at him in shock. "You don't know what it was like—to be married for so long, and she was never interested, and so I would watch stuff online, and that was all rough stuff. It made me want rough stuff myself."

"But...I'm a virgin," she managed to say, and her hopes of a beautiful first time were fading fast.

"I know," he rushed to say. "That's why I want your first time to be sweet and slow...special. We don't have to actually have sex yet to do fun things, Leah."

He said this matter-of-factly, as though he was the teacher, and she was the student. And in a way, that's what it was. She nodded slowly.

"Okay."

He raised an eyebrow. "Yeah?"

"Yeah. Sure. You won't...you won't hurt me, right?"

He was quick to reassure her, and she believed him. He would never hurt her. He was falling in love with her.

"You're falling in love with me?" The words were foreign on her tongue. No boy, or man, had ever said them to her. Not in this way.

"Yeah," he said, as though he were sharing a secret. "I am. You're precious to me, Leah."

She swallowed back her exhilaration and her joy. "I want to make you happy," she announced. "We can do whatever you want."

He smiled, because it was just what he wanted to hear.

"Okay. I brought these ties. I'm going to tie your hands and your feet, don't worry, it won't hurt, and then I'm going to use my mouth. On you. You'll like it."

Her eyes were wide, and she nodded mutely. She was nervous. What if she smelled down there?

He smiled and knelt down to tie her ankles. "Your knees will grow weak," he said. "But I want you to keep standing. That's your challenge, okay?"

She nodded again.

"If you ever want me to stop, don't say 'no.' Say…'coconut.'"

"Why coconut?" she giggled.

"That way I'll know you're serious."

"Okay."

He knelt down, and sure enough, within a minute, Leah's knees were weak enough to collapse. She had the first orgasm of her life, and she never uttered the word *coconut*.

Hello, she typed into her blog a few hours later. It's late, but I can't sleep. Maybe someone is up out there, too?

I met Ry tonight. He…um…we had oral for the first time. I mean, he performed it on me, and I'd never had that happen before. I was self-conscious, but it was amazing. I had an orgasm, and he knew exactly what to do.

When he was done, he kissed me on the mouth.

I could taste myself and he loved that. He got very, very excited. So excited that he almost got carried away and wanted to have sex right there at the construction site. I said no, though, and he agreed. My first time is not going to be on dirt and rocks.

He told me tonight that he's falling for me.

I can't believe it. I don't know what he sees in me, but I love it.

I don't want to lose him. I don't want to lose this.

I do feel guilty, though. We have to lie to everyone, and I'm a really terrible liar.

Her cursor blinked, and she decided that was good. She tagged it *fellatio, older man, forbidden, younger woman*.

When she went to bed, she splayed her hand on her belly, where the vibrations of her orgasm still lingered. Was it supposed to be that strong, that powerful? Should she still be feeling the ripple effects of it even now?

Lord, if so, how was she going to stop doing stuff like this? How did people ever manage to come out of their bedrooms?

CHAPTER TWENTY-THREE

August 29

Emmy is out in the garden when Derek stops by, looking windblown and healthy.

"Hey," she greets him. She can't quite look him in the eye, because she still isn't sure about him. Of course, to be fair, she isn't sure about anyone anymore.

"Are you going to the Fall Festival?" he asks her. He is tanned; island life suits him, she decides. "Why do you guys have a Fall Festival in August anyway?"

She grins. "We like to give the summer tourists the chance to attend before they all go back home. And no. I think I'll just stay around here." She cuts the dead head of a flower off, and lets it drop onto the ground. With her foot, she pushes it into the cuttings pile. She doesn't add her silent thought—that she doesn't have much to be thankful for.

"Come with me. I don't want to go alone. You'd be doing me a favor. Everyone always tries to match-make me. If I go with you, maybe they'll leave me alone for a while."

"So you're using me, then?" She arches an eyebrow and he laughs.

"If you want to look at it like that. I personally see it as a mutually beneficial situation."

"How so?"

"Well, you need to get out of the house and eat something, and I need to be saved from the female piranhas of this town."

She considers that. "I wonder if Mrs. Atchison has her booth with her fried stuffing this year?"

"Doesn't she always?" Derek cocks his head, waiting.

"Okay, fine," Emmy answers, pulling off her gardening gloves. "Because I can't resist that." Secretly, she figures she can use this time to observe Derek some more in a candid setting.

He laughs, completely unaware.

"Let me get my shoes."

She runs into the house and shoves her feet into her worn Sperrys. She flinches when she sees Leah's worn-out black Converses inside the door. Unlike her new white ones, Leah wore these hundreds of times, and so for that reason, Emmy hasn't been able to throw them out yet.

She closes her heart on that for the day, and goes back out to meet Derek. He's waiting patiently by the front gate.

He holds out his arm, and she hesitates for a scant second to take it. Did her daughter touch that arm?

She exhales and links her arm with his. They stroll into town, and the breeze is actually nice. It isn't too hot, which is a rarity on the island. Fall decor lines the streets, bales of hay, scarecrows, sunflowers, and mums, wreaths on the quaint streetlamps. Normally, she loves this festival.

Normally, she's here with Leah.

She ignores the pain in her heart, focusing instead on the smells of food.

Turkey legs, fried stuffing, pies, candied nuts. There are booths for practically everything, as well as booths with games.

"What do you want first?" Derek asks her. She doesn't hesitate.

"Fried stuffing."

He laughs and says, "Okay. I'll go get in that line. Will you get in the hot cider line?"

"Now you're speaking my language," Emmy tells him. They split and head in different directions. Emmy gets in the cider line, which is actually wasil. Apple cider, brewed with orange juice, cinnamon sticks, and cloves. It is practically the nectar of the gods.

She can't help but notice Hutch in a few spots ahead of her in the line. He's chatting with an elderly woman, Mrs. Fitzgerald…a nosy old woman whom Emmy actually detests. The old bat is always stirring up trouble, but Hutch doesn't seem to mind. She pats his shoulder, and glows while she is talking. He does seem to bring out the best in people. He gets his wasil, and leaves without noticing Emmy, which is fine by her. She isn't really here to socialize.

Within a few minutes, it's her turn, and she waits while they serve up two steaming cups for her. As she's paying, Mrs. Fitzgerald sees her, and Emmy flinches internally.

"Mrs. Fisher!" the old lady sings, pushing to get to her. People move out of the way, probably thankful that her sights aren't set on them. "You're looking so skinny. It's a good thing you're here. We'll fatten you up!" She pats Emmy's shoulder and peers into her face. "It was a terrible thing that happened to your girl. We're all sorry for it."

Everyone around murmurs or looks away. No one likes this situation, and most don't know how to act in it.

"I know there was some talk about Leah there in the end, but I for one didn't believe a word of it," Mrs. Fitzgerald announces. "Apples don't fall far from the tree, and while I did personally know your mother, and I know she was, well...unique, I also know that Leah took after you. I don't believe a word that they're saying, and trust me, Pastor Hutchins doesn't either."

Emmy is confused, and her face must reflect that. She takes the change that the cashier offers her, and she stares at the old woman's wrinkled face.

"I'm afraid I don't know what you're referring to," she admits, and she hates that she's taking the bait, but God, she has to, doesn't she?

"Well, the rumors, sweetie," the old woman said. "You know."

"I don't know," Emmy answers politely.

Mrs. Fitzgerald has the grace to be uncomfortable.

"Well, I don't want to speak ill of your girl, especially since I don't believe a word of that gossip anyway."

"You're speaking of it right now," Emmy points out. "Can you just finish?"

Mrs. Fitzgerald flushes and leans toward her, her old chin wobbling. "The talk, dear. The talk about how Leah was becoming a home wrecker, she was flirting with every married man in her vicinity. The pastor was counseling her in the end. At least, that's what my Amber said."

Oh, yes. Emmy forgot. The horrid old lady is Amber's grandmother. The apple truly doesn't fall too far from the tree. She fights to keep the bitterness and shock off her face.

"My daughter was most certainly not a home wrecker, Mrs. Fitzgerald," she says politely. "Anyone who says otherwise is simply wrong, and hateful."

The old woman takes a step back, patting her hair. "Well, that's exactly what I said," she answers. "I truly thought so, too."

"You shouldn't spread these lies," Emmy continues.

Mrs. Fitzgerald stares at her, her faded eyes a bit hardened.

"I'm not the one spreading them," she says with an air of importance. "I'm the one ignoring them. I simply wanted you to know that we all don't think badly of your daughter."

"You're the first I've heard speak of it at all," Emmy points out.

The old lady shakes her head. "I'm the first who has *said* anything to you, dear. Trust me, people are talking."

Emmy is stunned, and she looks across the street at

Hutch. He is standing in a circle of teenagers from his youth group, laughing and talking. Mrs. Fitzgerald follows her gaze.

"Truly, though, she couldn't have handpicked a better person to counsel her," the old lady says. "After his nasty divorce, the pastor is well versed in helping home wreckers."

"My daughter was not a home wrecker," Emmy practically spits out, but at the same time, she can't help adding, "and Hutch is divorced?"

That doesn't fit with her wholesome image of him. For some reason, she assumed he graduated from seminary a little later in life than most people, and moved straight to Key West. She never pondered what his prior life had been like.

"Oh, yes," Mrs. Fitzgerald rushes on to say, pleased she could spread even more gossip. "Apparently it was quite the scandal back in Chicago, where he used to live. His wife ran off with a friend of his, and she broke up his friend's marriage, to boot. A true home wrecker, if I ever heard of one."

Emmy can swear that the old woman is getting pleasure from this.

"That's terrible," she says quietly, and excusing herself, she takes the cider and weaves among the crowd to find Derek. As she does, she catches Hutch's attention and he waves to her from across the street.

She doesn't want to doubt her daughter, but she knows she is going to have to talk to the pastor. She doesn't know if he'll be able to tell her anything, what with confidentiality and all, but maybe he can.

She knows in her heart that her daughter would never be a home wrecker, but she can't help but imagine that everyone is watching her, already having condemned Leah in their own minds. Her daughter was only fifteen years old, for God's sake. There's no way she was such a monster. Emmy would've known.

But you didn't know her as well as you thought, her mind whispers to her, like a devil in the shadows. *Maybe you didn't know her at all.*

Was Liam right when he thought that Leah had been flirting with Derek? Maybe Derek had been upstanding and had rebuffed her, and then wanted to spare Emmy the humiliation of knowing about it. Had her own mother's genes passed down to her daughter? Could that even happen?

She is consumed with her thoughts for the rest of the festival, and Derek pretends not to notice. She watches him as he interacts with the townspeople, easily and politely. He is a perfect gentleman, and it's honestly hard to think of him as anything other than that.

As they walk back toward home an hour or so later, Derek catches her staring at him.

"What are you thinking?" he asks curiously. "You've been staring at me all morning."

She flushes. "I'm sorry. I didn't mean to."

"You didn't answer my question, though," he points out. "What are you thinking?"

She's hesitant, but she'll never get any answers if she

doesn't ask. "You know the other day, when I asked how well you knew Leah…" Her voice trails off. He nods, uncomfortable.

"Yeah."

"I need to ask…and you can tell me. Was Leah ever inappropriate with you?" The words hurt her throat and she can't believe she is even saying them. He stares at her.

"What do you mean, inappropriate?" he asks slowly.

"I mean, did she ever come on to you," she clarifies, and she is the uncomfortable one now. "Or flirt with you."

He's silent. "I think perhaps all girls her age flirt without meaning to," he finally answers. "I don't think she meant anything by it."

A weight slams into her, hard and fast. "So she did flirt?" *God oh God oh God.*

"Maybe a little. But she was just being friendly. And I don't mean to sound conceited, but a few of the girls in youth group have harmless crushes on me. Where is this coming from, Em?"

She stares ahead, at the horizon, anywhere but at Derek. "Mrs. Fitzgerald. She said that the whole island is talking about Leah. That she was a home wrecker or something."

Derek bursts out laughing. "A home wrecker? Leah? That's ridiculous. Look at the source, Emmy. That old woman is terrible. If there are rumors, you can rest assured that *she* started them herself."

"Maybe." And when Derek says it, it does sound preposterous. She allows herself to relax, just a bit. She feels ashamed that she let nasty words make her doubt her own daughter.

Her daughter was only fifteen, for God's sake.

She wouldn't have even known what the word *home wrecker* meant. She had probably been misunderstood by someone. Perhaps, like Derek said, she inadvertently flirted with someone, and the old woman witnessed it.

That's that.

She is stupid to have worried about that even for a second.

She thinks about her daughter's blog and flinches again. Something was going on with Leah, but Emmy would bet her last dollar that Leah didn't instigate it.

Someone took advantage of her.

The question is…who?

CHAPTER TWENTY-FOUR

July 27

"**H**ey, girl!" Skye hollered and waved as she walked up the stairs to the Black Dolphin. Her father waved and rolled his window halfway down.

"See you there, girls!" he called and drove off, his face plastered on the side of his SUV. Leah smiled. Skye hated driving in that thing.

"You ready?" Leah asked. Skye rolled her eyes.

"Have been for a week."

"Why is your dad gonna see us there?"

Skye rolled her eyes again. "Because Hutch asked him to be a chaperone. Apparently, he was low on adults." She glanced at Leah. "But don't worry. We'll stay far away from him, and his supervision."

Leah laughed and opened the door.

A week prior, Hutch had announced at youth group that he would be hosting a lock-in tonight from 8:00 p.m. until 8:00 a.m. the next morning. It was being held at the school, so they'd even be able to swim. Everyone they knew was going, and it was going to be amazingly fun.

"Your mom isn't going?" Skye glanced at her friend.

Leah shook her head. "I think Hutch asked her, but we've got a full house tonight, so she couldn't get away."

Which was for the best. They didn't need two of their parents there.

"What are you wearing?" Skye asked as they walked through the lobby.

Leah glanced down at her shorts and T-shirt.

"You are not," her best friend told her. "You're going to wear something cuter."

"Why?" Leah shrugged. "There's no one there I want to impress."

Skye humphed and tilted her nose. "I beg to differ. Evan Wallace is coming," she announced, and they both knew he was the most beautiful guy in their class.

"He doesn't even come to youth group," Leah answered, confused.

"Nope. But he's friends with Jase Cooper, and Jase is coming."

"Ohhh. Well, cool. I like Jase."

"And I like Evan." Skye waggled her eyebrows. "So we're all set."

"I didn't mean I like Jase like that," Leah groaned, and Skye laughed.

"Well, we'll see how you feel about that by morning."

They jogged up the stairs to Leah's room, where she finished stuffing things in her bag and rolling up a sleeping bag.

Through the window, they saw Liam walking by the water. He looked lonely, and Leah cringed.

"We should ask him," she told Skye. Skye hesitated.

"But if we do, all he's gonna want to do is hang out with you," she mentioned, and for the first time, Leah saw a bit of jealousy in her friend. She rushed to reassure her.

"Nah. It'll give him a chance to hang out with some of the island boys," she argued. "Then he'll have other friends besides me."

"That's true," Skye decided. She opened Leah's window and hollered down at the top of her lungs. "Hey, Liam! Come up!" She waved her arms, and Liam stopped in his tracks, his face tilted up. "Come up here!"

Liam nodded and disappeared around the corner. Within a few minutes, they heard his steps on the staircase.

He emerged into Leah's room, and seemed a little uncomfortable.

"What's up?" he greeted them, and stood awkwardly by the door. His black T-shirt and jeans seemed out of place in the sea of turquoise walls.

"Wanna go to our church lock-in tonight?" Leah asked him as she yanked a brush through her hair and pulled her hair into a ponytail. "It's gonna be fun."

"Okay," Liam agreed immediately. "I've never been to one."

"Oh, you'll like it," Skye told him. "We'll have the run

of the school. We can swim, pig out, you know. Good stuff."

"Okay." Liam shrugged. "What time?"

"Eight."

He pulled out his phone and sent a text to his dad. "What do I need to bring?"

"Have you never been to a lock-in?" Leah was incredulous. Liam rolled his eyes.

"Um, no."

"Well, just bring clothes and a sleeping bag, although you probably won't get much sleep."

Liam nodded and ducked back out to go pack. When he was gone, Skye turned to Leah.

"God, he's hot."

Leah stared at her. "You really think so?"

Skye nodded. "Oh, yeah. So sultry, like you're staring at him across a smoky bar."

"You've got a big imagination," Leah pointed out.

"Are you sure you've never been into him?" Skye asked hesitantly. "I don't want to step on your toes or anything."

Leah burst out laughing. "Um, no. You have my full permission."

Skye was satisfied with that, and pulled out one of Leah's shirts from the closet. "Can I borrow this? It makes my boobs look great."

"Sure." Leah sprayed her ponytail, and then glanced out the window. "Here he comes. That was fast."

When he emerged back into the room, he had his bag and was wearing a wrinkled scowl.

"What?" Leah asked immediately.

"My dad is gonna give us a ride. I don't think he believes me that I'm going to a church. Like I'm gonna burst into flames when I walk through the goddamned door or something."

The girls laughed, and Leah shrugged. "It's fine. We're not doing anything wrong. He can take us."

"Good, because he's getting the car and he'll be out front in a minute." Liam looked miserable, but the girls weren't bothered. They hefted their bags onto their shoulders.

Derek pulled up right after they walked onto the porch. He took their bags and opened the girls' doors like a gentleman. Liam scowled again, but his father ignored it.

When they were all in the car, Derek turned around.

"So, to the church?"

"No, to the school," Leah corrected him. He nodded, and within a few minutes, he was dropping them off.

"Hey," he told them suddenly as they climbed out. "I'll bring some pizzas later. Teenagers can't eat too much pizza, right?"

"You don't have to, Dad," Liam told him. "I'm sure there will be enough."

But Leah could tell that Derek perhaps wanted to check on them, so she nodded. "That would be great, Mr. Collins. Thank you."

"Why do you encourage him?" Liam growled to her as they went inside. She just shook her head.

"When will you learn, Li? Just go along with him sometimes. It will make your life easier. And bringing a pizza there isn't going to hurt anything. He'll be in and out, I'm sure."

They went inside, and immediately they were sur-rounded by laughter and chattering. Hutch waved at them from across the hall, and music was blaring. It was a party, and there was a ton of food and dumb games, and for the next couple of hours, they had a great time.

It wasn't until after an intense game of dodgeball that Skye noticed Leah wasn't around.

"Hey, where's Leah?" she asked Liam, wiping sweat out of her eyes.

He looked around. "I don't know. Maybe the bath-room?"

She shrugged, and then narrowed her eyes. She had Liam all to herself for a minute. She knew exactly what to do. She turned on her charm.

"I can't stay in here long," Leah told Ry, listening ner-vously. They were in an empty classroom, next to the door. "Skye will come looking for me."

"This won't take long," he answered, and he pulled her to him, inhaling her neck, and then following his nose with this lips. "You smell so good."

She melted then, into his arms, his compliments turn-ing her knees to jelly. He held her up, tightening his grasp.

"I've been thinking," he said softly, his hands running up and down her back, gripping her hips. "There's some-thing I want to do."

Butterflies took off in Leah's stomach and she stared up at him.

"What is it?" She was almost nervous, and also excited.

He smiled. "My feelings for you almost scare me,

Leah. They're so powerful. So real. I don't know when it happened…when I allowed myself to feel this way about you. But now that I have…I've opened the floodgates."

Leah waited, curious as to where he was going with this. She also listened for noises in the hallway. The last thing they needed was for someone to find them.

"I want you to come away with me," he told her. "Just you and me."

She startled, frozen. "Now?" she finally managed to say.

He paused. "I haven't worked out the details yet. Maybe later. Maybe sooner. Just promise me you'll think about it. All that really matters is how we feel about each other. We can work everything else out."

He was intense, and his eyes glistened in the darkened room. Leah actually felt a little uneasy, as though he wasn't really thinking rationally. It wasn't very possible. It was illegal, for one thing. And it was so soon, for another. They'd just started this relationship.

But he was waiting on her, and she didn't want to disappoint him. She could deal with the practicalities of everything a different day.

"Okay," she agreed. "I'll think about it."

He hugged her so tightly that she almost couldn't breathe. He smiled when he noticed.

"Do you like that, little Kitten?" he whispered, and he slid his hand up to her neck. He squeezed there, his fingers on each side, cutting into her soft flesh ever so slightly.

She was uncomfortable with that, and she moved away, trying not to make a big deal of it.

He pretended not to notice.

His shirt had somehow come untucked, and he fixed it, his hand sliding down the front of his pants. "You should go on out first," he suggested. "I'll follow in a minute."

"Okay." She started to obey, but he stopped her at the door.

"Behave yourself with Liam," Ry said, and she started to roll her eyes, but then realized he was serious. He was jealous.

She sighed, then turned and left.

CHAPTER TWENTY-FIVE

August 30

I didn't like his hand around my throat. It was suffocating, and just a little nerve-racking, to know that if he tightened his grip even a little, I wouldn't be able to breathe. More than that, though, it was the look in his eyes that I really didn't like. It felt like he was getting off on it. Like he enjoyed the thought of hurting me. Or maybe just being rough with me. I don't actually know. But this isn't the Ry that I have fallen for. When he got that look in his eye, he felt like someone else entirely.

I read my daughter's words, and I think back to the church lock-in. I hadn't gone, and it kills me to know that he was there, and if only I had been there, too, maybe I would've noticed something happening.

If only.

I find myself saying those words so often. Too often.

My phone rings, and it's startling. It's too early in the morning for anyone to be calling. I plunge my hand into my robe pocket and pull it out.

It's my ex-husband.

"I'm going to kill the son of a bitch," he growls.

I grimace. "You've been reading her blog?" I guess. I'd texted it to him last night, the website. "You said you had no interest."

"I changed my mind," he says bluntly. "I'm booking a flight. We're going to find the guy and put him in jail."

"I'm not sure we can," I point out. "No one ever saw him with her."

"Someone had to have," he argues. "Skye. Or Liam. Someone."

I shake my head. "They say they didn't. I believe them."

"Someone has to know something," he insists. "I'm booking a flight."

He hangs up abruptly, and I sigh as I pad down to the kitchen and start some coffee. As it brews, I watch the sun coming up over the water, an array of oranges and reds and golds exploding on the surface.

When the coffee maker beeps, I pour a cup and sit on the veranda in my rocking chair. I haven't been out here much since…*it* happened.

The sea breeze is chilly this morning, blowing my hair away from my face. I rest my feet on the porch, feeling the wood against my skin. The water laps at the sand on the shore, dragging with it ragged shells, dead jellyfish, and seaweed.

Bo romps out at the edge, and for a minute, I'm resentful of him. He never has gone in the water. If he'd been less of a chicken that night... I shake the thoughts away. I can't keep doing this.

"Bo," I call quietly. He's getting too close to Derek's bungalow, and at any given moment, he'll probably start barking. He digs in the sand, oblivious to me, and I call again, a little more firmly this time.

The big dog purposely ignores me, and continues to dig, furiously now, the sand throwing behind him like a storm.

"Goddamn it," I grumble, setting my coffee down. I stomp down the porch. The last thing I need is for the dog to wake up my last remaining guest. The sand is still cool beneath my feet and I sink into it as I stalk toward the dog. He glances up, sees me coming, and continues with his digging, unbothered. His hackles are standing up, the way dogs do when they feel threatened.

Curious now, I quicken my pace, and I kneel beside Bo just as he pulls up his prize.

It's a sweater...a cardigan. Dark green with pockets. It's dirty now, since it was covered by the tide, buried in sand. It looks as though it's been here awhile. I roll my eyes at the dog.

"Bo, you're crazy," I tell him. Things wash up here all the time. But he's still sniffing at it suspiciously, and his hackles are still up. "It's just a sweater."

But he growls at it.

I pat him, and it doesn't placate him. I examine the sweater again. Men don't usually wear cardigans in this day and age. I think the only one I've seen wearing one is Hutch, and he's a pastor, so he can get away with bad fashion choices. You never know, though. The tourists that come in and out have some pretty bad fashion decisions, too, sometimes.

I stand up, taking the sweater with me to throw in the garbage. As I lift it, though, something falls out of the pocket, fluttering to the ground at my feet.

Glancing at it, I freeze.

It's a photo, and it's grainy and dirty, but the image is clear.

It's my daughter, half-undressed in front of her window.

I pace in the main dining room, up one length and down the other. The dirty cardigan lies on the table. I eye it as I circle around it.

Whose is it?

Finally, I pick up my phone and call the police station, my heart pounding a mile a minute.

I get Detective Keaton. I'm surprised to be put right through to him, but then again, this is a small place and I doubt he has much to do. I stammer a little as I explain the situation to him, the blog, everything.

He knows who I am immediately, of course. He listens, and when he finally answers, he seems a little bit like he's humoring me.

"I understand your grief," he tells me. "My niece died a few years ago."

That's not the same, but I don't tell him.

"I'm not crazy with grief," I insist. "My daughter was involved with an older man. I have a sweater here that the guy must've been wearing, and he was spying on her. There's a picture in the pocket of her in her room—half-dressed!"

My voice fractures at this point, because the idea of someone lurking in the shadows watching her under my very nose is excruciating.

The detective sighs. "Okay. I'll stop by later today and take a look at it."

I can tell from his voice, though, that he's not taking me seriously.

I hang up the phone with more force than necessary.

"Bad morning?"

I look up to find Derek in the doorway, an empty mug dangling from his hand.

"I ran out of coffee," he tells me. "Can I borrow some of yours?"

"Of course," I answer. I try not to notice that his hair is bed rumpled, and his shirt is unbuttoned. I can easily see the thin dark trail of hair that runs downward from his lower belly into his pants. I swallow. There's something sexy about that, and I shouldn't be thinking that way. Not now.

He smiles. "Thanks."

He crosses the room and pours himself a cup. He sits at the table, inviting himself, and stares curiously at the tattered sweater.

"New centerpiece?" he asks, one dark eyebrow lifted.

I shake my head. "No. Bo found it on the beach." Unfortunately, the photo is lying there, too, and Derek zeroes in on it.

"Is that…" His voice trails off and he peers at the photo. "Oh, my God. Who took that?"

He seems very sincere and very confused as he stares at me.

"That's a very good question," I finally answer. "It appears that someone was spying on Leah."

"It couldn't have been Liam," Derek answers quickly. "He's been up north, and he'd never wear…that."

"Liam never crossed my mind," I assure him. "It has to be someone older. I don't think many younger men wear cardigans."

"Actually, I have one," he replies. "It was a Christmas gift a few years ago from my ex. I should've burned it, now that I think about it."

"It's never too late," I tell him. He nods.

"Yeah. Good bonfire material."

I try to picture him in a cardigan, and fail.

"What color is yours?" I ask.

He narrows his eyes. "Not green," he answers defensively.

Bo pads into the room, his toenails clicking on the wood floor, and he growls once again at the sweater.

"He has something against it," I tell Derek unnecessarily.

"I see that," he answers. "Maybe he knows who wore it."

His words click into place like puzzle pieces and I'm stunned that that didn't occur to me.

"Oh," I say limply.

"Dogs are also very good judges of character," Derek tells me as he scratches behind Bo's massive ears. I think he might be making the point that Bo approves of him, so therefore he's a good guy. He's good-looking and charming, I'll concede to that.

"You should probably call the police," he mentions. "They probably won't do much since Leah's…gone. But they should at least know about it."

"You don't think they'll do anything?"

He shakes his head slowly. "I haven't lived here my whole life like you have, but I've been here long enough to know that islanders stick together. Leah is gone, and that guy is still here. They probably won't want to stir up trouble."

It's sad because I know Derek's right.

I nod. "Yeah."

"But you never know. You should call," he adds.

"I already did," I tell him. "They'll be over sometime today. I doubt they're in a hurry."

He sips his coffee. "I should go," he says quietly, and I find, deep down, that I really don't want him to.

It's startling, and I try to shove that emotion away. I don't want to feel it.

But his eyes are soulful and deep, and they seem to look right into my heart.

"I make you uncomfortable, don't I?" he asks bluntly.

I answer honestly by nodding.

"Why?"

He examines me, his eyes thorough.

"I don't know."

He lifts an eyebrow.

"It's nothing bad," I assure him. "I just… You just… You stir up… I don't know."

I'm at a loss for words and he laughs; his teeth are white and they flash in the sunlight.

"Okay. As long as it's nothing bad."

But I can see on his face that he already knew that. His grin tells me so. I grimace. I don't have time for this. I don't deserve to be able to do this while Leah can't.

"I've gotta get to work," he tells me. "I have a conference call in half an hour. If you need anything today, or if you want me to come back when the police arrive, just text me."

"Thank you," I tell him and I'm sincere. He smiles again, and he's gone. Out the back veranda and down the trail to his bungalow. I watch him go, his broad shoulders swaying in the morning light.

He pauses at his door and looks back.

His eyes meet mine.

It's hard to see from this distance, but there seems to be a million things in his eyes…sympathy, gentleness, hope… and something else. Something I can't put my finger on. I can see the sparkle in them from here, the way the sun hits them just so. My heart skips a beat and the corner of his mouth tilts upward, ever so slightly, like he *knows*.

That's when I know.

I've got to guard my heart around him.

My heart is not whole anymore, and it's not in good enough condition to give to anyone.

With a sigh, I take another drink of coffee and wait for the detective.

CHAPTER TWENTY-SIX

July 26

"I don't like any boys here," Leah told her father, holding her phone between her chin and her ear. She poked through her closet as she talked, picking out clothes to wear the next day.

"None of them?" Her father was doubtful. She laughed.

"None of them. They're all dumb." She pulled out a red shirt and white shorts. "And not cute. At all."

"Not even Liam?" her father asked.

Leah paused. "Liam is cute, but I don't like him in that way."

"Huh. Okay," her father relented, and changed the subject. He talked about his job, and the heat in Phoenix, and the next time Leah would come visit.

"You can come for Christmas," he told her. "I ordered new bedding for your room. It's teal, your favorite color."

"You didn't have to do that, Dad," she answered. "But thank you."

"How's Bo?" he asked, and it sounded like he was chewing on something. Leah cringed. For some reason, chewing noises grated on her nerves.

"He's good." She eyed him, where he was sprawled next to her bed. He opened one eye to look at her, but didn't even lift his head. "He's a little spoiled."

"I figured. Your mom still mad at me about it?"

"You know she is," Leah answered, grinning.

"Okay, kiddo. I have to go. Think about Christmas and lemme know."

"Love you, Dad," she said before she hung up.

When she put the phone down, she saw three text messages, all from Liam.

Hey. Wanna hang out?

Leah!

Are you ignoring me?

She rolled her eyes and picked her phone back up.

No. I was on the phone with my dad. Come on over.

He was knocking on her door a few minutes later. She motioned him in. She was sitting in a circle of photographs, all prints that she had taken and developed herself.

Liam sat down beside her, cross-legged, and started picking them up and examining them, one by one.

"This one is good," he said, holding one up of Skye. It was a close-up of her face on a day at the beach. The wind was blowing her hair across her eyes and she looked into the distance.

"Yeah, I like that one. I'm gonna frame it and give it to her."

"Ohh, this one of me is rad," he said, picking it up. He was all in black and sitting on her porch steps, his legs sprawled out, his hair shaggy. It was a black-and-white print, stark contrasts. "I look bitchin'."

"Very rock-and-roll," she agreed, stacking the ones of Bo separately.

"Who's this?" Liam picked up another, a picture of Leah's black Converses next to a pair of gleaming male dress shoes. She was standing next to someone, but only showed their feet—a contrast of their size difference. His feet were large, hers weren't.

Leah almost flushed. "Just a guest. I liked his shoes."

"They're nice," Liam agreed, putting it back down. As he did, there was a faint buzzing. He looked up, but didn't see anything to make the noise. He looked around.

Nothing.

The noise stopped.

He continued sifting through pictures, but the buzzing happened again. Leah's phone, however, was in her lap.

"What's that noise?" he asked. It annoyed him that he couldn't find it. "Am I losing my mind?"

Leah looked up. "I guess so. I don't hear anything."

Liam scowled and stood up. "Can I use your bathroom? I had too much Red Bull this morning."

"You've gotta stop drinking so much of that stuff," she told him. "It's not meant to be drunk by the pack."

As soon as he was gone, Leah scrambled to the seat under her window. She lifted the board and pulled her secret phone out of the hollow space underneath.

There were several texts.

She sucked in a breath when she saw them.

I'm thinking about you.

I can't get you out of my head.

Do you want to see what you do to me, sweet girl?

Then there was a picture of his erect penis. Leah's cheeks flared as she examined it. It was fairly large, she imagined, as penises go. And very, very rigid.

She thought it was probably supposed to make her hot and bothered, but honestly, it didn't. It was exciting, that he'd send it to her, but just looking at it did nothing for her. Maybe that was why men were visual and women weren't so much.

"Your bathroom is a mess," Liam said, emerging. Leah shoved the secret phone into her pocket.

"I know," she answered. "I've got to clean it before my mom sees it. In fact, I'd better do it. Wanna give me an hour or so and then meet me at Nico's for lunch?"

"Sure." He stood up. "See you there."

He ducked out and she gathered up the photos. She took

the one of the shoes and put it in the pillowcase on her bed, along with a stack of other private ones. Lord, that was close. She didn't realize it was out in the open.

She stacked the others on her desk, and set to work on her bathroom. She took off her shirt so that she wouldn't splash bleach on it, and twenty minutes later, she was scrubbing out her tub in her sports bra, track shorts, and a pair of rubber gloves. The water was running by her ear, so she didn't hear the knock on the door.

She didn't hear it the second time either.

That's why, when she saw a flash of movement out of the corner of her eye, and then saw someone standing in the bathroom doorway, she gasped.

"Calm down, it's just me," Ry told her. He was dressed nicely, as though he was going out. Leah did a double take.

"What are you doing here? Oh, my God. If my mom sees you…"

She was frozen in the bathtub, kneeling on the porcelain, and Ry laughed.

"I'm not stupid, sweet girl. I just saw her in town. She's running errands."

"If anyone sees you here," she murmured, and her hands fluttered to her chest, as though she could still her pounding heart with only her fingers.

"You worry too much." He took a step inside, and held out a hand to assist her out of the tub. "I came in the back door."

He eyed her up and down as she stood in front of him.

"You look beautiful," he said softly. She flushed and tucked a tendril of hair behind her ear, something she did whenever she was nervous. He noticed and smiled. "Don't be scared," he told her. "I'd never do anything to hurt you, or to get you into trouble. Do you trust me?"

She nodded immediately. Of course she did.

"Good." He smiled again.

He peeled off her gloves, one by one, and tossed them into her sink. Then he took a step toward her. He couldn't help but stare at her track shorts, and how they barely covered the curve of her rump. He reached out a hand and traced that curve. It was firm and tight, the effortless body of the young. He swallowed hard, and shifted his weight. His groin was already tightened against his pants.

"Come here," he said to her. She nervously glanced at the window, but did as he asked, her heart pounding and her cheeks pink.

He grabbed her and kissed her hard, his hands splayed out against her back. He walked her backward until they were in her bedroom, where he fell onto the bed with her, careful to shield her from his weight. His head grazed her dream catcher hanging directly above the headboard, and he reached up to brush it away.

"I hope this doesn't block any dreams of me," he said with a smirk. She shook her head.

"No, it only catches bad dreams."

"And I'm good?" he asked, burying his head in her neck.

"Very."

He pushed against her, rubbing, rubbing. He was so hard, and rigid, and Leah almost couldn't breathe from nervousness and excitement. Was today going to be the day? Right here in her bed?

She let her hands wander and she touched him all over.

Over his back, over his shoulders, and then, then…he guided her hand into his pants.

She closed her eyes and felt the velvety skin. It was moist at the tip and the wetness smeared on her hand.

"No, I haven't come yet," he told her, grinning. "That's pre-cum, sweet pea. It means I want to come. But I'm holding out."

That was when he put his hand down her panties and she arched into him.

God, this couldn't be bad.

It couldn't be. It felt too good.

He had her shaking in his palm a minute later. He was so good at it. He knew just what to do.

"Do you want more today?" he whispered into her neck, and he smelled so good, like trees and musk. She nodded, clinging to him. She wanted everything. It was terrifying, but she wanted it.

He nodded, too, and reached to shove his pants down, but then Bo was barking downstairs.

Leah sat up abruptly, and looked out the window. Her mom's car was in the drive, her mom digging in its trunk.

"Oh, my God, you've got to go."

She shoved him toward the door, and they ran down the stairs. He paused for a scant moment at the back door.

"Don't worry, Kitten. I'll still be close. I'll be watching you."

She startled at the odd choice of words, but he didn't hesitate. He ducked into a nearby alley, where he'd stashed his car.

It was a close call, but oddly enough, Ry liked it…the thrill of almost getting caught.

He liked it a lot.

Ramblings from the Island

I don't want to whine, dear readers.

I really don't. But something feels off.

I feel like I might be out of my depth.

Ry appears to enjoy the element of possibly getting caught. That seems weird to me. Wrong, even.

Does he really like me at all? Or does he just like the idea of me? The idea of getting caught? The idea of doing something wrong?

I don't know anymore.

And that makes me wonder how much I ever knew in the first place.

He said he'd be watching me.

What the hell does that even mean?

A week ago, I'd find that endearing. Maybe protective. But now...

It feels a little threatening.

Maybe I'm crazy.

I'm probably overreacting.

Tags: paranoid, older man, younger girl, dark romance, afraid, sex, watching.

Responses (1)

SammySea32: Girl, you need to break it off. He sounds dangerous. At the very least, he's a predator. It's not dark romance. It's starting to sound criminal!

CHAPTER TWENTY-SEVEN

August 30

I find myself down at bungalow three after the police leave. I didn't plan on going, I just simply find myself standing in front of the door.

Derek answers before I even knock.

"How did it go?" he asks immediately, opening the door wide for me to come in.

"As we expected." I sigh. We go in and sit at his table. He pours me coffee and pushes the cup to me. My fingers brush his, and I can't stop the explosion of warmth that shoots into my belly.

"So they didn't do much." He urges me to give details. I shake my head.

"No. I get the feeling that since Leah is gone, they aren't

going to look into it. Justice is just an illusion in this country, I guess."

"I wouldn't go that far," he answers. "It's just this island. They don't want to stir things up."

"I guess."

He furrows his brow, his slender fingers circling his mug. "Hey. Let's get out of here today," he suggests. "You need a break."

"What are you thinking?" I ask before I simply reject him out of hand.

"Let's go for a car ride. We can grab some sandwiches and just feel the wind in our hair."

I should decline. Nate will be arriving later.

I should go back up to the main house and do a hundred other things other than a drive with Derek Collins.

But I don't.

I say yes instead.

He's pleased when I do. He clears up the coffee mugs and even gets me a sweater.

"It can get chilly in the convertible," he explains, and before I know it, we are sailing down the road, the top down, and the wind in our hair. The road hugs the coast, of course, and so the scenery is panoramic as we drive.

I stare at it, at the blurred sand and sea, and my mind is a million miles away.

That's why, when Derek reaches over and grasps my hand, letting our intertwined fingers rest on my thigh, I don't see it coming, and I don't react.

Instead, I enjoy the warmth and strength of his hand. It feels good.

I close my eyes and enjoy the sun on my shoulders, and for once, for the first time in forever, I try not to feel guilty.

Derek drives on for minutes and minutes, and finally, the car comes to a stop. I open my eyes, and we're parked on the bluffs. I know exactly where we are, but I honestly haven't been here since I was a kid.

"Do you know the history of Black Caesar?" Derek asks me. "I'm sure you do."

I nod. "He was a pirate who used to bring his female prisoners here and hold them captive in catacombs beneath the island."

"Historians have never been able to prove that, though," Derek adds to my statement. I nod.

"They haven't. But islanders know it's true."

"I wouldn't doubt it."

We're sitting atop the entrance to some of the catacombs. They are too dangerous to enter since half of them have caved in with the sandy soil and high water table of the island.

"Everyone thinks it's a romantic dark history," I say. "But he was keeping them prisoner."

"They say, though, that he didn't do anything but love them," Derek points out.

"Uh-huh. But that could mean anything. That could mean that he raped them, or God knows what else. If they wanted to be here, he wouldn't have had to force them."

"True," Derek agrees.

We get out and stand on the bluffs, overlooking the sea. From here, the water seems to stretch on forever, rippled blue glass glistening in the sun. Anyone would think that

Key West was a paradise without tragedy...anyone who didn't know better.

We walk along the beach, hand in hand, for the longest time. The gentle breeze caresses our skin, and for just a little while, I'm able to focus on something other than Leah. I'm able to focus on something good. Something pleasurable.

Derek turns to me when we reach an inlet.

"Thank you for coming with me," he says quietly. "I know you aren't getting out much, but I'm honored that you would choose to come with me."

I want to roll my eyes, but I don't. He's sincere.

I eye the tall, gentle man in front of me. I think about his nasty divorce, and the way his ex-wife screwed him over. I think of how he has to share time with his only son, and how up until now, he's been practically a recluse, afraid to trust anyone. After what his wife did, I can't say that I blame him.

"Thank you for trusting me," I tell him instead of rolling my eyes. "I know it's hard."

He shields his expression, his eyes darken.

"You're not like most women I've met," he says. "You're real. You say what you actually mean. You don't play games, and you don't expect anyone else to either. You should watch that. Someone is going to take advantage."

"They haven't yet." I shrug. "I am what I am. I'm not gonna change it now."

"Good," he says.

That's when he cups my face in his hands, and he lowers his face to mine...and he kisses me.

It's without pretense, without preamble. His lips are gentle and soft, and I kiss him back, slowly and sweetly.

When we pull apart, I say, "Well, my grandmother is turning over in her grave. I'm not supposed to make friends with the guests."

"Too late," Derek observes. I nod.

"Yeah."

I'm shivering from the sea breeze, so we head back to the car and Derek wraps his sweater around me. It smells like him, like Old Spice or something similar, and I inhale it as we drive home.

The tires crunch on the gravel driveway when we arrive, and I find, quite unexpectedly, that I'm not ready to be home yet. The inn looms large and empty, and it is a reminder of what I have lost. The daughter that lived in the house.

"I've always worked too much," I muse aloud. "If I could go back, I would have worked less and spent more time with Leah."

Derek looks at me, his gaze sympathetic. "You did what you thought you had to do. You were trying to provide for her. She knew that."

"I hope so."

I reach for the handle and as I do, a tiny flash of turquoise catches my eye from the floorboard. Bending down, I reach for it. A white feather attached to a turquoise bead. I've seen it before…somewhere…and I stare at it as I try to remember.

When it hits me, it hits me with the force of a thousand bricks.

It's from the dream catcher on Leah's wall.

CHAPTER TWENTY-EIGHT

July 28

Leah was sitting on her bed when the text came in.

It was a photo.

This time, it wasn't of a penis, or abs, or anything sexual at all. It was of Ry's hand, and in the palm, there sat a feather.

It was white, attached to a turquoise bead, and Leah knew it immediately.

She twisted around to view her dream catcher. Where there used to be at least ten feathers, there were only five now.

Why did you pluck my dream catcher? she asked, and she felt herself growing annoyed.

It's something I can keep in my pocket and look at. I like to think about you.

Her belly fluttered with something she couldn't place. It was a tiny bit excitement, but more like…apprehension. Annoyance. Was that what instincts felt like?

My dad bought that for me, she replied, with a rolling-eye emoji. I didn't even see you take them.

I only have one left, he replied with a frowning-face emoji. The others blew away on accident.

So you desecrated my dream catcher for nothing? she asked. What's going to keep me from having nightmares now?

A beat went by, then another, before he answered.

I will. I'll take care of you. Always.

What once would've felt comforting and safe, now felt smothering.

Leah put her phone away, and held her dream catcher in her hands. Maybe she could fix it. She could buy some more feathers and attach them herself.

But her real issue, she knew, wasn't the dream catcher.

It was the man across the island who was focusing on her. More than she ever thought, more than she felt comfortable with now.

She was out of her league.

She should never have begun this. The question now was…how to get out of it?

CHAPTER TWENTY-NINE

August 30

I dangle the feather in my fingers and turn to Derek, my blood ice in my veins.

"Why do you have this?"

He stares at it blankly. "I don't know what it is," he admits, and I desperately want to believe he's lying. But there's no way.

"This is from a dream catcher that hangs above my daughter's bed. It is now in your car. Please tell me how it got here."

My heart pounds and pounds, and I think it might explode.

"I've never seen it before," he says slowly. "I'm serious, Emmy. Why do you think it is in here?"

"I don't know. All I know is...you had her anklet and

now you have this. It seems like too much of a coincidence."

I open the door and get out, the feather in my hand.

"Something isn't right here," I tell him. His face is open and hurt.

"Emmy, the last person who sat in this car was Liam, when I took him to the airport. Leah hasn't even been in here since I took them to the lock-in."

"Are you saying Liam had this?" I hold it up, and Derek shakes his head slowly as he climbs from his car.

"I'm not saying anything like that. I'm saying maybe it was stuck on his shoe, or... God, I don't know. All I know is, I didn't have anything to do with it. *At all*."

I stare at him, and I want to believe him so much, so damned much, but that would be dumb. The signs point to him.

"You were the one," I say simply. "You were the one my daughter was involved with."

Derek's head snaps back, and before he can say a word, someone is speaking from behind me.

"What the fuck?"

My ex-husband suddenly appears and charges past me and slams into Derek. The two of them roll over the hood of the car and sprawl into the dirt, punches flying.

"You son of a bitch," Nate spits out, and blood splatters. I rush to try to break them up, but someone, and I don't know who, elbows me in the mouth by accident. I taste blood, and they roll over again.

They grunt and groan and I shriek for them to stop.

They finally do. They each sit back, blood and dirt on their faces, glaring at each other.

"What the hell is happening?" Derek barks. He looks at Nate, and then he looks at me. "What the fuck is going on?"

"You were fucking my daughter, you sick bastard," Nate says as he wipes his mouth with his sleeve. Blood smears on his cuff. "I'll see you fry for this."

"I was not." Derek stands up and he turns to me. "That's disgusting. Emmy, you can't think that's true. I would never."

"Then explain why you have her things," I say simply. "I don't want to believe that you would do something like this, Derek. But nothing makes sense." I look at Nate. "When did you get in?"

"About an hour ago. You weren't here." He's almost accusatory. He looks from me, to Derek. "What's going on?"

"Nothing."

"I'm going to call the police," Nate says. "I read through all of Leah's blog posts on the plane—every last one of them. If this guy did it... I'll fucking kill you."

He turns to Derek again, but honestly, Derek looks genuinely confused.

"What blog posts?"

"Leah had a blog," I explain. "She had an older boyfriend. Much older. She blogged about it."

"Really?" Derek rubs his temple. "I thought she and Liam might actually get together."

"Shut the fuck up, liar," Nate interrupts. I put my hand on his arm.

"Nate. We don't know anything yet."

He glares at me. "Nice of you to defend him." He stalks off toward the house. Derek and I watch him go.

"Well, that was fun," Derek says. I glance at his bloody lip.

"You need to put some ice on that."

"Do you really think I could do something like that?" Derek asks me, and he sounds so, so hurt. I shrug.

"I don't know. I don't know *who* could do something like that."

I walk away into the house, trailing after my ex-husband. I feel Derek staring at me as I go, every step of the way.

I find Nate pacing in the den, like a caged animal.

"Emmy, she was fucking him," he growls. "Our baby girl."

"Actually, as far as I could see, she hadn't yet," I answer tiredly. "It doesn't say that they ever actually…"

"They did enough," Nate snaps. "He had his hands around her neck."

"I know." I sit in the chair, tucking my legs beneath me. "I told you that. A while ago. Why did you suddenly decide to pay attention?"

Nate looks pale. "I don't know. I didn't want to believe it. But it's true. And that bastard has to pay for what he did."

"We don't know if it was him," I remind him.

Nate looks away, his expression hard and jaded. "The police can decide."

He picks up his phone and calls them.

I close my eyes, wishing that none of this was real. It was bad enough to lose my daughter, but to have this taint her memory. It seems too cruel.

"I need wine," I tell Nate, standing up. "Do you want any?"

He nods and sits, his big hands restless.

"What were you doing with that guy anyway?" he asks when I come back, a bottle and two glasses in tow. I shrug.

"We went for a car ride. I needed some fresh air."

"Emmy, you live on the ocean," Nate reminds me wryly. I shrug again and pour the wine. I swirl mine around in the glass before I take a drink.

"He's Liam's father," I say, more to myself than to Nate. "He wouldn't."

"We don't know what he would do," Nate answers. "You know that."

I can't help but remember Liam's own reservations about Derek. But I also have to keep in mind that Liam resents his father in the first place. Boys often don't get along with their dads at that age, just as girls butt heads with their mothers.

We drink our wine in silence, and Nate goes to the kitchen to make a platter of olives, cheese, and crackers. We snack on them, drink more wine, and sit in more silence. It is dark when my phone rings.

I pick it up to find Derek on the other end.

"Don't hang up," he says quickly. "I want to tell you something I just told the police."

"The police were here?" I ask in surprise.

Nate's head snaps up. We didn't see them drive past.

"Yeah. Listen. I'm wondering…and I don't want to start stuff or instigate rumors. But I've been looking at Leah's blog, and since I know I'm not the one she's writing about, I've been racking my brain. I called Liam, and we talked about it, too. I wonder…"

"Just say it," I tell him bluntly. There's no need to pussy-foot around.

"I wonder if it's Hutch," he answers simply.

I burst out laughing, but he protests. "Don't dismiss it

without checking," he cautions me. "Listen, I know he seems like a good guy. But, I've seen him wear cardigans, and he certainly had access to Leah. It's not unheard of for a pastor to go bad, Emmy."

It's a sobering thought, and my heart thuds.

"Maybe," I say uncertainly.

"Well, I mentioned it to the police," Derek says. "So hopefully they'll look into it."

"Thank you," I reply. I don't know what else to say, or how I'm supposed to act now. I still can't rule him out.

"I guess I'll talk to you later," he mumbles, and hangs up.

Nate stares at me.

I relay to him what Derek had said, and Nate looks uncertain.

"Surely not."

I shrug. "I don't know. Do we really know anything anymore?"

He has to give me that.

We don't.

Ramblings from the Island

Dear readers,

I've been avoiding Ry for a couple of days now. I don't know what to do.

I could tell my mom, but I'd be in so much trouble. She'd never forgive me for being like her mother. I really thought those genes didn't run in my veins, not the bad ones. But here I am...and I'm faced with the same decisions that Lola was faced with.

Lola chose death rather than facing the people she harmed. That seems extreme but honestly, I can't stand to think of the disappointment on my mother's face if she knew.

Everyone on the island knows Ry.

They know me.

It would be such a scandal, such an embarrassment for my family. It would maybe even affect the inn sales. My mother would never forgive me for that.

I'm in a bind.

I truly don't know what to do.

Do any of you have any thoughts?

Tags: scared, abusive relationships, bad decisions, older men, bad genes.

Responses (2)

SammySea32: Your mom surely wouldn't be mad at you for this. You made a mistake, but this guy sounds creepy. Maybe even crazy. You need to tell someone!

SammySea32: Can you message me with your phone number? You can talk to me. I don't know if you're actually considering it, but suicide is never the answer. You can talk to me.

CHAPTER THIRTY

August 7

Leah lay on the beach alone, watching the foam roll up on the shore. It came in and out, in and out, lapping at the sand over and over. It was rhythmic, and something she could count on. The pull of the ocean would always be there, ever the same, never changing.

"Hey," a soft voice said from behind, and Leah turned to find Liam approaching. He was in shorts and a T-shirt, and although the company was welcome, it was also a little distracting.

She had serious thinking to do.

Decisions to make.

"Hey yourself." She hid her frustration, patting the sand next to her. "Have a seat. I've been saving it for you."

Liam laughed and sat next to her. He bumped her shoulder with his own. "How long have you been out here?"

Leah shrugged. "Awhile."

Liam lifted a dark eyebrow. "Any reason why?"

She shrugged again. "Can't a girl sit by herself?"

Liam stared at her doubtfully. "You're never alone," he pointed out. "Ever."

"Well, I am today." She sighed. "What are you up to?"

"I was just doing laundry. So I could pack."

Leah startled, then realized what day it was. "Oh, my God. School is getting ready to start. You have to leave."

Liam looked at her like she had two heads. "Um, yeah. Just like every year at this time. What's up with you?"

"Nothing," she told him. "Everything. I don't know. I don't want you to leave, I guess."

Liam rolled his eyes. "While that is flattering, you were bothered before you realized what day it is. Remember? What's up?"

Leah stared out to sea, at the clouds, at the blue where it kissed the water. She thought about telling him…all of it. But it would hurt him. Deeply. She knew that, and she'd never do that to him.

"Have you ever done something that you regretted?" she asked him bluntly, instead. He lifted an eyebrow.

"How much regret are we talking about? Losing your virginity in a drunken stupor to a stranger, or something less?"

She rolled her eyes.

"I'm still a virgin."

She could've sworn he exhaled.

"Seriously. Have you ever done something and then wished you could take it back, but you were so caught up in it that you didn't know how to even get out of it?"

"Of course I have," he said quietly. "When my mom and dad got divorced, I should've stayed with my dad. But I felt guilty for letting my mom go off all alone, even though it was her fault in the first place."

"And you regret that now?"

Liam nodded. "Yeah. I'd rather be here. But I know I hurt my dad by not wanting to come in the first place, and sometimes, things can't be salvaged."

Leah put her hand on his arm. "Liam, your dad wants you here. He told me."

"Really?" His eyes were wide. "Sometimes, it feels like he doesn't like me at all."

"He loves you. He probably just doesn't know how to act sometimes. We can all relate to that."

Liam narrowed his eyes and examined his friend.

"What is going on with you? Are you in trouble?"

Her heart beat once, twice, three times while she again considered telling him. She could tell him without names. Couldn't she?

"I...I might've gotten involved with someone I shouldn't have," she finally said. He started to react, but she held up her hand. "It was stupid, so stupid. And I can't even stand to look at him now. I'll figure it out."

Liam asked a hundred questions all in one breath, and Leah shook her head. "You don't need to know the details. I've got it handled. Or I will anyway."

"If you need me, I'm here," Liam assured her.

"Until tomorrow," she pointed out wryly.

He rolled his eyes. "I'm here for you, even if I'm across the country. Is this guy someone I know?"

Leah looked away. "He's a little older. More mature. It's done, Liam. Don't worry about it."

"How mature?" Liam looked concerned. Leah shook her head.

"Not criminal. I'm of the age to consent, Liam. But it's not necessary. It's over. Please, stop worrying."

The wounded look on his face hurt her heart and she wished she'd never said anything.

"Let's change the subject," she suggested, and Liam obliged.

He started chattering about stuff back home, and Leah stared out to sea once again. She didn't mean to tune out her friend, but all she could think about was her current predicament, and what she should do about it.

That was when her phone started buzzing. She ignored it at first, but then it buzzed again, and again, and again.

Sighing, she glanced at it.

I miss you.

I need to see you.

Look what you do to me. With this one, he had included a picture of his penis, erect and red. She had to fight the urge to shudder. It was no longer exciting.

"Who is it?" Liam asked curiously, watching her face. "The guy?"

She shook her head. "No, it's fine." She slid her phone back into her rear pocket, and so she didn't see the next text until later.

Leah, don't ignore me.

CHAPTER THIRTY-ONE

August 31

I have an idea as I'm washing up in the kitchen.

I rush upstairs, and grab Leah's laptop, and pull up her blog.

I don't know a lot about blogging, anything really, but I'm smart enough to figure out how to make a new entry.

Hello out there.

My daughter used to write this blog. I don't know how many of you follow it, or will even see this. But I want you to know that she died.

She drowned.

And while I know that nothing will bring her back, I'd like to find the person who was victimizing my daughter.

Please. If any of you have any information at all, contact me. My name is Emmy Fisher.

I list my phone number and email, and then push Publish and wait.

Nothing happens.

No replies, no phone calls, no texts, no emails.

Damn it.

Then…then…a reply.

SammySea32: I had a feeling something bad was happening. You know me, Mrs. Fisher. I'll text you.

Two seconds later, a text pops up on my phone.

It's Amber Fitzgerald, Ms. Fisher. I'm so sorry about Leah. I commented and told her to end things.

I see that, I answer. Did she ever reach out to you?

No, she answers immediately. But I didn't tell her who I was. I knew that if I did, she wouldn't listen to me. We didn't exactly get along. I thought that maybe she might respond to my anonymous comments, but she didn't. I don't know who she was talking about. I don't know who the man is.

My hopes, which were tenuous and fragile at best, are dashed as they fall to the ground.

My heart is heavy as I stare at the laptop, at the blinking cursor and my waiting text messages.

We'll never figure out who it is, I realize in a heartbeat. We'll never know. It's a thought that feels like it will torment me to the grave.

I never knew what my daughter was feeling, what she was doing…and I can't even help her now.

I feel more helpless than I've ever been.

CHAPTER THIRTY-TWO

August 9

On Liam's last day before he returned to NYC, they lounged in her room, music playing.

"You have to call me when you get there," Leah told him. "I need to know you're safe."

He smiled. "It's nice to know you care."

His tone was weird, and she eyed him. "Of course I care."

He hesitated. "Leah... I..."

She waited.

"I like you. I know you're just breaking up with someone, but..." His voice trailed off, and he flushed.

Stunned, Leah's mouth opened. Then closed.

"I'd like to be more than friends," he clarified, his cheeks bursting into a thousand shades of red.

She took a deep breath. This wasn't what she needed, or wanted. Not today, of all days.

"Liam, I love you. Like a brother," she added gently. And he stood up, his eyes glossy.

"Don't friend-zone me," he groaned, and she cringed.

"You *are* my friend," she answered quietly. "One of my very best friends."

"But why can't you give me a chance for something more?" he asked urgently. "We'd be great together. I know it."

She thought on that for a minute. They probably would. They were the same age, he got her sense of humor, he was good-looking.

But the chemistry just wasn't there.

At least, not for her now.

"I know you're messing around with someone you shouldn't be," he said hesitantly. "I saw some weird texts pop up on your phone on the beach. I'm good for you, Leah. You wouldn't have to sneak around."

"You don't know anything," Leah argued, and she was relieved that Liam didn't notice she was using a separate phone. But even still, Liam could see on her face.

He was absolutely right.

His expression fell. He stormed out, without another word. She tried texting him, over and over, and he didn't answer. She saw his dad's car leaving a couple of hours later and she knew Liam was leaving without saying goodbye.

She met Skye for lunch to distract herself.

Skye chattered about mundane things, and Leah found it

hard to concentrate. When Skye asked what she was wearing for the first day of school, she shrugged, unconcerned.

"I'm just gonna wear white jean shorts and a maroon top," she told her best friend. Skye rolled her eyes.

"You're so basic, Leah," she giggled. "You would be drop-dead gorgeous if you just put some effort in." At Leah's face, she backtracked. "Not that you aren't now, but you could be ultraglam, if you wanted."

Leah sniffed and pushed a fry through some ketchup. "I don't. It seems like too much work."

Skye rolled her eyes yet again. "Girl, if I had your eyes, I'd be rocking a smoky eye every day of the week."

"Well, you know what they say," Leah said glibly. "Yesterday's eyeliner can be today's smoky eye if you believe in yourself."

They giggled, and ate their lunch.

"Liam asked me out today," Leah finally said. Skye stopped eating.

"You're kidding."

Leah shook her head. "I wish. I said no, and he left to go back to New York and didn't say goodbye. He's gone now."

Her eyes swam with tears, but Skye was annoyed and stared overly hard at her almost-eaten hamburger. "You knew I liked him," she said angrily.

"And I said no to him," Leah answered. "I didn't do anything wrong."

"You must've led him on," Skye growled. "If you truly gave him all the signs that you weren't interested, he wouldn't have asked."

"That's crazy," Leah snapped. "He's my friend. I never did anything wrong."

"Whatever," Skye snapped back, standing up. "I'll see you later."

She flounced away, utterly pissed, and Leah sat stunned.

What even just happened? She was trying to confide in her friend, and all hell just broke loose.

She looked up again to see if Skye was coming back, but she wasn't. Instead, she saw two teenage boys, tourists, staring at her from across the court. They smiled at her, but she ignored them. Why did it feel like her life was tumbling down around her shoulders?

Things only got worse when her phone buzzed. Her real phone, not her secret one. Glancing at it, she found a text from an unknown number.

Those boys are eyeing you.

She glanced around to see who sent it. She didn't see anyone.

Who is this? she answered.

You don't know your own boyfriend? I'm using a throwaway phone.

She felt a surge of anger. What the hell was he doing watching her? This wasn't a movie, this was real life. And in real life, it was stalkerish.

Why are you spying on me?

He answered immediately. I'm not. I was here in the square and saw you. It was a coincidence.

Leah's gut said otherwise, although she didn't have any proof.

She didn't answer that text, and instead, she left for home, glancing around to make sure Ry didn't stop her in public. She needed some time.

When she got home, Leah sorted through her pictures again, the ones she'd taken this week. Ry texted her a few times, and she didn't even look after the first one.

Do you want to hang out tonight?

No, she didn't. She still felt unnerved, and as though something was wrong. Maybe she had made a mistake. Ry was far too old for her. He shouldn't even want to be with her. Didn't it sort of make him a pedophile?

She condemned herself for thinking that, though. She definitely had a woman's body. She wasn't a child.

But still.

The relationship felt too intense.

When she heard her mom rattling through their apartment, she came out. Maybe she could talk to her mom about it, in a roundabout way. She definitely couldn't tell her everything, but she could dig around. She needed advice. She didn't know what to do, but she knew she didn't want to get anyone in trouble. Not when she'd been a willing participant.

Her mother was rummaging around for dinner, and she and Leah ate in silence. Leah, because she was trying to think of what to say, and Emmy, because she was thinking about inventory at the inn. They were each lost in thought.

After dinner, her mom grabbed a glass of wine and they sat together on the porch for the first time in a long time. Emmy dangled her arm around the back of the seat and Leah leaned into it. For tonight, she was enjoying the feeling of being a little girl.

When her mom started talking about her mother, Leah's grandmother, it was her chance. She listened while her mother talked about Lola, explaining that she was different, and wild. And then Leah asked, "Do you think she dated older men?"

Emmy shrugged. "I don't know. She could've. If she saw someone she wanted, it didn't matter to her the cost. She just went for it."

Her grandmother had killed herself, and after feeling so icky for a couple days, Leah could see how maybe someone could get to that point. Her grandmother must've felt so guilty, because she must've known, deep down, that her behavior was wrong.

Just like Leah.

Her behavior was wrong.

And she was going to have to stop.

She talked her mother into letting her go night swimming just for a little while, and then she jogged upstairs to change into her suit. Bo waited patiently by the door, and as an afterthought, she paused and grabbed her secret phone.

I need to talk to you, she texted, without reading all of

his previous messages. I can't do this anymore. It's wrong. Can we go back to the way we were before?

She re-hid her phone, grabbed her board, and went back outside. She plunged in. The water was cool, refreshing, and dark. The stars were twinkling, and with nothing to obstruct her view, the sky seemed endless. She sighed and stared at the moon, losing herself in the rich, yellow light. It caressed her skin like gold, like fairy lights, and she straddled her board, floating.

On the sand, Bo flopped down, his giant head on his paws. He was such a chicken. She laughed at him, and he stared forlornly at her.

She closed her eyes and imagined a place far from here. A place where life was perfect. Was there anywhere like that?

Ashore, she heard Bo growl, and then a soft splash.

She opened her eyes, and while her dog was standing, barking, his hackles raised, there was nothing there.

"Bo, you goofball," she called. "It's fine. Calm down."

The water around her was a sheen of ripples. She put her finger in one, disturbing the perfect ring.

She was watching the ripple effect when something bumped into her underwater. Before she could even think, she was grabbed hard by the leg and yanked under the water.

She didn't even have time to scream.

CHAPTER THIRTY-THREE

August 9

When Leah opened her eyes, her entire world was black.

There was no light.

Her head was pounding, and her ankle was on fire.

She tried to scratch at it, but her hands were bound.

She squirmed, and realized that her feet were bound, too, so tightly that she couldn't feel her toes.

She was tied to a chair, in the middle of a black room.

The gravity of the situation hit her all at once, and she tried to scream, but there was duct tape over her mouth. Only a weird moan came out.

She was alone.

She tried to see, but the void of light made it impossible. Her heart pounded, and she was still in her swimsuit. She racked her brain, trying to remember what had happened, but there was nothing there.

Something had hit her in the water. Dragged her under. Then there was a sharp pain in her temple, and now she was here.

Anything that had happened between then and now was simply gone.

How long had passed?

Where was she?

Was she going to die?

All valid questions, all things she didn't have an answer for. Instead, her pulse bounded erratically, and the fear was almost too big to think around.

It was so black that she couldn't tell a difference when her eyes were closed or open. Listening, she tried to see if she could hear anything. It seemed almost as if she were in a seashell…with the vague sound of the ocean coming from somewhere.

She craned her ears.

It was definitely the ocean. But there was no other sound. No traffic, no people.

She struggled again, and decided that her hands and feet were duct taped, as well. Not tied. There was no way she was getting free.

She knew one thing, though. She was in grave danger.

With a moan, she dropped her head.

CHAPTER THIRTY-FOUR

September 2

Nate accompanies me to church on Sunday.

Not because we're overly religious, but so that we can gain some access to Hutch without arousing suspicion. We have to do some digging, some probing. Even if it's just being around him, to judge his character. I've never paid that much attention to him before.

During the sermon, I steal glances toward him. He's sitting among the youth group, and he's poised at attention, his eyes focused on the pastor speaking.

The sermon is on forgiveness.

I find it ironic, because once I find out who defiled my daughter, I'll never forgive him.

Nate drapes his arm behind me on the pew, out of habit, I'm sure. I absorb his warmth and his strength, and it is so familiar. Once upon a time, I could've leaned on him without question. Now I have to be careful. If I lean too much, he could take it the wrong way. I don't want to reconcile. We're better apart.

Nate's finger taps restlessly against the wooden back, and from time to time, I reach over to still it with my own. He glances down at me, his mouth tilted into a small smile. He has nervous energy. I get it. I do, too.

We stand to sing a hymn, then sit for the benediction. Then we're released. I try to casually make my way over to where Hutch is standing. Skye is next to him, standing close, and for a split second, my heart leaps into my throat.

Was it him? Has he moved on to Skye? Is he grooming her?

"Jesus," Nate mutters, and I know he's thinking the same thing. Skye sees us at the same time, and starts waving.

She barrels into my arms, and then she hugs Nate, too. "I haven't seen you in forever, Mr. F.," she says to him excitedly. He squeezes her shoulder.

"It's good to see you, kid."

"You guys have to come over for lunch. Mom is making her famous BBQ brisket. Pleeease say yes."

"Yes," Nate says promptly. "We'd be honored. But you should probably check with your mom first."

Skye nods and bounds off to find Christy, and we're left standing in front of Hutch. I have no idea whether the police have contacted him yet, but when he turns to me, he doesn't act any differently.

"Hi, Emmy," he greets me warmly, reaching for and grasping my hands. His fingers are cold. "It's so good to see you." He looks at Nate. "Nate, you, too."

Nate shakes his hand, but he's stiff.

"Did you enjoy the sermon?" Hutch asks politely. I nod.

"Yes. It was enlightening."

The police must've spoken with him. He seems oddly polite. Oddly formal. Or has he always been this way?

I look at his hands. Were they really stretched around my daughter's neck? I can hardly fathom it. He's a man of God.

"How's youth group going?" I ask, at a loss for what to say. He smiles.

"It's really growing. We're finishing up the Habitat for Humanity project, and we're raising money for autism. I'm really proud of the group this year."

"As you should be," Mrs. Fitzgerald breaks in, coming up to shake his hand.

I've never been so happy to see her in my life. She distracts Hutch, and Nate and I slip away.

Skye and her mother find us in the parking lot.

"Are you coming?" Skye asks eagerly. "Mom said it's fine."

Christy smiles at us. "Please come. If you don't, we'll have leftovers for days."

I find myself agreeing, and in the car, Nate turns to me at a red light. "We've got to tell them about our suspicions...about Hutch. They've got a daughter in that group."

He's right, and I know he's right. But God, how awkward that will be.

"What shall we say?" I ask slowly. "I'm sorry, but your daughter might be carrying on with the pastor?"

"Maybe something a little less direct," he suggests, and

I almost smile. "Skye did seem to be comfortable with him," he adds.

I cringe. "They're all comfortable with him," I tell him. "They love him."

"Unfortunately, that's the *in* that most predators need," he answers grimly. "They put themselves in positions of authority, like teachers, pastors, policemen. The kids automatically trust them because of that."

"That's sick," I say. Nate agrees.

I stare out the window, at the passing scenery. It seems like only yesterday when I was in the car with Leah, and we were shopping for back-to-school clothes. She was laughing, switching radio stations, and I was annoyed and telling her to stop.

I shake my head. That time is gone.

We pull into the Haydens' driveway, and Nate opens my door, ever the gentleman. Skye meets us at the front door.

"Come in, you guys." She pulls us in, and her house does smell like amazing BBQ.

Jason catches me inhaling with my eyes closed. "Right?" he laughs. "She slow-bakes them for hours and hours. Trust me, they'll melt in your mouth."

"Leah told me about them," I say, and abruptly, the mood in the room shifts to uncomfortable. "I'm sorry," I say sheepishly. "I..."

"Don't be," Jason says warmly. "Leah did love Christy's barbecue."

He turns to Nate. "Do you guys need a drink? Wine? Vodka tonic?"

"A vodka straight up for me," Nate says.

Jason turns to me. "Red for you?"

"Perfect," I murmur. He smiles and leaves.

Skye hugs me. "I love you, Mom," she tells me. And once again, the *M*-word cuts me. I even feel Nate stiffen beside me. But it's okay. If I tell myself that enough, it will be true.

I force my shoulders into relaxing. I hug her back.

"I have something to show you," she tells me, and she tugs me into her bedroom.

There is an easel in the middle of the room, with a drop cloth underneath. A giant canvas is displayed there, a work in progress. A jolt runs through me, at all of the pictures of she and Leah. It's a giant collage, featuring pictures from kindergarten to present. I swallow, then swallow again, before I can speak.

"It's beautiful, honey," I manage to say. Skye gazes at it.

"It is, isn't it?" she whispers. "I loved her so much. I'll never have another friend like her."

I trace my finger along some of the photos. I stop on one where they were around five years old, each in pigtails and with red Kool-Aid mustaches. "I love this one," I tell her. "We went to the beach that day. I remember."

She nods. "We rode the banana boat."

I smile. They'd wanted to ride it forever, and finally they were tall enough. "I have a picture of you guys on that thing somewhere."

Her eyes light up. "Can I have a copy of it?" she asks hopefully. I nod.

"Of course, babe."

I look at the collage again, and I wonder if I should say

something to Skye about Hutch. Would that be appropriate? Or should we discuss it with her parents?

That problem is solved for me. When Skye and I rejoin everyone else in the living room, Nate is already discussing it with Jason and Christy.

"We really do have reason to believe he might've been involved with Leah," Nate is saying earnestly, leaning forward in his seat. "We don't know for sure, but it stands to reason that you might want to use caution with allowing Skye to be around him."

Skye is frozen to the ground, and she looks up at me. "Who is he talking about?"

Her parents look like deer in the headlights, and Nate looks to me for help.

"Um, they're talking about Hutch, honey."

"You think he was involved with Leah?" she speaks slowly, as though trying to wrap her head around it. "That's impossible."

"I thought so, too," I agree. "But I don't know anymore. The police are going to look into it."

"The police?" Skye's shock is palpable.

I nod. "Yeah. We'll leave it to them to try to figure out what was going on."

"But why does it even matter now?" Skye asks. "Leah's gone. It won't make a difference. We're just gonna ruin some guy's life because he happened to get involved with Leah?"

Her shock has turned into outrage. Her mother handles it. "Skye, whoever she was involved with...it wasn't legal.

The guy was a predator. He needs to be punished so he won't do it again."

Jason nods in agreement. "Skye, honestly. It will be for the best. Don't worry. If he didn't do it, he won't have anything to worry about."

Skye looks from her dad, to her mom, to me. "But you know how this town is," she says indignantly. "Even with just an investigation, the gossip is going to fly. It will ruin his life. Even if he didn't do it."

"Don't you think Leah deserves justice?" Nate chips in softly. He looks at Skye beseechingly, begging her to understand. "We don't want to hurt anyone. We just don't want anyone else hurt."

"If Leah participated in it, then she wasn't hurt." Skye's voice wavers. "She was actively participating. She gave her permission. She never said anything to me, so that tells me that she knew what she was doing was wrong, and she chose to do it anyway. I doubt she'd want him to get into trouble either."

"Skye, Leah wasn't of the age to consent to something like that," Christy tells her firmly. "If Hutch did this, it was grossly wrong. If he didn't, then it's like your father said. He doesn't have anything to worry about."

"Then none of you understand this town at all," Skye cries, and runs out. Her door slams closed one second later.

We all stared awkwardly at each other. I fight the urge to go after her.

"She just doesn't understand," Christy says. "She'll come around."

"You know, we shouldn't stay," I tell her. "I don't want

Skye to feel uncomfortable. Let's let her process this in peace."

Nate agrees with me, and stands up, shaking Jason's hand, and then hugging Christy. "Thank you for the invitation. Maybe next time."

Jason shows us to the door. "Don't worry about Skye," he tells me gently. "She won't stay mad long."

I nod, and Nate and I drive back to the inn.

"Do you think we're making a mistake in pursuing this?" I ask as we get out and climb the front porch steps.

"Absolutely not." Nate is firm. "The guy is a monster. He needs to be prosecuted."

"If it's him," I say uncertainly.

"*Whoever* it is," he corrects himself.

I nod, and when we get inside, I find myself walking up to Leah's room once more. I sit on the bed, and look around at the bedroom of a little girl.

"We haven't changed this room for years," Nate says from the doorway.

I shake my head, my eyes welling up. "No. But she added things. Pictures and stuff."

Nate nods, and crosses the room to look at the news clippings and photos hanging on the twine stretched across the wall, hanging on little clips. Leah thought it made it look like an art studio display.

"Nothing we do is going to bring her back," he points out. "But I still think the guy should pay. Whoever it is. Do you agree?"

A lump is in my throat, heavy and thick, but I nod. "Yeah."

"Okay, good. We're in agreement. I'm gonna go for a walk on the beach to clear my head. You interested?"

I shake my head again. "No. I think I'll lie down in here for a little bit."

Nate presses a kiss to my forehead on his way to the door, and then I lie down in Leah's bed. Her pillow still smells like her, and I breathe it in. I ball the edge of it up in my fist, and I squeeze for everything I'm worth, until my fingernails cut my hand.

I fall asleep among Leah's things, and her scent, with Bo on the floor beside me.

I don't know how long it is until I wake up, only that when I open my eyes, it is dark outside. My phone is ringing.

I answer it groggily.

"Emmy," Derek says quickly. "Liam is gone. He ran away from his mom's. If you hear from him, will you let me know?"

I'm instantly awake and agreeing, and as we hang up, I am stunned in the dark.

What the hell?

CHAPTER THIRTY-FIVE

August 10

Something dripped nearby. Leah could hear it. She perked her head up, listening, but there was nothing else.

She was still alone.

She'd learned hours ago that struggling was futile. The tape was tight around her ankles and wrists, and she'd only made them sore by wiggling against it. Her mind raced a million miles per hour. *Why am I here? Who is doing this?*

On the same token, she was confident that someone would find her. Her parents would hunt to the ends of the earth for her. Of that, she was certain. She just had to survive until then.

How long did it take to starve to death? Or dehydrate?

There was a sound, all of a sudden. It sounded like an echo from down a hallway.

She froze, listening. The silence made her ears ring, but there was certainly a noise. She tried to yell, but her voice was muffled.

Then there came a laugh, low and derisive, from somewhere near her.

A man.

She protested against the duct tape, and it bit into her. It tasted like glue.

He laughed again.

"What do you think that's going to do?" he asked calmly from behind her, and she froze at the sound of his voice.

She knew him.

She struggled more frantically, and suddenly, hands were on her shoulders, and the tape was ripped off. It was harsh, it was sudden, and it hurt like hell. She wished she could rub her mouth, soothe her stinging lips, but she couldn't. Instead, she started to scream.

Ry waited patiently until she wore herself out.

"Why are you doing this?" she finally asked and her voice was hoarse and tired. "Why? I thought you loved me."

"If you loved me," he said harshly, in a tone she'd never heard before, "then you wouldn't have broken things off."

"I just asked if we could go back to the way things were before," she said in confusion. "What we were doing was wrong. I felt too guilty."

"Love shouldn't make you feel guilty," Ry said sharply. "So you didn't really love me. Did you really think you could lead me on that way and nothing would happen? I wanted you, Leah. I wanted you for so long, and I waited and waited for you. For you to become a woman. I watched you, you know. I made sure you were safe every night, that no one was disturbing you."

"You watched me?"

"Oh, yes. I stayed on the beach out of sight, in the sun, in the rain, at night. I lost my favorite sweater while I was watching over you, even."

He made it sound like it was her fault, and she swallowed hard. "I'm...sorry," she said limply.

"You should be."

He slapped the tape back on her face, and some of it got in her hair, pulling sharply. Her words were muffled again, so she stopped speaking them. It wouldn't do any good.

She was slack, her shoulders drooping.

Ry laughed.

"I'll be going now, Kitten. I'll come back a little later tonight, after you've had a chance to consider your new circumstances. You'll be giving me your first blow job, by the way. That should be fun."

She fought against the tape and he laughed again.

"Don't wear yourself out," he cautioned. "You're going to need your energy."

She froze.

"You will be a good girl and do everything I ask of you, or I swear to you, I'll bring Skye here, too. Do you want her to go through this?"

Leah immediately shakes her head.

"Good." She hears shuffling, and then it stops.

"Oh, and one other thing."

She waited.

"Everyone thinks you drowned. So no one is going to come looking for you."

She started screaming again from behind the tape, and Ry laughed as he left. She heard him walking away, then nothing more.

She was alone yet again.

CHAPTER THIRTY-SIX

September 2

Detective Keaton sits at the kitchen table, with me across from him, Nate beside him.

"Listen, I'm just going to say this," he breaks the ice bluntly. "We've looked at your daughter's blog. We've looked at the sweater you found in the sand, and the photo. The thing is, even if we tracked this man down, without your daughter's testimony, we wouldn't have any evidence. There's nothing substantial here, no paper trail. If you had a photo with a face, that would be different."

"So you're telling us that there is a predator on this island, and there's nothing you will do about it?" Nate asks slowly.

"It's not a matter of *will*, it's a matter of *can*," the detective says quietly. "I have kids in the school here. If I could figure out who it is, and then have the evidence to put him away, that would be perfect. But that's not the case."

"But Leah's blog…" I say.

"Hearsay," he says with a nod. "I don't make the laws, Emmy. I just follow them. There have been several cases I've worked on over the years where the end results weren't to my liking simply because of lack of evidence."

"What if I could find more evidence?" I ask suddenly.

He narrows his eyes. "How would you do that? By poking around? Nothing good will come of that."

I look away. The end will justify the means. I don't have to ask permission. I'll ask for forgiveness later. Isn't that the way it goes?

"I mean it, Emmy," he insists. "Don't go poking around people's lives. That's invasion of privacy. If you find something in Leah's room, by all means, show me. But that's as far as you can take it."

I don't agree to that. I think he notices, but he doesn't push it.

Nate stands up. "Well, thank you for coming out to tell us," he says curtly. He shows the detective to the door.

He leaves, and Nate and I stare at each other.

"You should probably head back to Phoenix and get back to work," I tell him quietly, moving to clear up the coffee cups. I feel him staring at me.

"Are you serious, Em? I'm not giving up. This is ridiculous." He paces for a minute. "I'm going to go look through her room again. There has to be something there."

I've already been through her room with a fine-tooth

comb, but I don't say anything. He needs to feel like he's doing something. I understand that.

I'm washing the baseboards in the den to stay busy when there's a knock on the door. With a groan, I consider not getting up off the floor to answer it. But there's a second knock, more urgent this time.

I haul myself up, and Bo beats me to the door. Oddly enough, he doesn't bark.

He knows whomever it is.

I open the door to find Liam on my porch.

I gasp, and stare at him. He's dressed in black, like always, but he's skinnier, with circles under his eyes.

"Liam! How did you get here?"

"I flew."

"I figured they'd be watching the airport," I manage to say. "Your parents are looking for you. The police, too."

He sighs. "Can I come in?"

I glance outside, as though the police will be descending any moment. "Yes. You need to come in while I call your dad."

"No." He yanks his hand away from the door. "You can't call my dad. That's what I need to talk to you about."

He's flushed, his brow furrowed, and he's very serious.

"Um. Okay," I finally say. "I'm just gonna call my ex-husband down from upstairs. Go ahead and wait at the table."

"Please don't call anyone," he pleads. "I have to talk to you about something important."

"Okay," I agree. I go to the stairs, call for Nate, and then rejoin Liam. He's fidgety and jumpy.

Nate comes down, and startles in surprise. I put a hand on his arm.

"Liam needs to talk to us about something important. He just got here."

Nate stares at me hard, but I nod slightly. *Let's give him a minute.*

Nate sits down. I join him. Together, we stare at the boy in front of us, waiting.

He blinks. "Okay, I know what you're thinking."

"I doubt it," Nate answers drily. Liam gulps.

"I know you're thinking I'm just a runaway spoiled brat. But I've got reasons."

We wait.

"Mrs. Fisher, I know you were wondering if my dad was inappropriate with Leah."

I start to interrupt him, but he continues.

"And I want you to know, I think he was. I've been digging ever since our conversation about it."

"Liam," I manage to break in. "I don't think it was your dad."

Nate's head swivels, but I ignore his stare.

"Honestly, I'm going with my gut on this one, but I don't think it's him."

"But is it just because that's what you *want* to believe?" Liam asks. "Because I've got proof."

He pulls out a crumpled paper.

I take it from him and smooth it out on the table. It's a printed-out email.

"I hacked his account," Liam says. "I sifted through, and I found this."

"It's between him and Leah," I say aloud to Nate. My ex-husband moves closer to me so we can read it together. "It was from about two months ago."

From: Lili24@Jupiter.com
To: Derek.Collins@RenproFinancial.com

Derek,
Talking to you last night was so nice. I feel like no one understands me here, and that I'm so alone. You seemed to know exactly what I was going to say before I even said it, and you really listened to me. I can't tell you how nice that was. Liam is so lucky to have you. Can we hang out again sometime soon?
Thank you again,
Leah

To: Lili24@Jupiter.com
From: Derek.Collins@RenproFinancial.com

Hi Leah,
I'm glad our chat helped. You're a great girl who just needed an ear. No need to thank me.
    I'm always available to you. You know where I live!
Best,
Derek

I read it through three times before I sit back in my seat. On the one hand, Derek didn't disclose this.

On the other, he signed it "Best, Derek."

"It sounds almost like a business email," I say uncertainly.

"Yeah, except the recipient was fifteen," Nate mutters.

Liam leans forward. "Yeah. But the weird part is, I asked my dad about Leah. I asked if he was ever alone with her, or if anything odd had ever happened, and he said no. He never said he emailed her, or that she had had some heart-to-heart with him."

"Liam, I agree it's odd, but…"

Even Nate is uncertain. Liam is shaking his head.

"Look, you don't understand. Something was going on with them. I know my dad."

"Liam, you ran away from home," I say bluntly. "For what? To come give us this? You could've just called me."

"I have to figure this out," he says stubbornly. "I have to do it in person. I owe Leah that much. I didn't step in when I should've. I left without saying goodbye. I'll never forgive myself for that."

So he feels guilty. I get that. I feel it, too.

"Liam, she knew you loved her," I say gently. "There's no need for you to feel guilty *at all*."

"What's your goal, Liam?" Nate asks directly. "You came here to confront your dad? Is that it?"

"I don't know," he answers, his cheeks red. "But I felt like whatever I need to do, it should be in person."

"Well, you'll have that opportunity," I tell him, pulling out my phone. "We've got to tell your dad that you're here."

Liam doesn't even argue. I text Derek.

He's at my door in one minute flat.

I open it, and he stalks in without a greeting.

He walks straight to his son. "What the hell are you

thinking?" he demands. "Your mom is going to have a nervous breakdown."

His vein is throbbing in his temple. I understand, though. When we couldn't find Leah... For just a minute, I'm back in that night.

Standing on the porch, while the red-and-blue lights of the Coast Guard searched the ocean. I wouldn't wish that kind of panic on my worst enemy. I was numb for two days, unable and unwilling to believe that she was just gone.

It happened so fast.

"Well, the important thing is, he's here now," I say aloud, almost without meaning to. Derek looks at me.

"Yes. He is. Go down to the house," Derek tells him. "Now." He gestures toward the door, but Liam doesn't move. Instead, he shoves the email toward his father.

"Can you tell us what this is?" Liam asks politely.

Derek grabs it, reads it, and then stares harshly at his son. "How did you get this?"

Liam doesn't answer.

"Did you break into my personal email?" Derek is incredulous, and Liam doesn't blink.

They stare each other down, until I interrupt.

"Um. You never told us that this happened," I tell him. "Why is that?"

Nate is steely faced, and Derek looks at him, then at me.

"It's completely innocent," he protests. "I didn't bring it up because I knew it might look bad. But honestly, Leah was out walking Bo, and she saw that I was up, and she stopped to chat. That's it. She lectured me on smoking, she talked about some of her issues, and that was it."

"Were you in your bungalow together?" I ask.

He shakes his head. "No. We were outside the entire time. In full view of the inn, to be honest."

"What kind of 'issues' did she talk about?" Nate asks.

Derek hesitates at that. I lift an eyebrow.

"She was talking about your divorce," he admits. "How much she hated it. How she never gets to see her dad, and how Emmy has to work so much that she never sees her either."

I flinch, and I think Nate does, too.

"To be fair, I always worked a lot, even before the divorce," I say raggedly.

Nate grasps my shoulder. "And how did you counsel her?" he asks.

Derek glances up. "I told her that divorce is tough. That I definitely know that. That I wish I could see Liam a lot more, and that I'm sure you felt the same, Nate."

"That's very true," Nate admits gruffly. "I think she knew that."

Derek doesn't answer. Instead, he eyes his son, who is still steely eyed and has his arms crossed over his chest. "Don't believe me?" he asks softly.

"I don't know what to think," Liam replies. "I just don't."

"Well, that doesn't change the fact that you're in huge trouble with your mother," Derek tells him. "Let's go."

Then he says to us, "I suppose you'll be giving this to the police?"

I don't answer, and he turns to leave.

I listen for the door closing behind them, and then I say to Nate, "What do you think?"

He sighs. "I hate to admit it, but I think you're right. I don't think it's him."

CHAPTER THIRTY-SEVEN

September 2

Skye had been sitting by herself at lunch. She couldn't bear to sit with anyone other than Leah.

Other girls eyed her and then talked about her, wondering if Skye was losing it. She'd heard their whispers. And she didn't care. They didn't know what it was like.

She ate alone, she sat alone in classes and during youth group, she no longer even bothered with makeup. She didn't want the attention of anyone. She just wanted to be left alone.

At home, Christy glanced up when she came in the door.

"Babe, how was youth group?" she asked hesitantly. Skye dumped her bag in the hall and came to get a glass of juice. She looked terrible, and Christy didn't know what to do about it. If she said something, it might make Skye even more uncomfortable. She'd talked to Jason about it, and he wasn't worried. But men weren't as perceptive as women in situations like this.

"It was fine," Skye told her.

Skye poured apple juice into a small glass and downed it in two gulps. "I've gotta go study."

She walked out, ignoring her mother's other questions.

How are you feeling?

Are you okay?

She was tired of hearing them.

She grabbed her bag again and lugged it up to the Tree House. Her mother seldom went up there. She hated climbing the stairs. She was so pissed at her mom anyway. For being willing to ruin Hutch's life on some dumb idea?

When Christy called up that she was going to the store, Skye barely answered.

Curling up in a recliner, her feet tucked under her, she tried to focus on US history. She really did. But she kept finding her thoughts drifting away...to days in the sun with Leah, laughing and joking. She'd give anything to have those days back.

She would give anything to have someone to talk to about it with. Someone who wouldn't look at her with pity, or nervously like her mother. Someone who deserved a warning.

Hesitating, she pulled out her phone. Before she could change her mind, she texted Hutch.

He was walking through the door to the Tree House ten minutes later, concern etched on his face.

He headed straight for her, kneeling down next to the

chair. He opened his arms, and she collapsed into them, crying softly.

He held her while she cried.

He didn't judge, he didn't speak. He simply patted her back and let her experience her sadness. He sat with her, and he didn't tell her it was going to be okay. In his years as a pastor, he knew better. He knew that, for her, it didn't feel like it would be.

When she finally looked up at him with a tear-streaked face, she had no more tears left to cry. She was spent.

"Your life isn't over," Hutch finally said. "I know it feels like it is, but it's not."

"Leah didn't think hers was over either," Skye answered. "She was looking forward to the school year, plotting out what she wanted to do for college. And then, all of a sudden, it was game over. She wasn't expecting that. If it can happen to her, it can happen to anyone."

Hutch nodded. "That's very true. Tomorrow isn't promised to any of us. We should always remember that, and live each day without letting fear rule us."

"Does fear rule you?" Skye asked softly. She was still in his arms, and he was still patting her back.

"Sometimes." He nodded. "It's human nature. We do what we can to overcome it, but it will always be a struggle."

"You should know something," Skye finally managed to say. "They think you were involved with Leah."

Hutch was silent, frozen, his gaze connected with Skye's. His breath seemed to hitch, and then it released.

"Who?" he rasped. "Why?"

Skye shrugged, scowling. "Because it's a witch hunt. Leah was apparently involved with someone. She didn't bother telling me about it, but there are pictures."

"Of me?" Hutch was incredulous now.

For a scant moment, Skye was startled. Shouldn't he have immediately protested, or denied it?

She shook her head slowly.

"There isn't a face," she answered. "Just inappropriate pictures."

Hutch is still. "Leah was being inappropriate with someone," he repeated, as if trying to believe it. Skye hesitated. Could she believe him?

"Apparently," she answered. "And my parents think it was you."

"But why me?" Hutch was still confounded, and Skye relaxed ever so slightly.

"They're just using deductive reasoning, I guess."

Hutch looked absolutely appalled, disgusted. The appropriate things for an innocent man to feel. Skye relaxed entirely. She knew she could trust him. She knew him far better than her parents did.

"Don't worry about any of this," Hutch told her. "I'll get it cleared up. It's fine. Everyone is grieving. No one knows what to think."

"Well, they shouldn't try to hang an innocent man," Skye bit out, in defense of her beloved pastor. He smiled.

"You're a loyal girl, Skye. But don't worry. I'll get this cleared up."

With that, he released her. She sat back in her chair, and he sat down in the seat next to her. "You know you have a lot of people who you can talk to, right? Me, your mom, your dad, Emmy. So many people love you."

"I can't really talk to Emmy," Skye told him. "It feels silly that I complain about my sadness when she lost her daughter."

"Your pain doesn't diminish hers," Hutch said. "If anything, you are kindred souls. I'm willing to bet that you could talk to Liam, too. He's grieving, as well."

Skye nodded. She knew.

"I'll be right back," she told him. "I've got to use the restroom."

She hurried down the stairs and through the kitchen.

She used the bathroom, washed her hands, and returned to the Tree House.

Hutch was shooting pool while he waited, bent over the red felt table and accurately knocking the yellow striped ball into the corner pocket.

"You look like you've had experience," Skye said.

He looked up, grinning. "There was a pool hall down the street from the seminary," he answered. "It was cheap entertainment."

They spent the rest of the afternoon playing a game of pool and talking. When Hutch left two hours later, Skye felt immensely better, as though a weight had been lifted. She didn't realize it would make her feel so much better to simply talk to someone about her pain.

As she walked Hutch out to his car, she noticed that a light was burning in the Tree House window. She'd forgotten to turn it off. After she'd hugged him goodbye and thanked him, she jogged back up to turn it off.

That's when she saw the photo on the floor, by the edge of the rug next to the chair.

Curiously, she bent to pick it up.

As she studied it, she almost dropped it.

It was a photo of Leah, her best friend, bound and gagged in a chair. Something sticky and white was splattered on the picture—she didn't want to know what it was.

Her friend looked so thin. Her eyes were blindfolded with a necktie, and the photo was black-and-white, grainy.

Was this... Oh, God. Leah had been into bondage with the guy?

She'd never imagined that Leah could be into something like that.

Why hadn't she ever confided in her? She almost felt like she'd never known Leah at all.

And why was the picture here now...after Hutch had been in this very room?

Was it Hutch? Had her parents been right?

Anxiety clenched at her gut as she tried to process.

Hutch's face was so sincere when she questioned him.

Was he really that much of a liar? Could he really be? He was a man of God, right? She was surely wrong.

But there was no other way that photo could've gotten into this room.

Chills ran down her spine as she thought of the implications of what Leah had been doing.

With a shaky sigh, she sank back into the chair, the photo in her lap. She didn't know what to do...or who to tell...or even who she could trust anymore.

CHAPTER THIRTY-EIGHT

September 2

Water dripped somewhere around her. She'd been here for so long that she'd lost count of the days. One turned into the next, and time ceased to exist.

She'd prayed to die, only to fall asleep, then wake up again each time.

It was never ending.

She knew there was water on the floor. She could feel it with her toes. The circulation in her legs felt cut off, but she could still feel the water.

Leah was terrified of Ry coming back. Never, in all the years she'd known him, had she thought he was capable of this. He had been so sweet and kind to her. Had he always had this evil streak?

She thought back to his hands on her throat that time, and how he had stalked her.

Maybe he had. She should've paid attention to her instincts earlier. She should've said something to someone.

But she didn't.

And now she was here.

Everyone must think she was dead. No one would still be looking for her. God, that must be killing her mom. Maybe her dad came. Did they have a funeral? She felt sick to her stomach at the idea of everyone mourning her, of Liam and Skye. Good lord, maybe Skye was in danger now, too. If she didn't do everything he asked of her, he would bring Skye here. She couldn't let that happen.

She waited for what seemed like hours, or days. She didn't even know. All she knew was, when he reappeared, she felt broken.

She could hear the sneer in Ry's voice, like he was mad at her, but she hadn't done anything. He asked for things, disgusting things.

She did everything he asked.

She had no choice.

When he was finished asking, and she was finished doing, he wiped the tears from her eyes. At least he hadn't raped her.

"That wasn't so bad, was it?" he asked softly. "Do you remember why you love me?"

She remained motionless.

He growled and slapped her face. Her head whipped to the side from the force of the blow.

"See what you made me do?" he raged. "This is all your fault, Leah. If only you hadn't pushed my buttons."

She remained motionless, trying not to react, even though she was terrified. Her pulse raced, her blood was ice-cold.

"I'm going to take your virginity, you know," he told her smugly. "I think I'll film it so I can watch and rewatch it over the years."

He was quiet.

"Of course, I'll have to kill you after," he added. "I can't let you live now. I hope you understand that I never wanted this. You forced me to do this. This is all your fault."

She screamed against the tape on her mouth, struggling against the binding.

"Do you want to know when that will be?" he asked her sadly. She stilled, waiting, her hair ratted and her hands raw.

"It will be soon," he promised. "Very soon."

And then he left her alone.

CHAPTER THIRTY-NINE

September 3

The inn is too confining.

I walk along the beach for over a mile.

It's chilly today, and the sun is behind the clouds. It's as though it understands that I can't be cheerful. I am gray, like my mood.

I don't want to talk to anyone, I don't want to listen. I just want to hear the ocean, and feel close to my daughter.

This is what she did when she was overwhelmed. She connected to the ocean. This is where she came.

I sit on the damp sand, unconcerned that it soaks into my shorts. I lift my face and smell the salt and close my eyes. If I focus hard enough, I can feel Leah here.

I love you, Mama, she'd say. *I made a mistake. Don't judge me for it.*

I don't judge you, babe, I'd answer. *I just want to know what happened.*

You don't. She would turn to me, and her steel-gray eyes would stare into mine. *Trust me, you don't.*

I'm not sure that she's not right.

As I get further and further into this, I dread finding out the truth. I dread finding out who defiled my daughter, and what exactly he did with her.

But I also don't think I can live with not knowing. It feels like an insult to her memory.

"I'm sorry," I whisper to my daughter. The sea breeze grabs my words and carries them over the water.

For what? she would whisper back. I can almost feel her by my ear.

"I don't know," I answer aloud.

"Emmy!" a voice calls. I turn to find two figures walking toward me on the sand. I squint my eyes. It's Liam and a girl.

When they draw closer, I see it's Amber Fitzgerald. My head perks up. Maybe she remembered something.

"Emmy," Liam calls again. This time, I greet them.

Amber looks at me warily, and I'm probably doing the same to her. I check myself, putting on a blank pleasant face. I can't help but be annoyed with her, for reading my daughter's blog and knowing someone was in trouble, but not doing anything about it. I, of course, can't put that kind of guilt onto a teenager.

"Hey, guys," I say instead.

"Amber has something you might find interesting,"

Liam tells me. "She texted me about it this morning and, once she found out I was in town, brought it over."

This is intriguing. I turn to her and she's hesitant, nervous.

"I'm sorry," she says slowly. "I didn't know if you'd want to see it. Especially after you found her blog posts, and...I just didn't know what to do with it."

I wait, and she produces a picture.

Another damned picture.

I blink hard when I see the grainy, slightly unclear photo. It's my daughter, sitting in a chair, restrained.

The photo is shadowy, and it's clear that she didn't take it. If she had, it would be good. Instead, it's low quality and blurry. But I can see that it's definitely Leah.

She has the same tie wrapped around her eyes, the ugly one with shamrocks.

I can't tell where she was, because the photo is too grainy, too dark.

I squeeze my eyes closed. Why would she have allowed herself to be drawn into that? She always said she was a feminist. To be degraded like that... Someone had to have done some smooth talking to convince her.

Or she was very vulnerable.

I swallow hard.

"Where did you find this?" I manage to ask.

"In the girls' room at school," she says quietly. "Lying on the sink."

"What?" I'm confused. "How?"

Who would've had this at the school?

"I don't know who had it," she said, as if anticipating

my next question. "I'm sorry. I didn't really know what to do with it, but I didn't want to leave it there."

"You didn't even like Leah," I remind her, a little bitterly, too bitterly. That doesn't even matter now.

She looks stricken. "No. But no one deserves to be thought of like…this…after they're gone." She glances at the photograph painfully. "I'm really sorry, Mrs. Fisher. I should've called the police." She seems genuine, and I think I might believe her.

"We should call the police and give them this picture," Liam tells me firmly. His mouth is set, he's determined. I glance at him.

"I will. Shouldn't you be going back to the city? You've got school."

"I'm staying with my dad," he tells me. "I want to. I've got to figure this all out."

"You don't have to change schools for this," I say immediately. "The police will—"

"The police won't," he answers. "You know it."

"*I* will," I amend.

"And I'll help." He stares at me for a moment, and then he and Amber turn around and walk away. She glances over her shoulder once, and then they're gone.

I still have the photo in my hand, and I stare at it once more.

My daughter's slender shoulders are slumped, dejected. Her head is dropped. She's dressed only in a sports bra and panties… I suck in a breath and force myself to keep looking.

My eyes freeze on the image.

That isn't a sports bra.

That's a swimsuit top. The same red top she was wearing the night she drowned.

Liam said she was upset that night. Is this the reason why? Was she bound and gagged and it scared her? Is this the last photograph ever taken of her alive?

I clutch it to my chest, and my heart pounds against it.

I take it back with me to the house, and I sit at the dining room table, putting it along with the other things I'd found. The anklet from Derek's bungalow, the feather from the car, the cardigan with the first photo, and now this picture.

They all mock me, staring at me with their secrets.

Nate comes in and presses coffee into my hands, and I tell him about my new finding.

He immediately picks up the phone and calls the detective. He's firm, he's insistent.

"He'll be here soon," he promises me when he hangs up.

We wait at the table, and he reaches over to hold my hand.

"It will be okay," he assures me. I do a double take.

"Yeah? What about this is okay?"

"You know what I mean. We're going to figure this out, and then you will get back to your life and you will put this behind you. You're strong, Emmy. You're going to be fine."

"We'll never get over losing Leah," I announce incredulously.

"No. But every day, we'll figure out how to handle it

better. That's what you do. You handle things. I'm not so good at it, myself."

It's now that I notice how tired my ex-husband looks. He's lost weight, too, and he seems so tired, like he's aged five years.

"You don't look good," I say suddenly. He smiles wryly.

"Gee, thanks."

"You know what I mean. You need to start taking better care of yourself. You know, like you told me."

"And did you listen?" Nate lifts an eyebrow.

"I plead the fifth." I sigh.

"Yeah, it's easier said than done. I know."

Bo whimpers next to me, and I look down, scratching his ears. He drools on the floor, and with a sigh, I get up to grab a paper towel.

It's when I'm wiping at the floor that I think of it. How could I have forgotten?

My hand lingers on the floor, and I stiffen.

Nate glances at me. "What is it?"

I jump up and run for Leah's bedroom. I hear Nate following me, but I don't look back. I burst into her bedroom, and drop to my knees next to her window seat.

"This has a hidden compartment," I tell him, feeling for my fingers to loosen the board. "It's not meant to, but the board comes off and on. Leah found it years ago and she told me that if we ever had a home invasion, that's where she would hide. I haven't thought about it in years."

My fingers find the groove and I pop the board out. It falls away, and we're left staring into the most convenient hiding place a girl could have…right next to her own bed.

CHAPTER FORTY

September 3

Skye opened her eyes, staring at her ceiling.

The picture she'd found yesterday was unsettling, and she was even more uneasy now that she'd misplaced it. Her fingers tapped, tapped, tapped on her headboard, and she listened in the darkness.

She'd taken it to school, intent on going to see the principal and giving him the picture. He'd surely know what to do with it...to get it to the police so they could question Hutch.

But then...she'd lost it.

And now, she didn't know what she'd do.

All she knew was that she felt such a jagged hole in her heart. She'd trusted Hutch. She thought he was good, and he wasn't. She felt utterly betrayed.

She knew she didn't have the evidence anymore, but still. She could do *something*. She picked up her phone and texted her youth pastor, regardless of the late hour.

I know what you were doing with Leah.

She pressed Send, and there was no going back.
He answered almost immediately.

Skye? What are you talking about?

I saw the picture you left in my house, you monster, she answered. You were having sex with Leah. With a minor. With someone in your youth group. It's wrong. And when I tell everyone...

Her phone started ringing immediately. It was Hutch.

Skye let it ring and ring, and then go to voice mail. There was no way she was answering that. She was safe here, in her house, and tomorrow, she'd tell the world.

Skye, I don't know what you're talking about, but pick up your phone. If you found a picture of Leah, the police need to know.

It wasn't me, he added. I would never do something like that.

Never.

Isn't that what anyone would say when they've been caught? she asked. I don't believe you.

You can trust me. I'll call the police myself and let them know that you might have something they want to see. I want to do everything I can to help. Leah deserves that.

The beginnings of doubt etched away at Skye. She did think that Hutch was a good man. Could she really have been so wrong? She'd been with Leah and Hutch together many times, and she'd never caught even a bad vibe that something had been wrong, or off.

But there had been a few other times, with someone else, when something hadn't felt right.

A touch that lingered, some stares that had lasted too long. She'd always explained it away to herself and never allowed herself to truly question it because the very notion was just too...sick.

But Leah deserved for her to examine it.

It was possibly the very last thing she could do for her best friend.

Her mother was sleeping. She should hear tiny snores coming from down the hall. Her father was out late again, which was for the best. He was a light sleeper and would hear her poking around.

She crept out of bed, down the hall, and through her parents' bedroom into their closet. Using her phone as her light, she sifted through her father's ties. She didn't see it.

The shamrock tie that she'd given to him last year for Christmas. He was a Notre Dame fan, and she knew he'd love it.

It was the same tie that was wrapped around Leah's eyes in the photo. She'd bet her life on it.

She kept digging, and kept coming up with nothing.

Where the hell is it?

It wasn't here.

She rocked back and leaned against the drawers, resting her head on a handle, thumping it against the metal as she thought. Where would it be?

Her gut told her to keep looking.

Turning, she pulled open the sock and underwear drawers, rifling through them.

Nothing.

The tie wasn't here. Maybe she'd been wrong.

With a sigh, she gave up and tiptoed back out. Her mother was still snoring, undisturbed.

She quietly walked down the hall and paused. Instead of returning to her room, she continued down the hall to her father's office door.

She turned the handle to find that it was locked.

It was never locked.

A bad feeling was building in her chest, like an avalanche waiting to happen.

She remembered something. The locks in her house all used the same weird straight-looking key. She had one on the doorjamb over her room.

She rushed to get it, reaching up on her toes, feeling with her hand. She grabbed it and ran back, shoving it into her father's lock.

It turned, and the door opened.

There was a lamp on the desk, and she turned it on as she opened up drawers, sifting through them. She didn't find the tie, or anything else suspicious. She was almost feeling stupid as she finally sat in his chair and stared out the windows.

What exactly had she been suspecting her father of? Of having an affair with Leah? That was ridiculous. He and her mother had a great relationship. They never fought, they were always laughing together. What had made her doubt that?

She was getting paranoid, or maybe her grief was getting to her. Maybe she even needed medication, or something.

As she was getting up, she bumped his keyboard, and his computer came to life.

Stunned, she found herself staring at what seemed to be video footage from a surveillance camera...grainy images like the photo she had found yesterday. Only the footage appeared to be live.

It seemed to be in some sort of stark stone room, and there was someone sitting in a chair, the hands and feet bound. Long dark hair fell around the face, but Skye would know her best friend anywhere.

It was Leah.

Confused, she squinted at the numbers on the footage. The date, the time. It was a live feed, happening right this minute...only that was impossible.

Leah was dead.

But there she was, sitting in a swimsuit on a chair with her father's tie around her eyes. She was shivering, but she was alive...almost a full month later.

Leah was alive.

She sucked in her breath and leaped to her feet, spinning to run from the room. Instead, she spun into her father's chest.

He grabbed her arms, his thumbs biting into her flesh.

"What are you doing in here?"

She stuttered, "Looking for... There was a noise..."

His gaze touched on the screen over her shoulder. "I see."

She was silent, and his eyes were hard.

"Now what am I going to do?" he asked her. "You've seen this. I can't just let that go. Why did you have to do this, Skye?"

"Is that Leah?" she asked unnecessarily. She knew it was.

Jason stared at her, unflinching, unreacting.

"You've had her this whole time?" Skye's pulse was bounding now, an erratic cadence, and her feet were frozen in place. What should she do?

"You don't know anything," he told her coldly, and she'd never heard him use that tone before. It was almost emotionless. "You don't understand."

"Were you having an affair with Leah?" she asked bluntly. "It's an easy question."

"It's not an easy answer," he said stiffly.

"Is Leah alive?" she asked, her voice shaking. "Please, Dad. Tell me the truth."

He yanked her toward the door in long strides. "You can see for yourself," he told her, and dragged her out the front door and tossed her into the passenger seat of his car. She should've run. As soon as the car took off, speeding down the road, she realized her mistake.

Now the doors were locked, and her father was being erratic.

The car wove dangerously along the coastal highway, and she pleaded with him to stop. He ignored her.

"You asked for answers," he reminded her. "Now you're getting them."

He slammed the car into Park a few minutes later when they were parked on the bluffs, overlooking the sea. She recognized the place.

When he dragged her down the trails to the shore, she fought at him.

"No," she begged him. "Please, Daddy."

"You wanted this. You wanted to know."

He pulled her into the catacombs, and down the long, wet corridor. When they reached the end, it opened into a wet, dark room.

They burst into it, and Leah was suddenly there.

"Leah!" Skye exclaimed, and it was surreal.

She thought her best friend was dead. She had grieved her. She had cried. And now, here Leah was, struggling against duct tape restraints, covered in filth.

Alive.

"How could you do this?" she asked her father. He tossed her into the room, and she slammed into the wall.

Leah struggled so hard that her chair toppled over.

Jason allowed her to lay on the floor, her hair soaking up the dirty water. He grabbed a roll of duct tape and taped his daughter's hands and feet, too.

"Why are you doing this?" she asked him, tears streaming down her face. He didn't answer. He just slapped a piece of tape on her mouth, and left the two girls alone.

CHAPTER FORTY-ONE

September 3

Jason's blood boiled as he got back into his car and the engine roared to life. This wasn't meant to happen. Everything was spinning out of control, and he wasn't sure what to do about it.

Now his own daughter was down in that fucking hole, and what was he going to do about that? Kill them both? The idea was neither pleasing nor displeasing. It just was.

He'd long suspected that he might be a psychopath.

When he was a teenager, he realized that he didn't have sympathy for things. He'd quickly learned to pretend that he did. He didn't have attachment to anything; it was like he was missing some sort of sensitivity chip. He pretended to be normal, though. To love, and to be happy, and to act sad when the situation demanded.

There was only one thing he'd ever loved, one person, and to this day, he wasn't sure if he'd actually loved her, or if he'd simply loved how she'd made him feel. When Lola Casey had set her sights on him when he was only twelve years old, it had been the best day of his life.

He remembered it like it was yesterday.

He'd been at the pier with his friends, fishing off the edge, their feet dangling. Lola had come up the steps in her red dress, hunting for her daughter, for Emmy.

Her lips were fire-engine red, her full hips were swaying, and her eyes had widened when she'd seen him.

He'd hit a growth spurt that summer. He'd come into his own all of a sudden, and he knew he was handsome. He knew he would be a knockout someday, a lady-killer.

She'd whispered that very thing into his ear a few nights later when she'd taken his virginity in the very place he was holding Leah and Skye now. He'd plunged into her hungrily and she'd laughed when he came within twenty seconds. He was embarrassed, and then angry at her laughter, even as she'd stroked his back.

"It's okay," she'd said. "It's always that way your first time. Rest a minute, and we'll do it again."

They did, and that time he'd lasted much longer.

They'd met in the catacombs twice a week for most of that summer, and then one day she didn't show up. He'd walked back to town, where he saw her in the café, sitting at a table with a man her own age. She was flirting and twirling her dark hair, her lips as red and full as cherries.

She'd seen him at that moment, and her eyes had met his, and hers sparkled. She deliberately looked away, back at the other man, and Jason had known right then that she was done with him. She'd used him and dropped him when she was done, like a piece of dirty laundry.

He seethed and seethed, becoming angry and distant to everyone close to him.

He'd begun spying on her, then. On Lola.

He'd watched her coming and going, and he saw exactly what she was like. She was a dick-tease. She led men on, right and left—married men, single men, older men, younger. It seemed to him like she was trying to fill some empty hole inside herself. He recognized that need. He felt it sometimes, too.

So one night he followed Lola out to the pier after one of her many dates. She was alone, and had a bottle of whiskey and a cigarette dangling from her slender fingers.

When she saw him, she laughed in that husky voice she had.

"Whatcha doing here, kid? Didn't you get your fill of me?"

Her breasts were straining against the fabric of her red shirt. He was mesmerized and remembered when those nipples had been in his mouth. He'd hardened instantly, and she noticed, a grin forming.

"Look at you, kid," she'd said, taking an elegant puff of her cigarette. "That's what I love about your age. You're always ready."

He smiled, thinking that she was going to fuck him again, right there on the pier. The idea was exciting and completely arousing. He was hard as a rock.

But then she laughed again.

"But we're done, kid," she'd said instead. "Find someone your own age. I just wanted to see what it was like to be with a virgin. And, Jason Ryan Hayden, you're my daughter's age, for God's sake. I can't be with you anymore."

He saw red. He was humiliated, disappointed, and enraged. He didn't even know what happened next, but the next thing he knew, he was alone on the pier.

The next morning, Lola Casey's body washed ashore. Everyone said she'd committed suicide.

He knew that wasn't true. He didn't remember the specifics because his rage had blinded him, but he knew he'd killed her. He felt it in his heart, and it was a place of no return.

He also knew now that he was capable of more than he'd ever dreamed. He could take care of business when he had to, and he'd never get out of control again.

He lived up to that promise until he'd seen Emmy's daughter.

He first saw her in kindergarten, and he knew as far back as then that she'd be a stunner.

He'd watched her grow up and by junior high, she looked like a dead ringer for Lola Casey. She'd set his blood on fire even then, but he was patient and waited.

It was this past year, when she started responding to his overtures, that his patience paid off.

Soon, he'd take her virginity and dispose of her like he'd disposed of her grandmother.

The problem now was what to do with his own daughter?

CHAPTER FORTY-TWO

September 3

Emmy's hands tremble as she pulls the secret phone out of the cubby.

"What the fuck?" Nate breathes next to her.

She powers up Leah's phone, and it comes to life.

She clicks immediately into the text messages.

They were from only one person.

Her daughter referred to him as Ry, and they said salacious things to each other, wildly inappropriate things, led by Ry.

There are photos...of their daughter naked, and Nate looks away.

"Jesus," he mutters.

Emmy steels her heart. She keeps looking.

There are more pictures, of a hard penis, and a thread

of texts with him telling Leah what he wanted her to do with it.

She gulps.

There are pictures of their limbs intertwined, and even a picture of his penis in her daughter's face.

"Son of a bitch, who is this guy?" she murmurs frantically. There are more pictures of his penis, of her daughter's breasts, of his hands on her breasts, squeezed so tightly her skin was red.

Emmy's stomach is rolling; she feels she can't breathe.

She hands the phone to Nate and sits on the bed, arching her back to open up her airway.

"Focus on the room, Emmy," he tells her. "Focus on the colors. Tell me what you see."

She lists off pieces of furniture, and shoes.

The room spins, but she manages to calm herself, to center herself by focusing on the tangible objects around her.

Finally, she exhales.

"I don't think I can keep doing this," she tells him. "Let's take that phone to the police and let them figure it out. I can't look at another picture. It's killing me, Nate."

He nods. "I know, honey. Take a few minutes, and we'll go. I'll go if you want. Or I can go alone."

"Thank you."

He reaches over to grasp her hand, and for the hundredth time this week, she wonders why they ever got divorced.

"You've always been my rock," she whispers. "I've always loved you, Nate."

"I've always loved you, too, Emmy."

He hugs her tight, and he smells so good.

She never felt whole without him. She never had.

She tells him so, and he agrees.

"I've tried, too, Em," he says. "But I haven't either. You're a part of me. I don't want to be without you. We can weather this storm together, can't we? You and me."

She nods and tears stream down her face.

He holds her tight, and finally, he pulls away.

"I'm going to take the phone to the detective, okay?"

She nods agreement.

"And then I'll come straight back."

She nods again.

He gets up, clutching the phone in his hand. Against his will, he finds himself looking at it as he rushes down the stairs.

He freezes when he sees the face.

"Emmy!" he calls, his voice wooden.

"Yes?" She appears in the doorway.

He turns the phone around so she can see.

Emmy gasps as she looks into the face of Skye's father, Jason Hayden.

CHAPTER FORTY-THREE

September 3

In his anger and haste, her father had made the mistake of taping Skye's hands in front of her. Skye lifted them and managed to pull the tape off her mouth. She rolled to the wall and, using it as a brace, she was able to stagger to her feet.

The cavern smelled of excrement and the tang of urine. She didn't want to breathe it in, but she had no choice.

Hopping on uneven legs, she reached Leah and pulled the tape off her mouth and the necktie off her eyes. Then she lost her balance and fell to the floor. Her head hit the stone, but she shook it off.

"Leah, are you okay?" she said, and her lips stung from the tape.

Leah nodded. "I'm okay. I'm so sorry, Skye."

Her voice was husky, thick. She hadn't spoken in weeks.

Skye was able to study her now. Leah was so thin that her ribs protruded from her back. "Has he been feeding you?"

"Only a little," Leah said. "Every few days. Mostly water."

And semen. She didn't mention that.

"My father is a monster," Skye said aloud. "How could I not know that?"

"No one knew it," Leah answered bitterly. "He hid it well."

"How did you… I mean, what happened?"

Leah shrugged sadly, her shoulder painfully bony. "It happened so fast. I don't know. I'm sorry. Our relationship was sick, and I can't believe I allowed myself to be drawn in… It wasn't me. I mean, it wasn't like me."

"Why didn't you tell me?" Skye asked, and her voice was shredded with hurt. Leah flinched.

"Because he's your dad," she answered simply. "Skye, he said he was going to kill me. We've got to get out of here."

They look around, at the stone walls and then at each other, helpless.

"Can you try to get my hands free?" Leah asked. "Maybe we can get the tape off and run."

Skye rolled to the back of the chair, shoving with her feet. As she looked at the tape that looped thickly around Leah's ankles, her heart sank. "There's a lot," she said aloud.

"Just try," Leah urged her. "Your dad will be back."

Skye tugged at the tape, inching the edge farther and

farther back. It was difficult with her own hands bound, and an achingly slow process.

"How's my mom?" Leah asked as Skye worked.

Skye was silent.

"Skye?" Leah urged.

"She's grieving," Skye finally said. "She's lost without you, actually. She came to talk to youth group…we had a memorial service. God. I can't believe you're here. And you've been here this whole time. You're alive. You're really alive."

"It's okay," Leah said quietly. "You didn't know. He meant to do it this way. He didn't want anyone to find me."

"How'd my father do it?" Skye asked. "We thought you drowned. The Coast Guard said there was a shark…"

"I was floating on my board," Leah said, remembering. "Something rammed into me, and I thought it was a shark, too, honestly. There was a sharp pain in my head. So he must've knocked me out somehow. He was waiting for me. I had texted him earlier and told him I couldn't see him anymore…that it was wrong. I think he came to my house, and when he saw me outside, he came for me. I didn't see him coming."

She squeezed her eyes closed, but she was so dehydrated that tears couldn't form. Her throat was hot and thick.

"This serves me right," she continued. "I deserve this. I can't believe what I did, Skye. You must hate me."

Skye paused. "I don't know what I feel," she said honestly. "I love you. You're my best friend. I don't know what happened, and I don't know if I want to think about it. What I do know is, I hate my father. I can't understand how he could be so sick."

"I hate him, too," Leah admitted.

"What has he done to you?"

Leah's mouth pressed together. "I can't tell you," she managed to say. "You can't know. You'll never look at me the same."

Skye focused on the tape again, her hands shaking. "I'm sorry, Leah," she said raggedly. "I'm so, so sorry."

"So my mom's not doing too good?" Leah continued, changing the subject and biting at her lip. Everything hurt. Her face, her hands, her legs. Her stomach stopped aching from hunger days ago. That couldn't be a good sign.

"She's struggling," Skye admitted. "But she's okay. Your dad is in town right now."

"He is?" Leah was surprised. "Why?"

"To help your mom, I guess. She knows that something bad was going on with you. She was trying to figure out who you were involved with. She found your blog…"

"Oh, God." Leah was stricken.

"Yeah."

"Keep working the binding," Leah told her. "We've got to get out of here." She looked around. "I had no idea where I was this whole time. I should've guessed."

"How could you know?" Skye said, working on the tape as best she could.

"The sound."

Beyond them, outside of the stone, the ocean crashed relentlessly against the shore.

CHAPTER FORTY-FOUR

September 3

Liam and Derek paced on the beach, keeping an eye on the big house on the shore.

"The detective was just there," Liam told Derek. "Something is going on."

Derek nodded. Something was going on, and Emmy's ex-husband was there to help, instead of him. He didn't know how he felt about that. After his own ex-wife had been unfaithful, he didn't think he was in any position to be with a woman who was as close to her ex as Emmy was to Nate. He would have liked to believe he could do it, but he didn't think he could.

"I'm glad you're here," Derek told Liam. "I know you're probably just moving here to help figure out what was going on with Leah, but I'm still glad you're here."

"And I'm glad you weren't part of it," Liam said honestly. Derek was startled.

"So, you believe me now?"

Liam nodded. "I don't think I ever really thought you would do something like that, but everything got muddled up…and…"

"Don't worry about it," Derek said quickly.

They heard shouting, and both turned at the same time. Emmy stood on the porch of the Black Dolphin, waving her arms to get their attention. They rushed to her, anxious to see what was happening.

"Have you seen Skye?" Emmy said to Liam.

He shook his head. "No."

"Have you heard from her today? A text, anything?"

He shook his head, and Emmy bit her lip. She pulled out her phone and texted someone.

"What's wrong, Emmy?" Derek asked quickly. Emmy was clearly upset, clearly anxious.

"It was Jason Hayden," Emmy said bluntly. "He was the one who molested my daughter. And now Skye isn't home. No one knows where she is."

"Jesus," Derek said. "Jason Hayden? I left him a voice mail…to find me a house. I'm speechless."

"Is Skye in danger?" Liam asked. "Would he hurt his own daughter?"

"We don't know," Emmy said honestly. "We don't know what's going on in his mind. Apparently, no one ever really knew him at all. The police are trying to find him right now."

★ ★ ★

Across the island, Jason rushed into his garage and dug in his locked tool chest. He kept it locked for a reason. Triumphantly, he pulled out his Glock 9mm, sticking it in the waistband of his pants. Before anyone could see him, he got back into his car and peeled out, anxious to get back to the catacombs.

He sped through town, and was quickly on the coastal highway. Glancing down, he laid the pistol on the seat next to him. When he looked back up, there were red-and-blue lights in the rearview mirror.

"Son of a bitch," he mumbled, looking down at his speedometer. He wasn't speeding. Confused, he looked up to find a police car blocking the road in front of him, as well.

Son of a bitch.

They know.

He knew it in his gut. He pulled the gun onto his lap, as yet another police car fell into place behind him.

They definitely know.

He pulled off to the side of the road and stepped out of the car, his mind reeling.

A cop stood behind his open car door and yelled into a megaphone.

"Lower your weapon!"

Jason stood still, the gun dangling in his hand.

His gaze darted around his periphery, checking his options. He could run, but he wouldn't get far. They knew his name now.

They knew what he'd done.

"Lower your weapon!" the officer shouted again, louder this time.

He held it, without raising or lowering it.

"Where is your daughter?" the police officer yelled.

He thought of Skye and Leah, bound in the stone room by the sea. *They'll die there together.* His path forward was clear. The knowledge of where they were would die with him. No one would find them until it was too late.

He didn't have any compunction or guilt.

"You'll never find them."

He raised his gun, and amid the rapid firing of the policemen around him, he shot himself in the mouth. The back of his head exploded onto the car behind him in a splatter of crimson and gray.

He was dead instantly.

From behind the policemen, his wife, Christy, screamed, and someone had to restrain her. "Where's my daughter?" she screamed. "What has he done?"

No one knew the answer.

CHAPTER FORTY-FIVE

September 3

Christy rests on the sofa in the Hayden home while Nate, Derek, Hutch, and Liam gather in the kitchen around the table. I make chamomile tea to take back in to Christy, and the men watch me nervously.

"Where should we look for Skye?" Liam asks, anxious to be doing something. It has been two hours since the police sent us back here, and we haven't heard anything since.

"We should stay here in case she comes home," I tell them, dunking the tea bags. My hands are shaking, though. I know this mother's pain. I've been there.

"I can go look," Liam insists. "We don't all need to be here. Dad and I can go."

"The police told us to come here," Derek says hesitantly. Liam stares at him.

"They also never took Emmy seriously when she went to them with her concerns about Leah and…Jason."

He says the name aloud, reluctantly. No one has said it since Jason killed himself in the street.

Everyone is still shell-shocked, maybe me most of all. When I think of all the times I allowed Leah to spend the night in this house, that close to a pedophile…it chills my blood. It reminds me that you can never truly know someone.

"Did he ever act strangely in front of you?" I ask Liam. I know he hadn't been around him a lot, but he was still there some. Liam shakes his head.

"Not at all. I never would've known."

"Me either." Christy speaks from the doorway, pale and shaky. "I never knew."

"Come on…let's get back in and lie down," I tell her, rushing to support her elbow. But she yanks away angrily.

"Don't touch me!"

My head rears back, and Nate stands up. "Your daughter was carrying on with my husband," Christy spits out. "Now he's dead. I don't want you here."

"You shouldn't be alone," I tell her quietly, trying to calm her. "You're upset. This isn't my fault."

"No?" Christy shrieks. "My baby is gone. *Your* daughter caused all of this. If she hadn't chased after Jason, none of this would've happened. I saw the way she traipsed around here in her sports bra and shorts. She was begging for attention."

She collapses into a crying heap and I have to restrain

myself. I look pleadingly at Nate, and he and Hutch help her back to the living room. Liam awkwardly trails behind.

"She's wrong," Derek tells me. "This isn't your fault."

"No, it isn't," I agree. "I lost my daughter, too. Her husband was to blame. He was the adult. My Leah was a minor. What he did was criminal. Christy just can't process it yet. She needs to blame me instead."

"You're very understanding," he observes.

I shake my head. "No. I just know her pain. And I didn't have anyone to blame but myself. Until now."

Now I have a face to focus on. Jason Hayden's.

If only I was there to see him blow his brains out. That would've been gratifying.

"Are you and your ex getting back together?" Derek asks me quietly, his eyes knowing.

My hands still. "I don't know," I answer honestly.

He nods. "Okay. That's fair."

"You're a great guy," I rush to say, but he holds up a hand, rolling his eyes.

"Oh, God. Please don't," he says quickly.

I smile. "Okay. But truly, you are. I'm sorry I doubted you."

"It's okay," he assures me. "I would've done the same in your shoes."

I don't know if that's true, but I can't feel guilty. I have to look at all the options.

"Does knowing help?" he asks, his hand on my shoulder. I think about that.

I think about my baby, her innocence gone...all of the

pictures I've seen, the words I've read…and now, to have a face to put with the crime.

"I don't know," I answer honestly. "It helps that he's dead. Is that terrible?"

"*I* don't think so," he says. "I don't blame you at all." He takes the teacup from me. "I'll take this to her. Why don't you go get some air? Your cheeks are flushed."

I nod and let him take it. Then I head out the back door, stand on their porch, and listen to the ocean.

Their private beach abutts their house, and it is only steps until I am standing in the sand, staring at the outline of the moon. It is only early evening, so it isn't fully dark, but it's dark enough to feel the chill of the water. I gather my sweater more tightly around my shoulders.

I feel my daughter out there.

In the middle of the chaos, among the white noise and the chatter, there is a stillness there, a safe space. It is the eye of the storm where my grief is silent, and the world no longer speaks to me. This is where I hear her. On the beach, my feet in the sand.

This is where she loved to be.

"I miss you," I whisper. I imagine my words being carried on the breeze, up to Heaven where she can hear them. "I miss you so much."

Somewhere in my periphery, I see movement, and I shift my gaze to the beach, a few hundred yards away. A couple walks, one of their arms wrapped around the other. For a minute, I watch them, thinking they are lovers. Lovers come here often.

But the closer they get, the more I can see that one is

holding the other up. One's legs are dragging in the sand. And they are both women.

Something…

Something…

Something…is familiar.

It can't be.

It can't be.

My heart seems to freeze, and I find myself walking toward them, then running. I don't know why, only instincts tell me I should.

I am only a few feet away when I see who they are.

Leah and Skye.

My daughter is hanging on to Skye, her legs weak. She is practically a skeleton, sallow and gray, but her eyes move, shifting up to mine, and that is when she smiles a haunting, slow smile, And the impossible is standing before me.

My heart…

My heart.

It pounds in disbelief.

Leah is alive.

Disbelief floods through me, but she says, "Mom, it's really me."

I grab her to me, and her bones are so fragile, her body so thin. She smells terrible, but her heart beats against my own. I am shocked. Overwhelmed. Confused.

"Oh, my God, oh, my God," I keep repeating. Leah can't stand up on her own. I have to hold her up. "Is this real? Where have you been?"

"In the catacombs," Skye tells me. "My father took me

there, too. He was holding us there. We've got to call the police. They've got to get him."

I freeze, my arms full of my daughter, and I stare at Skye, her best friend. She sees the look in my eye, and she blinks.

"They have him already?"

I don't know what to say.

"Is he dead?" she asks quietly.

I nod.

"Good," she answers.

Then she helps me hold Leah up, and together, we walk into the house.

CHAPTER FORTY-SIX

September 4

It's been a full twenty-four hours since Leah and Skye walked up the beach, alive but not well.

Leah has been in the hospital ever since for extreme dehydration. Nate and I haven't left her side. Liam has been here, too. Holding her hand, getting her ice chips. He looks at her with tenderness, even though she flinches at his touch. After what she's been through, it's expected.

I'm still in shock that my daughter is alive…that she'd been alive the whole time and I didn't know it. I could've been searching for her, if only I had known.

If only.

Damn those words.

From out in the hallway, I can hear the commotion of

the hospital…beeps and squeaks and the intercom. But in here, in this room, the three of us are an island.

Nate squeezes my hand. Leah is sleeping peacefully, and she already looks better. The IV that feeds her fluid has given her color.

"She's okay," he tells me, for the hundredth time today. "She's okay."

I nod, unable to speak. I feel as though if I do, I might jinx it and it won't be real.

My daughter is alive. My life has meaning again.

"Mom." Leah opens her eyes. I grab her hand, and it's cold. I rub it to warm it up, careful not to bump her IV line.

"Yes, baby?"

"I'm sorry," she says yet again. She's been apologizing since last night. We took her in the house, wrapped her in a blanket, and I held her until the ambulance came. She apologized the entire time. She's been asleep almost the entire time ever since, thanks to sedatives administered in the IV.

"I'm so happy you're okay," I answer. "That's all that matters."

"Is Skye okay?" Leah asks, her eyes darting around the room. Her father nods.

"Yes, honey. She's good. Everything is going to be all right."

"Where's Liam?"

"He's been here for hours," I tell her. "Derek made him go home and shower. He's been right here, sitting next to the bed, even when you were sleeping."

She nods, apparently happy to hear that.

"I thought he'd hate me now," she whispers, and her eyelashes are black smudges on her cheek.

"Oh, honey." I shake my head. "He could never hate you. You were taken advantage of."

"I knew what I was doing, at least in the beginning," she sniffs. "I just didn't realize what the consequences would be. I was really stupid, Mom. So stupid. Just like Grandma Lola."

"You are *not* your grandma Lola," I tell her adamantly.

"Listen to me," her father tells her, pulling her into his arms, IV tubes and all. "You are a young girl. You had no idea what this would turn out to be. You made a bad choice. We all make those sometimes. You'll learn from this, and you'll move forward. That man was evil. He was a predator, plain and simple. He said all the things he knew you needed to hear. He planned it all. He orchestrated everything. Make no mistake about that."

Tears streak down her cheeks, but it's okay. It means she's hydrated now. Before, she was almost wrinkled from lack of fluid.

"We love you," he says. "We always have, we always will. No matter what. We'll get past this, honey. You, me, Mom. All of us."

"Will you stay?" She looks up at her dad. "Will you stay here with us now?"

He pauses, and looks at me. "I'll do anything for you and your mom. I made some bad choices, too. My career isn't the most important thing. You guys are."

A knot forms in my throat and while he's holding Leah,

I notice something I hadn't noticed before, the entire time he's been here.

He's still wearing his wedding ring.

My own eyes fill with tears at the discovery as he pulls me in with his other arm. The three of us are huddled together when the doctor comes in minutes later. He clears his throat, and I wipe my eyes as I step back.

"Leah, how are you feeling?" he asks my daughter, coming in to check her vital signs.

She nods. "I feel much better."

"Good." Then he turns to Nate and me. "I think she's well enough to go home," he tells us. "She needs rest and a calm environment, of course. And there will be a counselor getting into contact with you for aftercare."

I nod immediately. "Of course."

He leaves to get the paperwork ready and we all stare at each other.

"Ready to go home?" I ask her.

She nods eagerly.

Two hours later, we walk up the steps to the inn.

Bo sees her from across the living room, and without hesitation, he barrels toward her, as though he knew all along she would come back.

He'd been waiting, after all.

She squats down and loves on him, hugging him around the neck, letting him hold her up. Tears form in my eyes again as I watch their reunion.

When Leah stands up, I walk with her up the many stairs to her bedroom in our private quarters. She's shaky, but determined. When finally we reach her doorway, we stand there a second while she stares into the room. Bo is glued to her side, her hand buried in his fur.

"Can we change this, Mom?" she asks as she slowly walks to her bed. Her muscles are still weak, deteriorated from being confined. "Can we change the color, and all of it?"

"Of course," I answer immediately. "It's due for a change anyway."

She smiles at me weakly and crawls into bed. "I'm so tired," she says apologetically. "I can't seem to sleep enough."

"You've been through a lot," I tell her. "You need to sleep."

She closes her eyes and I pull the blankets up over her. Bo rests next to her bed.

"Mom?" she asks as I turn to go out. "Can you open a window? I want to hear the ocean."

"Of course."

I open the window by her bed. She opens her eyes.

"And can you leave the door open?"

She looks so vulnerable, so young, so afraid. I bend and press a kiss to her forehead.

"Yes, honey. You're safe now. Don't be afraid."

She nods, but her knuckles are white as she clutches her blanket.

"How about I sit with you until you fall asleep," I tell her. She's instantly relieved, and I take a seat by the bed. I hum and hold her hand, and it doesn't take her long to drift off.

I sit with her for a while longer, and then I tiptoe out and down the stairs.

I find my husband in the living room.

"Is she sleeping?" Nate asks knowingly. I nod.

"Out like a light."

"Come sit with me."

He opens his arms and I sit next to him, his arm around my shoulders.

"We're very blessed," he says aloud, as though he'd been doing heavy thinking. "In every way. We've been given a second chance…with our daughter, with each other. I don't want to blow it this time."

"We won't," I agree.

"Do you want me to stay?" he asks quietly, his husky voice so warm. I hesitate, and his face clouds over. "You don't?"

"No, it's not that," I say quickly. "I want to be with you, Nate. I truly want us to try again. I think we can do it this time. Our priorities were skewed before. We've been reminded of what is important again."

"Then what is it?"

"I don't know that we should stay here," I say softly. "It has such bad memories for Leah. Everywhere she goes… she'll be reminded, and people will always know what happened. They'll gossip and it will follow her everywhere."

"Leah is strong," he says firmly. "If you want to stay here, she'll be fine. Skye is here. Liam is here. It's not like Leah to run from anything."

"True," I agree. "She would definitely see it that way."

"I think that after all of this, the last thing we should do is take her away from her friends," Nate adds.

He's probably right.

"I love you, Em," he says, softer now. "She's going to be okay. *We're* going to be okay."

We fall asleep together on the couch. Nate's strength and warmth suck me into oblivion, letting loose all of my worries and cares. I don't know how long we sleep, I only know what wakes me.

Leah.

"Mom." She shakes my shoulder. "Mom."

I open my eyes and sit up. It's dark outside.

"Are you okay?" I ask her.

She smiles. "Yes. I was wondering…if we could go float on the water?"

I suck in a breath, and I almost automatically say no. I can't believe she is fearless enough to go out there again so soon. I had thought she drowned out there, in the night, and I can't let that happen again.

I have to forcibly remind myself that none of what I thought was reality ended up being true. It never happened. I steel myself, and finally nod.

Leah smiles beatifically. "One of the things I kept thinking while I was in that cave was that I was floating. Imagining that I was floating helped me stay sane."

"Okay," I say immediately. "Go get your board."

She spins around and I wake up Nate. He thinks I'm crazy, until I explain.

"Fine," he grudgingly acquiesces. "But we're going, too."

"Obviously."

He and I grab pool floats from the back deck of the inn, and we all meet on the beach in our swimsuits. The moonlight turns our skin silver, and I have to admit my pulse is pounding. Leah has her board, and she barely looks strong enough to lift it now that she's lost so much weight. But she does, and I watch her wade into the water. Bo sits on the edge for a moment, and then he wades in, too.

Leah and I stare at him, shocked.

"Mom!" she exclaims. "Look!" Bo paddles toward her, his big head bobbing.

"I see!" I call. I turn to Nate. "That dog is never leaving her side again."

"Nope," he agrees. "It's a good thing I bought him for her."

I roll my eyes, and we follow her into the water. It's cold, but Leah is in her element, her safe place. We all float on our backs, Leah on her board, and Nate and I on our floats. The moon hangs heavy and full above us, and the stars twinkle overhead.

"This is where we belong," Nate says softly, his hand reaching for mine through the water.

"Yes," I agree, my fingers closing around his.

Leah glances at us happily. She's going to have a long road ahead of her to get over the trauma of everything that happened, but I know she can do it. She can do anything.

"Look, Mom," she says, holding up her arm. "Fairy lights."

She closes her eyes and when she does, I see my little

girl, the one she was before all of this ugliness. The one who believed in fairy dust and hope.

I see it in her again now.

I close my eyes, secure in the sudden knowledge that washes over me. I feel it in my belly, a mother's instinct. Leah will leave all of those ugly things behind.

She'll be okay.

The four of us, Nate, Leah, Bo, and me, float for hours in the dark with fairy lights twinkling on our skin.

Ramblings from the Island

Hello, dear world!

I'm sorry it's been a while.

As you know, I got involved in a situation I shouldn't have with an older man. I know now that I was taken advantage of, and I don't like to talk about it. I've been in therapy for months, so I'm working through it. It's been hard, and sometimes I still have nightmares about what happened.

But I'm getting better every day.

I've decided that I'm going to pick this blog back up and use it as therapy. I'm going to talk about things I love, things I like, and things I hate. Everything. I hope you don't mind.

My dad is here now. He's living here. My parents are back together, and my mother is hiring someone to help her run the inn, so that it doesn't take up quite so much of her time.

Skye is okay. She's had to deal with losing her dad,

AND knowing that he was a psychopath. That's hard, and truly there are days that I don't know how to help her, other than to just listen when she cries, and hug her.

Life, though...it goes on.

And here I am, sitting in my room, with a brand-new dream catcher. There are nights when it fails, because I have nightmares, but maybe it's the reason I don't have nightmares every single night. Maybe it catches the bulk of them. Who are we to say?

Now onto something else...something lighter.

Dear readers, there is a boy. He's been with me all along, and I pushed him away. But he's been here the whole time, in front of my face. His name is Liam, and now that he lives here on the island full-time, things are happening.

Sweet things.

Things that make my heart skip a few beats.

We'll go slow, because after what happened, I have issues. I get scared sometimes, but Liam is so patient. He loves me and, dear readers, I think I might love him, too.

I feel at peace now...with this.

This is the way the world is supposed to work.

Two teenagers, innocent and naive and drunk on love. Right?

I'm not as innocent as I used to be in some ways, but in other ways...I still am. I still need to experience those things in a normal, appropriate relationship...and, dear readers, I'm here to tell you that I can't wait...because it's Liam. I love him.

Life goes on.

And so do I.

Tags: happily-ever-after, teenagers, love, fresh beginnings, new starts, life, happiness.

Responses (1)

LiamRoadRunner1: I love you, too.

★ ★ ★ ★ ★